FINDING YOURSELF IN SEVILLE

Steve Carter

Steve and Julie Books

Copyright © 2012 Steve and Julie Carter

All rights reserved

The characters and events portrayed in this book are fictitious. Any similarity to real persons, living or dead, is coincidental and not intended by the author.

No part of this book may be reproduced, or stored in a retrieval system, or transmitted in any form or by any means, electronic, mechanical, photocopying, recording, or otherwise, without express written permission of the publisher.

ISBN-13: 9781481827010
ISBN-10: 1477123456

Cover design by: Steve C
Library of Congress Control Number: 2018675309
Printed in the United States of America

To

Julie, Nicola, Mum, Pablo and Johan

CONTENTS

Title Page
Copyright
Dedication
1 Unbelievable!   1
2 Should I stay or should I go?   10
3 Things that make you go…   20
4 Hippy Chick.   30
5 Happy Together.   38
6 Get ready for this.   46
7 Can't stop this thing we started.   56
8 Love to hate you.   69
9 Wind of change.   81
10 Everybody dance now.   86
11 These are the days of our lives.   96
12 Too blind to see it.   105
13 Even better than the real thing.   112
14 Everybody in the place.   125
15 Give me just a little more time.   137
16 To be with you.   143
17 Come as you are.   149
18 Let's get rocked.   160

19 Please don't go.	173
20 Como hemos cambiado.	183
21 Always the last to know.	196
22 Finally.	203
About The Author	209
Books By This Author	211

1 UNBELIEVABLE!

Extract from a letter sent to the Orkney Islands on the 14th of June, 1991.

'...so, I guess I need to say don't worry, Mum. It's all going really well for me down here. Me and Rachel are very happy, we've been talking about moving out of the flat and buying a house. Who knows? There might even be grandkids on the way someday. I know you don't think she's a great match for me, but you'll see how nice she is when you get to know her a little more. She's putting in lots of overtime at work and we're trying to get some money saved for a deposit on the house. At twenty-nine, I feel like I'm finally settling down, finally getting my act together, as Dad used to say.

Anyway, gotta go now, Mum, and, like I said, don't worry about me.

Love,

Andrew xxx'

It was unbelievable. The whole world knew, with perhaps the possible exception of a remote pygmy tribe that lived in an inaccessible part of Papua New Guinea.

Oh, and me.

"Andy, I'm not enjoying this," Doug said, leaning forward, schadenfreude written all over his unshaven, chubby face. "But someone had to tell you."

"But are you sure, though?" I asked again, "Like, totally sure?" I searched his face, desperately hoping to see a sign that this was a sick joke. But the only thing of note was a small bloodshot thread in the corner of his left eye.

"Mate, everyone knows," he sighed, picking up his pint. He took a mouthful, performed a loud, deep belly belch and said, "I bet even your mum knows."

"There's no way my mum knows," I replied, waving away his beer breath with a grimace. "How could she, living all the way up there?"

"News travels fast these days, mate. And bad news travels even faster," he nodded at me sagely. I didn't want to think about that, about the fact that my mum might know. My eyes slipped away from his face, and I stared at the grubby Woodbine ashtray on the beer-stained table, trying to comprehend the incomprehensible.

"And you reckon it's that gay bloke from the wine bar?" I repeated, looking up at him.

"The very same," he confirmed, then added, almost as an afterthought, "Anyway, it would appear that he's not quite as gay as we all thought." I tried to take that in as Doug snorted in delight at the irony. But I pressed him further.

"How do you know if your 'sources' are accurate?"

"Mate, I'd stake my life on it," he replied indignantly, slamming his fat fist on the table and making a small splash as he did so. I have to say right now that Doug's life was not the greatest stake anyone could put up for a bet, mainly because he didn't have one. That said, my mind was struggling to take it all in. It was racing around like a Ferrari that had just hit an oil patch, and, like that Ferrari, my life was taking a dreadful skid. It's not as though I'd had any idea about what had been going on, but I couldn't get to grips with the fact that it was with the guy from the wine bar. How was that possible? "Wanna 'nother?" I shrugged indifferently while he easily manoeuvred his stout frame out of the chair and ambled over to the bar for another round. In the background, someone hit the video jukebox, and EMF's 'Unbelievable' started to blare out from the surrounding screens. The irony was not lost on me, I can tell you. Meanwhile, I was still unable to comprehend the fact that my girlfriend was cheating on me with a guy who had the world's dodgiest haircut. Think of a Def Leopard eighties mullet crossed with a Rod Stewart seventies feather cut.

When Doug returned from the bar, I was resolved to get more

details. "I don't suppose your 'sources' know how long this has been going on for?" I asked this because Doug had made it clear that he wouldn't reveal his 'sources' other than to say they were like the News of the Screws: 'Well placed and highly accurate.'

"Andy, mate, don't go there. Isn't it enough to just know?" he asked, stuffing a fiver into his wallet before tucking it into his back pocket and sitting down. "Why would you want to know it all? Anyway, I always told you she was no good."

"What, after you tried to get off with her?" As soon as I said this, I regretted it. His cheeks flushed crimson under his unruly mop of jet-black, curly hair. He slunk back in the chair and looked sheepishly into his pint as an uncomfortable silence engulfed the table. I shouldn't have brought it up because it went with the territory; everyone tried to get off with Rachel.

It was true. Every bloke I knew had tried it on with Rachel Michelle Hayes. Only now, it seemed the gay bloke from the wine bar had actually succeeded. I didn't blame people for trying. I did blame people for succeeding, though.

The problem was that Rachel wasn't just attractive; she was stunning. The first time you met her, you'd be struck by her eyes. They were large, deep puddles of melted chocolate framed with long, exotic eyelashes. She stood at an elegant five foot nine in her stockinged feet, was a perfect size ten, and had the kind of breasts that plastic surgeons aspired to create. Finally, her tanned legs, honed on the finest sunbeds money could buy, seemed to go on forever and were more often than not barely covered by her trademark item of clothing—the shortest of short skirts.

When she first arrived in the office three years ago, the clamour to date her was only matched by the ones to get off the Titanic when the captain mentioned there weren't enough lifeboats to go around. In essence, Rachel's appearance in the office quickly became the equivalent of Mount Everest in the 1940s—everyone knew where it was, and there was a massive clamour to be the first to get on top, but, at that point, no one had yet managed it. So it surprised everyone then when I became the metaphorical equivalent of Edmund Hillary.

Don't get me wrong, before Rachel, I'd had my successes with the fairer sex. I rarely had any problems finding someone to date, but I always seemed to attract the wrong type. I had a penchant for spending too much on designer clothes, a nice car, and an expensive rented flat. All this, allied to a well-paid job, meant the odd attractive girl went with the territory. Place emphasis on the word 'odd' there.

But I had a track record of two and zero regarding serious relationships. My first serious relationship was with Gaynor Huggins, the head girl at school. We dated for two years before she left me to join the Army. The last time I heard, she'd moved in with a staff sergeant called Beryl. What made that particular failure all the more painful was the fact that my mother held me solely responsible for turning my ex-girlfriend into a lesbian, so much so that she tended to bring it up on every possible occasion. 'Is that Gaynor girl still a lesbian?' she'd ask me over coffee as if Gaynor had caught something from me that she might eventually recover from.

The second one, Alice Cooper (Yes, honestly!), finished with me after five years and married my previous best friend, I took the whole thing so badly that I've never mentioned my best friend's name again and he's only ever referred to in conversation as 'previous best friend.' Come to think of it, that's why I ended up with Doug as my best friend. So, Alice Cooper and previous best friend have a lot to answer for.

The road to being three and zero in serious relationship failures began one Friday evening. I was taking one for the team and working late on the New Balance account. Cruickshank wanted it finished days before and was giving me the sort of grief Hitler gave his generals when the Russians were two miles from Berlin. Worse, the walking piece of smarm had cleared off earlier than he should have to go for a 'facial.' Which pretty much sums the guy up.

I was seated at my computer when I got the distinct feeling I was being watched. "Doing anything important?" purred a silky voice from behind me. Not recognising the voice, I swivelled in my chair and turned to face it.

It was Rachel!

Whenever she wandered onto my floor, she would give me the odd glance but never a second. Instead, she preferred to sit on Cruickshank's desk and cross those ever-so-long legs. They were legs that all the men stared at and all the girls glared at. Now, here she was talking to me, and any previous convictions I might have had to keep my distance evaporated like early morning mist on a summer's day. "Yes, it's vital, top-secret stuff," I said in a Sean Connery voice. "It's strictly on a need-to-know basis, Moneypenny." I was trying hard not to stare, but my eyes kept wandering of their own accord. She was leaning casually against a filing cabinet, arms crossed under her magnificent breasts, a position that was causing them to spill out of her low-cut pink top. I hoped to convey indifference and the sort of laid-back manner that I guessed might be the only way to impress a girl like her. This was tricky to do, though, as I was struggling to catch my breath. She seemed to be having no difficulty breathing and was playfully looking me up and down.

"What if I needed to know?" she smiled, stepping into my office. She approached the chair nearest to me and placed herself on it with no little aplomb. "Could you tell me?"

"I could, but then I might have to kill you," I said, tearing my eyes away from her crossed legs and forcing myself to look up into her eyes. Now, I could see down the front of her top, and what was worse was the fact that she didn't seem to mind. If anything, judging by her posture and the way she was leaning forward, she ensured I had maximum visibility. She was enjoying the banter and winning any sexual side of the encounter, not that that was a victory to rank alongside the Battle of Trafalgar.

I tried to regain some control, reminding myself that I was just another bloke in a very long line of men she'd toyed with when suddenly she spotted something on my desk and leaned forward. She brushed her left breast lightly against my arm as she reached over. Did she do that on purpose? I think she probably did. She picked up my dilapidated copy of Catcher in the Rye. "Oh, wow! What a coincidence. I was only reading this again last week," she squealed, flicking through it. "We read it in the fifth year at school, but I can't say I really understood very much, so I thought I'd give it another go." I couldn't really think what to say to that so I laughed and said,

"Yeah, I guess it is a weird book."

"So, what are you doing after you've finished?" she asked, tossing the book back on the desk with a disdain I'd seen her dispense to over-keen male admirers and shaking her hair back in the same movement.

"What the book?"

"No," she exhaled loudly. "When you've finished all the top-secret stuff here?" It almost sounded like she was asking me out.

"Don't know, really," I said hesitantly. "Probably going to go home, eat a fish supper, and maybe read a porn mag."

"I was warned that you were outrageous," she said, with a glint in her eyes. "Well, can I save you from your boring night and take you to the pub for a quickie?" I was well versed enough in the flirting game to know when a girl was hitting on me, and what man in his right mind would turn down the chance of a quickie with her?

"Alright, Moneypenny," I drawled. "I'll have a Martini, shaken, not stirred."

"Whatever," she replied, uncrossing her legs slowly in the most delightful way before standing up in a clear invitation for me to follow. "But you're paying."

That was something I'd get used to. Two months later, she moved in with me.

When I returned to the flat later that evening, Rachel wasn't home. She'd told me she was working late, but I figured she was with the guy with the dodgy haircut. I felt hurt and angry, but I still loved her; at least, I think I did. I went to the fridge and was relieved to find a pack of Stella.

I wasn't completely drunk when I heard the door open an hour later, but I wasn't sober either. She entered the front room, shaking light rain from her jacket whilst simultaneously kicking off her shoes. She made her way towards the gas coal-effect fire like a heat-seeking missile. "Ooh, it's freezing out there," she shivered. "I can't believe it's June. Sorry, I'm back so late. How long have you been home?" I didn't reply. I placed my hands on the armrests and pushed myself up unsteadily from the chair.

"I know," I said abruptly, and, standing precariously opposite her, I knocked over an empty can that skittered across the wooden floor.

"Know what?" she frowned as the can rolled towards her bare feet. She turned her pouting face away from me and lowered herself onto the Afghan rug.

"Everything! So don't deny it, Rachel. At least do me a favour and have a little bit of respect. Something you don't apparently haven't done too much of for me lately." That last bit came out wrong, not so much a sentence as a drunken slur.

"You've been drinking," she accused me, pulling her knees up to her chest but not before putting the offending can next to the Chinese lamp with a grimace.

"And that's got precisely what to do with anything? You've been shagging, so my drinking is entirely understoodable given the circumstances."

"Oh!" her reply was barely audible. She wrapped her arms around her knees like a barrier to protect herself from my anger.

"Is that it? Is that all I get? An 'Oh', not even an apology?"

"I'm sorry," she said rather weakly. "I'd hoped you wouldn't find out from anyone else. I was going to tell you this weekend."

"Oh, you were going to tell me?" I gasped, my voice escalating. "I don't know what I was getting so upset about. Everything's hunky dory cos you were going to tell me!"

By now, I was standing in front of her, looking down at her upturned face. "You're being dramatic, Andy," she replied sullenly. "That's not what I meant at all."

"Well, you needn't have worried. It's common knowledge

apparently; everyone knew but me." Her head dropped down to the floor at this point. I wondered if she was going to cry. I hoped she wasn't. I hated it when she cried. I didn't have much of a defence mechanism for it.

"It's not what you think. He's more of a friend," she mumbled.

"Maybe I should shag Doug then!" I replied theatrically. She nervously picked at the hem of her skirt but didn't look up.

"How could you, Rachel? And with him of all people!"

"I know you don't like him, but he can be very persuasive," she said, finally looking at me. Her eyes were glistening with tears, and her chin had a slight tremble. Surprisingly, it had little effect on my anger.

"He must be persuasive because I thought he was gay!"

"Gay?" she looked shocked. "He's got a wife and a family."

"He's married? Him? With that haircut?"

"What are you going on about, Andy? What haircut?" she asked, crawling across the floor. She pulled a handful of tissues out of a designer tissue box that had been carefully positioned on the coffee table like a feature on the front page of Home and Garden magazine. She pushed it back into place before blowing her nose loudly. "I don't know what you're talking about. You know he's not gay; you went to the wedding."

"The guy who works at the wine bar?"

"Brian," she said, blinking at me.

"Brian?"

"Cruickshank." It took a few seconds before it sunk in—Doug and his 'sources!' It was my own fault for believing anything he says.

"You're shagging Cruickshank?" I blurted out.

"I prefer 'having an affair'," she said primly, dabbing at her mascara-smudged eyes. "Who did you think it was?"

"That bartender with the funny, early-eighties hair."

"Alain? He's gay—everyone knows that. He's just a friend. How could you possibly think it was him?"

"Sources," I said, turning around and knocking a second can against the coffee table. "Just get lost, will you, Rachel? I want you out of the flat in the morning," I slurred and staggered off in the direction of the bedroom.

2 SHOULD I STAY OR SHOULD I GO?

Extract from a letter sent to the Orkney Islands on the 4th of July, 1991

'...so just to set things straight: It really wasn't anything to do with Rachel. It was more that we started to drift apart. I'm perfectly fine about it. In fact, I couldn't be happier. We're both going about our lives with no regrets. I mean, we're friends and everything. And thanks for the offer to come and stay with you. But Orkney is a little too isolated for me at this time in my life. So all in all, I think it's best this way, and I'll let you know when I decide what I'm doing.
Love,
Andrew xxx'

When I woke up the next day, she'd done as I'd asked. I was relieved, although not surprised. I'd always told her I could forgive her for anything but unfaithfulness; she had the decency to go without a scene, which was something. There was a note on the fridge door held up with a Marge Simpson fridge magnet: 'Gone to my mother's. I know you don't believe me, but I am sorry about everything. If you can find it in your heart to forgive me, then give me a call. Despite everything that's happened, I really do care about you.' She could have said, 'I really do love you,' but I suppose she didn't have to lie anymore.

I looked at the clock; it was half-eleven. I should have been at work three hours ago, but that didn't matter anymore. Normally, I'd make a courtesy call, but Rachel would have already told him I knew about them. Instead, I phoned Doug. He answered on what seemed like the twentieth ring. "Hello," he croaked deeply into the phone.

"It's me," I said, looking out of the window at the binmen dumping wheelies into the cart.

"Wha d'ya want? My head's killing me."

"Well, meet me in the pub. That's sure to fix it. By the way, how did you get back last night?"

"I got a taxi. Cost me a tenner and got ripped off," he moaned.

"I'm not surprised. You were completely trollied."

"I know, but there should be some benefit to being in the police. Not getting ripped off by taxi drivers being one of them."

"Fair point. See you in half an hour?"

"Yeah, okay."

The phone dial tone beeped in my ears, and I slouched away towards a very much-needed shower. As the hot water pounded my head back into reality, I started thinking. I do a lot of my best thinking in the shower, and the beginnings of a plan—one that might rescue something for me out of this stupid mess—began to form.

Forty-five minutes later, I was back in the pub and opposite Doug, who had just returned from the bar with two lagers. "So," he said, putting them down before us, "It all worked out for the best then?" This was Doug all over and one of the many reasons I lamented the passing of 'previous best friend.'

"How on earth did it work out for the best?" I retorted, sliding the pint a little closer but still not having the courage to drink it. "My girlfriend was having an affair with my boss, and now she's left me? If that's your definition of it all working out for the best, I wouldn't want to know what your definition of it all going completely arse up was."

"Nah, mate. You kicked her out," he said far too cheerfully. His thick fingers expertly ripped open a packet of nuts. Tipping the contents into his open mouth, he continued in a muffled crunching tone. "You told her to do one. That constitutes kicking her out."

"What does it matter? I kicked her out—she's left me. I fail to see," I said, now holding the pint and forcing it towards my mouth with the sort of enthusiasm I'd have for one of those nasty little suction tubes the dentist uses during fillings. "How does that constitute it all working out for the best?"

"Because," he said, choosing his words carefully, "at least it wasn't that bloke with the dodgy haircut."

"Do you mean the bloke your impeccable 'sources' told you it was?" If he should have looked somewhat uncomfortable at that point, I have to tell you he didn't.

"Yeah, well, take it from me. I'll be having a word in certain ears about that," he replied solemnly.

"Oh, that's comforting, Douglas. I'd appreciate it if you would."

"Don't be sarcastic, Andrew," he said as his index finger rummaged around the bottom of his nut packet. He sucked the salt off his finger and discarded the packet towards a filthy, overflowing ashtray in the middle of the table. "I mean, she was at least shagging someone. So, my sources weren't totally inaccurate."

"Yeah, it was just my married boss and not a gay barman. See the difference? Boss, who I hate, and who likes women, and gay barman, who I don't even know and who likes…err…men! Or are your detective constable skills unable to cope with the incredible similarities in the case?"

With that, I looked down at our two pints and saw that they were both miraculously empty. I raised my eyebrow in the way of a question, and he tipped his head towards the bar. When I got back, he was in a more reflective mood. "So, what are you gonna do about work and stuff?" he asked, taking a small packet of dry-roasted nuts from my hand.

"I did some thinking in the shower this morning," I said, slumping into the seat. "I can't stay there. One of us has to go and it's more than likely going to have to be me. The thing is, I've had an idea, and if it pays off, it could help me to salvage something out of this whole mess."

"Sounds interesting; I'm all ears."

"I'll let you know how it pans out. I'm going into work after this to see Cruickshank, and my intention is to make him wish he hadn't been born." He spurted out his pint at this.

"You're gonna punch his lights out?"

"Metaphorically speaking, young Douglas, I am."

Brian James Cruickshank was seated in his office when I arrived five hours late. I was considerably more confident than I might have been due to my lunchtime alcohol consumption with Doug, but I was not drunk. No, siree, I'd been careful to limit my intake to the point where it was bolstering my courage but not affecting my reasoning—the old, two-pint maximum.

I was delighted to see that Crooky looked uneasy at my unexpected arrival. He'd probably figured he was safe after lunch and that I wouldn't make an appearance. The fake grin he usually wore was nought but a distant memory. He looked up from his desk as I strode through his door. I could tell by his demeanour that the man was as uncomfortable as a DFS sofa. He ran his fingers nervously through his black, manicured, Mr Whippy hairdo. His tongue darted in and out of his mouth like a lizard's as he licked his dry lips. "Andy!" he exclaimed, closing the door behind me. "Come in, come in. I'm glad that you came to see me. I think we need to talk."

"I'm not sure I agree with you there, Bri," I told him, ignoring his outstretched hand. "Because I don't think *we* need to talk. I think *you* need to listen." At this, he gave off the sort of laugh your mother would give if you mentioned condoms in front of the parish priest. He walked back to his desk and gestured for me to sit down. Coughing first to clear his throat and shifting a little in his seat, he eyed me carefully.

"Andy, let me say, first and foremost, I'm extremely sorry about this err…little misunderstanding," he started, whilst pretending to rummage for something vital in his drawer. I had to give him his due. The slimeball was quickly recovering from the initial shock of my unannounced entrance.

"A little misunderstanding? Is that what you think this is?" I asked calmly and crossed my legs while leaning back into the chair. My eyes bored into his. "Is that what your wife would think? That it's all just a little misunderstanding?"

There. I'd served up an ace. It was a slight gamble that he hadn't told his wife and had no intention of ever doing so. His reaction told me my opening serve had made it fifteen-love. "We need to think this through, Andy. Let's not do anything too hasty," he replied in a voice attempting to soothe me. "I'm sure we can sort this out amicably; we're sensible people."

"Of course we can, Bri," I said amiably, a smile stretched across my face, but my eyes were as cold as ice. I stood up and walked around to his side of the large desk. From the collar of his Armani shirt to his immaculately shaped eyebrows, a red flush spread across his face, and I wondered if his blood pressure was rocketing or if he was just nervous. I sat on the edge of the desk and looked down at him.

"We can sort this out like sensible people, Bri. Provided I leave here with exactly what I want." He remained seated, looking meekly up at me. This was undoubtedly thirty-love. When I'd played the scene out in my mind earlier that morning in the shower, I'd feared he might go all mano a mano on me, standing in my face and screaming: 'And what is it you want exactly?' But he was unusually passive. So I laid out my terms. "What I want is a payoff. I want out from this dump, and you're going to make that happen." He shuffled about in his chair, his hand reaching back up to stroke Mr Whippy again. It was a sure sign he was on the back foot, but I wasn't home and dry yet, as it was well known that Cruickshank would rather sell his mother than spend company money.

"Well, that's going to be a little difficult given the current climate," he postured, puffing his chest out, clearly stalling for time. I could almost hear his brain cogitating, working out a way to extricate himself. But I was on a roll. I was serving for the game, and there was no way he was getting off the hook.

"Shall I tell you something about the current climate, Brian? In the current climate, there's a big depression moving in, and it's going to rain down all over you and your life if you don't get me the money. You've made it impossible for me to continue working here, and now you have to sort it out."

Forty-love and very nearly game, set, and match. I just needed one more killer shot, and I was there. With that, I reached inside my pocket and pulled out a number I'd written on the back of a beer mat from the pub. I slid it on the desk towards him. He looked down at it and then back at me before picking it up with just the slightest tremble in his fingers. His eyes darted back at me, and then he flipped it over to read the figure on the other side. "You have got to be joking," he gasped, tossing the mat back onto the desk. To be fair to him, which was the last thing I intended to be at that moment, I was pushing my luck a little. But I'd figured it would be best to start high and see where he went from there.

"Hmmm, am I? Now then, Brian," I said firmly as I stood up. I picked up the beer mat and held it before his face. He glared at the figure I'd written but didn't say anything. I was about to make the final ball toss. "You see, I don't think I am joking. There isn't anything funny about your married boss screwing your girlfriend. And considering the unfortunate circumstances we find ourselves in and the seven years of hard graft I've invested in this place. I think that figure is quite reasonable."

"You think that figure is reasonable?" he choked. "I don't think head office will agree with you." Taking a deep breath, he attempted to compose himself and shuffled some more in his chair. After a few seconds, he beamed a smile second-hand car dealers learn on their first day on the job. And shaking his head sadly, like a father telling his child that he can't have an ice cream before dinner, he implored, "Look, I'm sorry, Andy, but there's just no way I can…"

"Now you listen to me, Brian," I said abruptly, cutting him off. "I'm not going to mention any of this to your wife because she's the other injured party in all this," He peered at me suspiciously through narrowed eyes and waited for the punch line. I was more than happy to oblige. "Let's just say that if I don't get garden leave from today, and if that payment doesn't hit my account by next month, I'm going to send a letter to London explaining that the teambuilding ethic they value so much in this company is fostered by a manager who goes around shagging his employees' partners." Brian opened his mouth to speak, but I held up my hand and continued with the even worse news.

"But more than all that, I'll be more than happy to discuss any concerns they might still have from the strange closure of the Burns account. I take it you do remember the Burns account?" The Burns account was a 140-mile-an-hour ace he never saw coming, and it whizzed past his head.

"Now st…steady on," he stuttered. "We agreed—"

"What we agreed about the Burns' account," I talked over him, "became null and void when you started an affair with my girlfriend! So here it is, Bri. I'm going on garden leave, despite the fact that I live in a flat and don't have a garden, and you are going to get me that figure. I have every confidence in you getting me that figure, as it was chasing extraordinary figures that got you into this mess in the first place."

I dropped the beer mat onto the desk. It was game, set, and match, and we both knew it. Yet, like the bad loser in the post-match press conference, he had the gall to huff and puff a bit. "I'll see what I can do," he said, looking down at the beer mat and sounding wonderfully downtrodden.

I smiled, did not wish him a nice day, and walked out of the office, wondering what on earth I was going to do with the rest of my life.

"What are you going to do with the rest of your life?" Doug asked me as he plonked himself onto my sofa, having just put 'The Unforgettable Fire' on the stereo.

"I haven't got a clue. But one thing I do know is I need to get away from here. Go somewhere, do something different with my life, and keep away from women for a while," I replied, flopping into the chair opposite him. "I can tell you something else too: I'm sworn off women for the next two years, especially beautiful women. I'm going to make it a golden rule. Golden rule number one: no women."

"Yeah, right," he said, throwing me a can of beer. "We both know that's not going to happen."

"What's not going to happen?" I asked, lifting the cold can to my lips and picking up a packet of cheese and onion crisps from the coffee table.

"Neither. You're never getting out of here, and you're not staying away from women, especially not from attractive, spoilt women. It's a pattern, mate; it's what you do."

"Well, I'm not doing it anymore, and if Cruikshank comes through with the money, I'm off somewhere nice and sunny. Like Spain. Remember how good I was at Spanish in school?" Doug pondered this for a minute.

"Andy, you were only 'good' at Spanish because you could say 'Hola' and the rest of the class couldn't. And, besides, Miss Kirby, like most of the female staff, had the hots for you."

"That's not true. She liked me, but, if anything, she preferred 'previous best friend'."

"Liked you? She was almost drooling across the desk if you even smiled at her. You'd have noticed it, too, if it wasn't for all the girls in the class drooling as well. Well, except for Gaynor, who just happened to be the only one you were interested in."

"Anyway," I ignored him, "I've been thinking about going to Spain and doing some sort of language course out there." He digested this information with black, bushy eyebrows furrowed together in contemplation. Then, his eyes opened slightly with the realisation that my move could benefit him.

"Yeah! I could come out on holiday. We could bonk some Spanish birds together. Well, not together at the same time. That would be weird. But I could definitely use a cheap holiday on the old Costas." With this, he leaned back, stretched his legs out, and looked skyward to take in some imaginary rays.

"Sorry to rain on your bonfire, but I'm not going to the Costas," I said, putting my feet up on Rachel's coffee table. "Remember when we did the geography project on Spain? The real Spain is not the Costas. If I go, and I'm seriously thinking about it, I'm going to the real Spain."

"A truly mint idea," he agreed, putting his feet up and, looking at me, he gained a wink of approval. "The real Spain. I could help you choose where to go."

About an hour later, he was pinning a map of Spain, one that we'd found in the back of one of my old geography exercise books, onto my kitchen door. I had a dart in my hand and, being a bit drunk, was trying to steady myself before throwing it at the map. Wherever it lands," he pronounced, shoving a drawing pin in the top to hold it in place, "is where you go. Are we agreed?"

"Absolutely," I said, taking aim through one eye. The fact that no professional dart player I'd ever seen used one eye to aim did not occur to me in my slightly inebriated state. I threw it clumsily, and the dart missed, hitting an empty beer glass left on the shelf to the side. The glass shattered into a thousand pieces, and even in my blurry-eyed, drunken condition, I knew it would be a ball-ache to hoover up the next day.

"The Atlantic Ocean," said Doug, handing me another dart and grinning. "You are going to learn Spanish in the middle of the Atlantic Ocean."

"Get lost, Doug," I said, feeling both amused and irritated by him as usual. I took aim again and, one-eyed, I threw the dart at the map. Being totally useless, I aimed at the top of the map, but it quickly lost flight and sank deep down, eventually hitting somewhere near the bottom.

"Get in!" he exclaimed and squinted to see where the dart had landed on the map. "Seville? Where's that?" I had to admit, I had no idea. But the dart had landed almost smack in the centre of the tiny dot that marked the city.

Sort of like destiny?

I had no idea the next day why my foot was throbbing when I woke up. Until I discovered that I had one of those annoying tiny shards of glass stuck in it. I reluctantly got the Hoover out and gave the whole flat a going over. After all, it wasn't as if I had a job to go to.

When I finished, I hit the answering machine button. There were three messages, all from Rachel, asking if she could come over and would I please return her calls.

I deleted them.

I picked up the phone, dialled work's number, and then asked for Cruickshank's extension. It went straight to voice mail. Good, I didn't particularly want to talk to him anyway. I left a message saying I didn't want a collection and that I wouldn't be coming into the office again. I also mentioned that I had some duplicate copies of files from a job we did together a year or so back. They were pertaining to the closure of the Burns' account. Would he prefer it if I 'posted them directly to you, Bri, or the London office'?

A week after leaving that message, a letter from London arrived telling me that, sadly, the firm was downsizing, and they would have to let me go. In respect of my outstanding service to said company, I was to be offered a month's garden leave and a payment, the figure of which was not much less than the one I had handed to Cruickshank on the back of the beer mat.

All in all, a result.

The next day, I wrote a letter to Seville University enquiring about their one-year intensive Spanish course for foreign students—entry September 1991.

3 THINGS THAT MAKE YOU GO...

Extract from a letter sent to the Orkney Islands on the 31st of July, 1991

'...been accepted into the intensive Spanish language and literature course. I had to make a few phone calls to the university, but it's incredible how flexible people will be when you tell them you have the money to pay upfront in full. The course starts at the end of September, so I will fly out in early September to get settled and find somewhere to live. It's going to be an amazing experience. I don't know what I'm going to find in Seville, but I'm sure that destiny is waiting for me. I can feel it in my bones, sort of like you do with your rheumatism. I have to go now as I need to book some flights—so I'm off to visit the travel agents!

Love,

Andrew xxx'

"Oh," said Rachel when I told her the news that I was going to live in Seville for a year. She looked underwhelmed at the idea of having the flat all to herself. Her shoulders visibly slumped, and, for a moment, at least, I almost felt sorry for her. In the last week or so, Rachel had bombarded my answering machine with so many messages that it ran out of recording time. I got fed up with deleting them, so I resigned myself to the fact that I would have to face up to the final breakup meeting that so many wrecked relationships insist on having. It was solely due to Rachel's persistence that we were 'talking things through,' but what she wasn't expecting to talk through was my imminent departure to Spain.

She'd come around after work on a Thursday. We were in the living room, and she was leaning against the fireplace in a photo shoot pose while I stood near the window, putting as much distance as possible between us. "I just can't believe this," she said, shocked by the developments. She'd stepped hesitantly towards me, her dark eyes fixed on mine as if trying to compute what I'd said. "I mean, I just can't believe it."

"Don't you want to move back in then?" I asked, retreating to the safety of a chair and sitting down. "It's close to work, and it will make a nice little rendezvous gaff for you and Crooky. By the way, has he told his wife yet?"

"Please don't do this, Andy," she groaned, sitting on the settee where all poise for the moment temporarily departed. Turning towards me, she spoke in a little girlie voice, which I used to find cute. "I was hoping we could still be friends, at least?" her eyebrows lifting slightly for emphasis. On getting absolutely no response from me with the 'cute' voice, she reverted to her own. "Anyway, he can't tell her right now. She's got an operation coming up in three months, and he wants to make sure she's recovered and strong enough to take the news. He's not all macho, you know; he does have a sensitive side."

"That guy is about as sensitive as a prison officer wielding a baton in a riot," I scoffed. "Anyway, what the two of you do is no longer my affair but your affair—in both senses of the word." She let out a half sigh, half moan, and then did it. What? What they always do. What they learn to do from the very moment of their birth as a method of getting their own way. Well, at least in Rachel's hands, it was. She started to cry.

"I am really sorry, Andy," she sniffled. "The thing is, I still really like you. I want to be your friend, not someone you hate. I don't want you to move away to a foreign country." I was on the verge of reminding her that moving to Seville was the direct result of her infidelity and that we wouldn't be in this position if she hadn't got in a few positions of her own with Cruickshank. But I knew in my heart that wasn't the whole truth. In some ways, she'd done me a favour. Rachel had given me the opportunity and the courage to start a new life. If I was being honest, I don't think I'd ever really loved her. I thought I had been in love with her, but I'd been in lust. I'd certainly enjoyed the kudos of seeing the envy in other blokes' eyes when she walked into a room with me. The sex and the fantasy, rather than the reality, had kept me in the relationship. Yet, I also knew I'd kept myself emotionally distant from her as I did with everyone. A sad legacy of my past, I suppose.

So, despite what she'd done, I felt sorry for her. I raised myself hesitantly from the chair. Not wanting to sit beside her on the sofa, I hunkered down and lightly touched a hand that was clutching at a soggy tissue. "Look, I know you're upset, Rachel," I said carefully, staring at the tissue. "When two people like us split up in the circumstances we split up in, we can't be friends anymore; we just can't." I looked at her face and was dismayed to see big, fat tears spilling from her eyes and rolling down her cheeks. A dark, wet patch was forming on her silky, low-cut top. Was this more than the usual waterworks show? It was impossible for a mere man to know. I squeezed her forearm briefly, then lifted myself onto the sofa. My hand hesitated before it rested on her trembling shoulder, and I wondered what the protocol in situations like this was. I had no idea, so I awkwardly slid my arm around both shoulders and gave a small sideways hug, like one you might give to any friend who was upset. She seemed to take this as an invitation and turned towards me, entwining her arms around my neck. Her wet face was warm against my cheek, and those oh-so-soft, full breasts were pushing against my chest. I realised that she wasn't wearing a bra, but before I could disentangle myself, she tilted her head back and looked hard into my eyes.

"Remember how we used to sit together and watch Eastenders, even though you hated it?" she asked, smiling weakly and giving a slight sniffle. I was feeling very warm now, and my right hand began to pull at my Lacoste polo shirt collar.

"Yeah, well, we both know why that was," I said, making a half-hearted attempt to extricate myself from the situation.

"Because you loved me?" she sniffled some more.

"No, Rachel. If memory serves me well, it was because I was always on a promise if I agreed to watch it with you." She ignored this, and her arms wound tighter around my neck. If this wasn't bad enough, her thigh started to press against my legs while her short skirt rose even higher. The skirt was working in direct contravention of the laws of gravity.

Oh no!

Then, somehow, and I'm not saying you had to be a professional wrestler to manage it, she flipped me over and climbed on top of me. "You're on a promise now, Andy," her warm breath whispered while her eyes glinted like a cat toying with its prey. Then her hot tongue found its way into my ear, and she was writhing and moaning on top of me. She didn't seem to be sniffling much anymore, and my hands had inexplicably moved onto her arse.

"Rachel, let's not do—" her lips stopped any further conversation as they pressed down on mine. I could have escaped that with an emergency exit roll to the right. But her right hand was fumbling into enemy territory and pressing in the place where only she knew how to press, which led to what I later came to see as 'the great mistake.'

When I climbed out of bed an hour later, Rachel was in the kitchen, dressed only in her tiny M&S knickers and a Wham throwback 'Choose life' T-shirt. She'd pulled this out of a set of drawers she was supposed to have been clearing out. There were no longer any visible signs that this would happen soon. No, Rachel was making coffee for me like she used to whilst singing a very bad version of some Whitney Houston song at the top of her voice. She was acting as if she'd never left and, worse, as if she had no intention of leaving. At the best of times, she had absolutely no taste in music and was tone-deaf, another example of God's little levellers.

I'd dressed and reluctantly entered the kitchen with my hands buried deep into my jean's pockets. I looked down at my Converse trainers, pondering my next move. In all honesty, I felt like a man who'd accidentally reversed his Land Rover over the Andrex puppy in front of the kids. I knew that what had happened was a terrible mistake; was it my fault, hers or both? I didn't know the answer, but I knew I couldn't let it affect my plans. I was being selfish, but I wanted my future in Seville, and nothing would change that. I decided it would be better for Rachel to know, sooner rather than later, that she could no longer be a part of my life. I moved sheepishly towards a stool at the breakfast bar.

"Here, I've made it milky for you, one sugar, how you like it," she grinned, passing me a steaming hot mug of coffee whilst dressed like an air hostess on Playboy Airlines. It's not easy accepting a cup of milky coffee from a lingerie model and telling her that what had just happened was a big mistake. I felt guilty I'd allowed it, but I reasoned she'd also had no small role in it. Worse, I couldn't understand her motives. Did she seriously want to get back with me? It appeared by the way she was singing *'I Will Always Love You'* that she might.

"Rachel. What was that about?" I asked, putting the cup to my lips and blowing on the hot, frothy liquid.

"What was what about?" she pulled out a stool to sit on, placed both elbows on the breakfast bar, and cupped her chin in delicate hands. Her perfectly manicured fingernails were hidden under a tumbling mane of dark, shiny hair. She looked beautiful; she was beautiful. She gazed at me expectantly as though she was only too aware of the image she was projecting. In Rachel's world, her self-assurance and calculating use of her sexuality was all it took to get whatever she wanted.

"The sex, Rachel. What was the sex about?" I asked forlornly. She shrugged her shoulders, her face a depiction of emptiness. Any guilt I was feeling disappeared in the wake of frustration.

"Rachel, I want to say this clearly so you understand me. What just happened was a mistake," I pronounced firmly.

"What do you mean a mistake?" she laughed lightly; her voice was calm and disconcertingly assured. "It wasn't a mistake. I'll tell you what it was if you really can't figure it out: it was what's called make-up sex. We're getting back together; it's what we both want."

"We aren't getting back together, Rachel," I said, pushing my fingers through my hair. "When a couple get back together, it's because *both* of them want to. But here's the problem, Rachel: I don't want to. So, we are definitely not getting back together. We haven't made up because I'm going to Seville, and you are going to sort your own life out. Your own life, Rachel. Which, remarkably, is in even more of a mess than mine; I have to at least give you credit for that." Her coffee cup stopped midway as she lifted it to her mouth. She peered over the top of it and then squinted as the penny seemed to drop.

"You have to be joking, right?" she said, her flawless cheeks draining of colour. She placed the cup very calmly on the Quartz countertop.

"Like I said, it was a mistake," I replied, holding her gaze. "A big mistake." In hindsight, it was probably a bit harsh, but I felt it needed to be done. Girls who look like Rachel get used to having things go their own way. When this trend is bucked, they are apt not to take it too well. With my cards now laid out on the table, her eyes turned steely cold. Without warning, she leapt off her stool and grabbed the first thing she could lay her hands on, which just happened to be a big wooden spoon next to the cooker. She turned to hurl it at me. Rachel has a very accurate hurl, but it hit a closing door on this occasion. I was already heading out of the room, having witnessed the steely, cold eyes and knowing what had followed on many previous occasions.

When I returned a couple of hours later, the flat was empty. In a temper tantrum, Rachel had smashed a few plates. A lot of stuff in the flat belonged to her, which seemed to have brought her to her senses. Rachel had bought art and furnishings because, unlike me, she was undeterred by minor financial imperatives, like not having any money in her bank account. She would purchase expensive furniture and put it on credit. This had probably been behind the restraint she might have otherwise not shown.

The next couple of weeks were spent doing the mundane everyday tasks that lead to a major life change. I managed to sell the BMW, which, when added to my cheque from work, gave me a nice fighting fund for Seville. There were letters to the landlord, rent payments, banking arrangements, airline tickets, calls to utility companies, calls to hotels in Seville and selling off my worldly possessions, all of which added a tidy sum to my savings.

Friday, the sixth of September, finally arrived. I was at Manchester Airport, standing outside of the entrance to Terminal One's departure hall. As much as I had told him I'd get a taxi, Doug had insisted on driving me there.

Considering I was going for nearly a year, I was travelling light and had packed one case containing most of my worldly possessions. As Doug pulled the case out of the car boot, it occurred to me that I was nearly thirty, jobless, homeless and clueless. U2 was blasting out, *'I still haven't found what I'm looking for'* from the tape deck, which seemed apt. Yet, strangely, I was as confident as ever that destiny awaited me in Seville.

"Here you go, mate," Doug said, putting the case down on the pavement. "All the best, Andy. I hope it works out for you."

"Cheers, Doug," I said, flipping up the handle of the case and setting it on its wheels. "I'll send you my address as soon as I sort myself out over there. You can come and visit me then."

"Deffo," he replied, using his huge palms to slam the boot on his Golf down like a WWF audition. He stood in front of me and opened up his arms wide, "Give us a hug then."

"I don't think so," I laughed, backing off. "You've been watching too many episodes of *Thirty Something*. That's what blokes from California do, not the North of England." He feigned a slight frown, dropped his arms, and broke out into a grin.

"Right then. I'm off," he said, changing the keys over into his right hand. "Give us a ring if they have phones and stuff over there."

"'Course they have phones," I laughed. "I'll call as soon as I'm settled, take it easy Doug."

"Yeah, I will. Better go, mate, before I get done for parking the car in these yellow bits." He turned back to the driver's side, eased into the car, and slammed the door, muting *'Angel of Harlem'* as he did so. I waved as he sped off and then got the most incredible feeling of loneliness despite the fact I was amongst thousands of people.

The flight to Seville via Barcelona was uneventful. After collecting my case at the carousel, I strolled through passport control and out of the terminal. Leaving the cool, air-conditioned building behind and stepping out into a blanket of dense heat and a blazing sun, I slipped my sunglasses on and ambled over to the taxi rank, joining the small queue. It didn't take long before I was speeding off in a yellow taxi on a twenty-minute drive to Seville. My companion was an old guy called Ramón, who was jabbering away about Real Madrid. As I could only pick up the odd word, I smiled and nodded while looking out the window at the vast open fields and farmland. It was so hot and arid that the grass was the colour of straw, very different to the lush green fields in the UK. Every garage we passed seemed to double up as a cafe where locals drank coffee and ate tapas in the shade—a sharp contrast to the drab BP petrol station back home.

Ramón dropped me at the end of a Calle in the Centro, pointed towards a square and said something unintelligible. I paid him four thousand pesetas, gave him a 'muchas gracias' and a phrase I'd practised from some Linguaphone discs, which meant 'keep the change.' On calculating the thousand tip, he slapped me hard on the shoulders, hugged me like I was his best friend, and jumped back into the taxi. He was soon lost in a myriad of yellow taxis whirling around the roads. For the next few minutes, I stood, with my case in hand, soaking up the city's atmosphere. Seville had a hustle and bustle similar to the northern cities with which I was familiar, yet, at the same time, it was utterly unique. The traffic darted around streets lined with orange trees and palm trees. Narrow, cobbled alleys jutted off in every direction. Decorative balconies from the baroque buildings hung over the heads of the passersby as the hum of animated chatter from the countless bars and restaurants filled the air.

Eventually, I broke out of the spell and wandered down a narrow, cobbled alley, searching for the Hotel Miramar, which I found fairly easily. The hotel had a large, panelled glass door and a beautiful blue and white tiled reception. No one was to be seen at the reception desk, so I rang the bell and waited. Waiting, it would turn out, was something one got used to in Seville. I would quickly come to realise that the Spanish concept of mañana was taken very seriously amongst the locals.

Five minutes after ringing the bell, a very pretty girl with a disdainful air made an appearance. She was probably in her early twenties but wore a scowl, which gave her a much older look. Her long, brown hair was tied loosely at the nape of her neck with a black hairband. She gazed at me through a pair of round John Lennon glasses from which her clear, brown eyes held the finest Spanish contempt. Looking me up and down, she issued a rather blunt '¿Sí?' with absolutely no 'Señor' attached.

I felt slightly intimidated by her sheer audacity and rudeness. Stuttering a reply in Spanish using the word 'reservación.' She pushed a pen and form towards me with instructions to enter my details in almost perfect English. As she watched me complete the form, she picked up a key and jangled it annoyingly against the brass key holder. The key was brusquely thrust towards me, followed by: "Room thirteen. It's at the top of the stairs. Turn left." With no further ado, she did an about-turn and went back inside, probably to continue her studies for a night-school diploma in rudeness.

I picked up my case and began climbing the narrow stairwell to my room at the top of the building. It was a gloomy contrast to the warm, bright streets of Seville. When I entered, it became clear why I was only paying twenty pounds a night. It was the smallest bedroom I had ever seen, containing a single, lumpy-looking bed and a dilapidated wooden wardrobe with a missing doorknob.

I pushed a door open to find a claustrophobic bathroom. There was a shower of sorts with a bright orange curtain behind the door. When I pulled it back, the tiles were so mouldy I figured getting any STD in Seville could be completely cured by standing in the tiny cubicle and inhaling for five minutes. I had already paid for ten days and decided there was no way I would be extending my stay. But even a cramped, not very clean hotel room couldn't quell my enthusiasm as I planned how to spend the next ten days in this incredible city.

Wasting no time, I escaped the confines of the stifling room and went exploring. It wasn't long before I came across a little tapas bar with a terrace overlooking a quaint square. I sat at an outside table and cherished the realisation that I was in no particular hurry to do anything.

I ordered Gambas al Ajíllo (prawns fried in hot garlic oil), two slices of tortilla, and a large glass of red wine from a friendly waiter who understood my order without too much difficulty. When the prawns arrived with freshly baked bread, even with oil dripping down my chin, I felt like I'd gone to heaven. I'd never tasted anything so good. The sun slipped below the buildings slowly and, in doing so, cast the skyline in a deep red twilight haze. I marvelled at the world and the twenty-degree heat that bathed my body. I lazily watched people enjoying their evening as I ate. Young men in cars honked at pretty girls and preschool children playing in the square while their parents watched. A middle-aged lady was sitting on a bench under one of the many orange trees and stroked the head of a small dog asleep on her lap. I ordered a second glass of wine from a waiter. He served espresso to a group of old men playing cards, smoking cigarettes and bantering like they'd known each other all their lives. I was munching and drinking and thinking and munching and thinking. Thinking: yes, I could quite easily get used to this.

4 HIPPY CHICK.

Extract from a letter sent to the Orkney Islands on the 13th of September, 1991

'...and so Mum, I have to tell you that Seville (or as we say here Sevilla!) is amazing. The sun's been shining every day; it beats Northern England and the awful weather you get up on the islands. I've been exploring and seen some fantastic sights. I went to the cathedral yesterday and the beautiful Moorish palace, the Real Alcázar, the day before. Tomorrow, I'm going to the Plaza de Toros and the Parque de María Luisa. There's so much to see. I can't tell you how glad I am that I came here.

So I don't think you need to be worried about me leaving my job and 'ruining my life' because I'm loving it here. Don't worry about me, Mum. I'll be fine!

Love,

Andrew xxx'

The main building for the University of Seville runs the length of the Calle San Fernando. It's a busy road with lots of traffic, and it's lined with bars and hotels. The university is situated inside what used to be the old tobacco factory. As I strolled through the ornate iron gates, I looked up to the roof to see marbled angels trumpeting my arrival. Once inside, it appeared even more grandeur, full of swirling staircases and enormous art deco rooms. It was the setting for Bizet's Carmen and retains the ambience of a grand eighteenth-century palace. I had no idea who the genius was who decided it would make a great university, but just walking around its enormous echoing corridors, looking for Professor Johnson's office, I wanted to shake them firmly by the hand.

After twenty minutes of meandering and enjoying myself immensely, I arrived at Johnson's office, which was on the upper floor, at the stated time. Immediately after I knocked, a booming voice bade me enter.

The door opened into a large, cluttered office. A bearded, burly figure dressed in a stereotypical knitted cardigan with leather patches at the elbows was sitting behind a desk. His suede-booted feet were propped on top in a pose straight out of Educating Rita. A few papers had spilt onto the floor unnoticed. He was on the phone, one hand cupping the top of the mouthpiece and the other making swirling gestures, which I interpreted to mean come in and sit down. On top of his fine, greying hair was perched a broken pair of one-armed spectacles. There was a chair directly in front of the desk, and I made my way towards it. As I was about to sit down, I heard a voice from behind the door.

"Hey, don't sit there. He's been on the phone for ages. Come and sit over here by me." I turned around and saw a small, strawberry-blonde-haired girl. She was dressed in something resembling a purple kaftan. A large matching headband swept across her head and held thick, wavy hair back off a pretty, freckled face. Her outfit looked out of place and probably would have anywhere—unless it was San Francisco in 1967.

"I'm Saffron," she squeaked in a voice that was only slightly louder than a whisper. She then looked towards the figure at the desk, who was now chatting away in Spanish to the mystery caller. "Please don't call me Saffie, though; I hate being called that."

"Pleased to meet you, Saffron," I replied with a smile. "I'm Andy. Please don't call me Andrew, though. Only my Mum calls me Andrew, and I hate that."

"Wow, that's so amazing," she shrieked, her pale blue eyes radiating excitement. "That's why I hate Saffie so much; my mum calls me that!"

"Mothers have a lot to answer for," I laughed, sitting on the small chair beside her. "Well, in my limited experience, they do, only ever having had the one."

"They certainly do," she agreed and raised her hand to her

mouth to stifle a giggle. The figure on the phone dropped the handset into its cradle and turned towards us, spilling more papers onto the floor as he pulled his feet back off the desk. "Sorry about that. You must be Andrew—"

"Please, call me Andy," I said, causing Saffron to giggle again.

"Andy McLeod?" he asked.

"I am indeed. Thanks ever so much for accommodating me. Dr Johnson, I presume?"

"Yes, sorry," he went on. "I'm snowed under at the moment with the new intake and all the accompanying nonsense."

"All the more reason to thank you for fitting me in," I said, standing up to shake his hand.

"And you've met Saffron, I see," he said, smiling toward the girl seated behind me.

"Yes, I have." I nodded.

"She's in the same boat as you," he bellowed, now picking the phone up and dialling again. "Doing the same course, and, like you, she needs somewhere to live."

"My mum's a friend of the family," she chirped from beside me. "So Roger…Dr Johnson…has agreed to help me find a flat and look after me while I'm here. It's going to be super!" She said in a way that gave me the impression she would probably find a parking ticket on her car windscreen 'super.' She was also looking at me in a very enthusiastic way as if she was finding me 'super' too. I was starting to feel a little disconcerted, especially since I had sworn off women.

"So!" Johnson said, breaking my disconcertion and slamming the phone down in a small display of frustration. "I put one and one together with you two and have some good news for you both. There's a flat over in Triana—on the other side of the river —which my dentist owns. He lets it on yearly rents, and I usually send students his way. It's very nice, with three bedrooms. You might need to find someone else to cover the rent for the third bedroom. Interested?" From my point of view, it didn't take a great deal of thinking about.

"I am, thanks very much. I'm sorry if I appear rude, but can I ask what the rent is?"

"Not at all," he replied. "Ninety thousand a month. That's fairly good at the moment. With next year's trade exposition, the rents are being pushed up throughout the city. It's merely a case of seeing what you think of it and whether or not you get on and want to share."

"Oh, I'm sure we will," Saffron piped up. "I get on with anyone, and I'm sure Andy does too." I felt a little press-ganged, but it also seemed like an opportunity I couldn't pass up. Saffron pushed unruly tendrils of hair back under her headband, and I tried to gauge whether I fancied her. I didn't want to break my golden rule by living with someone with whom I might make any more mistakes. I had to keep away from women and concentrate fully on my Spanish studies. It occurred to me that living with a pretty girl so soon was not the best idea. I caught her eyes, and they seemed to gleam a little too much. I decided that I didn't fancy her, but she seemed nice enough, if not a bit too enthusiastic about everything. In the meantime, Johnson was patiently waiting for me to say something.

"Yeah, sure," I smiled, "let's go and take a look at it."

"Great," they said in scary perfect unison.

"I'll make an appointment for you both tomorrow," he mused, pulling his glasses over his head and onto his nose. He wrapped the one remaining arm over a large, hairy ear and bent over the paper to write down the address. His glasses slipped off his nose and hung askew against his cheek. He absently reached up to readjust them back and returned to the task of writing. But his glasses slid off again. I glanced over at Saffron, who was biting her cheeks to hold her laughter in. I suppose it did look funny. After numerous attempts to keep his glasses in place, tears of laughter threatened to spill down her cheeks. I wasn't sure if she could hold it together. I caught Saffron's shimmering eyes. I had to admit she was pretty in that quirky, hippy chick way some girls have about them. I hoped I wasn't violating the golden rule.

"The owner won't be there, but he has an old woman who runs the local shop to manage it for him," Johnson said, picking up the phone again. "I'll give her a ring. Why don't you two go and get a cup of coffee in the bar and get to know each other better? Pop back in about half an hour, and hopefully, I'll have an appointment for you to go and see it."

At this, Saffron bounced out of the chair like Tigger on crack cocaine and flew out of the doorway faster than Carl Lewis. Once she'd got to the other side of the heavy door, Johnson and I could hear what sounded like faint whoops of laughter being choked back. Johnson looked puzzled as I rose, leaned over, and offered him my hand. "Err...I think she just needed to go to the bathroom. Thanks for all your help, Dr Johnson." He took my extended hand and shook it enthusiastically.

"Not at all. See you in class from time to time."

"I hope so."

Half an hour later, I was finishing my beer, and I'd learned a little about the life story of one Saffron Elizabeth Morley. She was from somewhere called Pinner in Middlesex, where, according to her, nothing much ever happened. She was twenty-three, a French graduate at Durham University, and was taking a year out before her master's to do some Spanish as a 'life type thingy.' Her dad was a pilot, her mum was a lecturer at the LSE, and she had no brothers or sisters. It was clear she was a smart cookie but there was an undercurrent to her that I couldn't figure out.

For my part, I'd given little away. I told her I was an only child from a small council estate in Northern England and that my mum now lived in Orkney without going into any of the painful reasons why she'd left. I condensed the last few years of my life into a demanding job and a relationship breakup, which was pretty much the truth of things, if not the bare bones. I was, in all honesty, still working out if I wanted to flat-share with this fizzy, nervous bundle of new-age energy. Something about her eagerness and enthusiasm was both endearing and off-putting simultaneously.

"What do you say then?" she asked me, putting her apple juice down and tinkering once more with her headwear. "Why don't we go and look at the flat tomorrow and see what we think?

Where are you staying?"

"I'm in a hotel in the Centro. Not far from the new M&S."

"Well, in that case, we could meet at the cinema near the San Telmo bridge, the one at the end of Constitución. Do you know it?"

"Yeah, I passed it on my way here. Why don't you see if Johnson's got a time yet? I'll get us another drink. Sure you won't have a glass of vino?" I asked, rising to my feet.

"No thanks. Juice will be fine," she replied, also getting up. "I'll see you in a minute then."

As I waited for my drinks, I marvelled at the idea of having a bar inside the university teaching area. A great idea, in my opinion. I decided to write to Doug later that evening and suggest he get a petition going for a bar in the local police station.

The barman handed me a beer and a glass of juice. I turned around without looking and collided with an arm, sending my beer flying. The glass shattered on the floor, and the barman, with raised eyebrows and shaking his head in an exaggerated fashion, went to collect a brush and pan. When I looked at the arm, it was completely covered in beer. "Thanks for that," the girl attached to the arm said in wry amusement.

"I'm so sorry! What an idiot," I groaned, turning to put down what remained of Saffron's drink on the bar. "I can't believe I did that. Well, I can. I'm always doing stupid things."

I stood lamely and watched while the girl tried to squeeze beer out of her sleeve. She was of medium height and not particularly skinny, but she was wearing tight jeans like she couldn't care less. Her hair was red, wavey and long. She had pulled it back into a ponytail, and a few escaped strands framed an open, pleasant face. Her brown, stained sleeve looked a mess, and squeezing it had only made it crumple and look worse. She grinned at me as she rolled it over her elbow. "Don't worry. No real damage done," she laughed, wiping her wet arm with a handful of napkins off the bar. "I never liked this top much anyway. And, what use is a long-sleeved top in Seville in this weather?"

"Well, I really am sorry," I repeated, relieved she wasn't upset. I caught the other barman's eye. "Can I at least buy you a drink?"

"You can," she said, grinning. "That will definitely help to make amends. And get one for my dad over there in the corner… the tough-looking Geordie." I looked in the direction she'd pointed and saw a stocky, red-haired man in his fifties, with a twinkle in his eye, holding a glass up to me.

The barman leaned over, and I said, 'Tres cervezas más' in something approaching a Spanish accent.

"Seems there's more English than Spanish in this uni at the moment, and, of course, we're all in the bar."

"Where else you gonna go?"

"Good point," she laughed.

"I'm Andy, by the way," I said, extending my hand.

"Maggie," she smiled, shaking it. "And that's my dad, Rob. He's not as mean as he looks. He's helping me move in before driving back to Newcastle tomorrow." The guy in the corner raised his glass again and tapped it. "I think you better get him that drink, or we could both be in for it." The barman placed three beers on the table, and I produced a thousand-peseta note. As he returned with the change, I handed Maggie her drinks, and that was when a squeaky voice said,

"Andy, our appointment to see that flat is at two tomorrow. Who's this?" I wasn't sure when I got married to Saffron, but it suddenly felt like years ago.

"This is err…Maggie," I said, feeling like I'd been caught doing something wrong.

"Hi. I'm Saffron," she replied haughtily, not holding her hand out.

"Maggie," Maggie countered, and unperturbed, she extended hers. Saffron looked down at Maggie's hand as if it were contagious. Ignoring it, she looked at me.

"We need to finalise our plans, Andy," she pressed. The girl, Maggie, gave me one of those fantastic looks where she managed to appear neutral to Saffron yet full of amusing pity towards me.

"Don't let me interrupt your planning," she said, her eyes dancing over at me. "It was nice meeting you both. I hope we'll all bump into each other sometime."

"Yeah," said Saffron, turning her back on Maggie. "Let's hope so," she replied, sounding as if it was the last thing on earth she hoped for.

"Nice to meet you too," I shouted after Maggie as she returned to her table.

"Oh…my…God!" Saffron scoffed dramatically. "A nice girl, but that bottom in those jeans at her weight is a definite no-no." She rolled her eyes. Saffron didn't appear to notice that I wasn't paying any attention. My eyes followed Maggie back to her seat. When she sat down, she turned back towards me and sent me the cutest little wave I had ever seen.

5 HAPPY TOGETHER.

Extract from a letter sent to the Orkney Islands on the 9th of September, 1991

'...but I'm managing okay. Thanks for the money offer, but I really don't need it. I have more than enough to live on.

I know you don't think that I've made enough of myself so far in life. I've made mistakes along the way, especially with women, as you keep pointing out. But you have to believe me when I say that's all changing. Anyway, I'm going to see a flat tomorrow, and I'll let you have a new address when I know it.

Sorry, this is only a quick letter. I'll write in more detail as soon as I'm settled.

Love,

Andrew xxx'

Even though I had some minor concerns about living with Saffron, I agreed to meet her near the cinema the next day. The upcoming exposition in Seville was pushing up rents everywhere, and there wasn't as much availability as there might have been. At the back of my mind, I knew I was ignoring my gut feeling, and that could be bad news in the long term. But the accommodation Johnson had arranged for us was cheap and meant I'd have more money to enjoy the city.

The flat was over in Triana, about twenty-five minutes from the hotel. We crossed the San Telmo bridge, and once again, I had to pinch myself to check I wasn't dreaming. The orange trees were a constant reminder that I wasn't dreaming; there were thousands of them, and I couldn't wait until their scent filled the air in spring. As we walked, my eyes took in the beauty of the city. It was in stark contrast to the almost constant stream of chat pouring out of Saffron's mouth.

"Aren't you excited, Andy? I am. We could be living together in our flat this time next week. Won't it be amazing? It will, won't it? I'll do the cooking. I love cooking anyway, so don't worry about that. It's all veggie stuff, but you'll like it. Everyone thinks veggie isn't tasty but it is. It depends on how you cook it. Do you know what? We can walk to the uni together in the mornings."

And so on.

She was grating on me by the time we reached our destination, a small grocery shop, Ultrámarinos on Calle Trabajo. This was where the woman who managed the flat for the dentist lived. Johnson had mentioned to Saffron that her name was Maria and, according to him, she was 'a bit quirky.' We shuffled into the shop, which was a hive of activity. A group of the local old lady brigade was standing at the small glass counter, chatting furiously with each other; everyone seemed to be shouting all at once. A short, dark figure dressed in black buzzed up and down behind the counter. She picked up a cloth and began polishing the sparkling glass in a rapid circular motion, all the while carrying on a conversation with her customers. She stopped briefly to wave her cloth at one of the older ladies and shouted something I couldn't understand. She was in her mid-sixties but looked like she had the energy of someone half her age and reminded me of the Tasmanian Devil in the Bugs Bunny cartoons.

We stood awkwardly in the doorway, not wanting to interrupt the heated exchanges. After a few minutes, the shop owner saw us and stopped polishing the counter. The rest of the group all turned around and went quiet as they stared at us. They have made staring practically an art form in Seville, and this motley crew of ladies were highly skilled artists. The squat lady in black behind the counter then rudely ignored us as she climbed up some step ladders to reach for a packet of fresh coffee on one of the higher shelves. Whilst doing this, she harangued the locals in a language mainly unrecognisable to me but approximating Spanish to some.

The truth is the Sevillanos are the Glaswegians of Spain. They do talk Spanish, but not as we know it, Jim. Their accent is so strong that if it were a cheese, it would be very runny and completely inedible. The worst of their language traits is to ignore the letter 's' at every given opportunity as if it were the linguistic equivalent of a binman with hygiene problems. When the ferocious little figure finally decided to acknowledge us, she turned from her regulars, frowned her big, bushy, dark eyebrows our way, and issued a wonderfully disdainful, "¿Qué?"

I tried in my best Spanish to say we were there to see her about the flat, but this merely elicited a long, unintelligible reply. Thankfully, Saffron interrupted at this point and rescued the situation. "She's going to take us up to the flat and show us around," she said, slowly backing out of the door while pulling me along with her arm. "We need to wait outside for five minutes. I think that's what she said anyway." We both smiled and waved at her to show that we understood, and she scowled back. The rest of the onlookers watched us with mild interest as we retreated through the door.

"Wow! How did you understand that?" I asked, putting my hands in my pockets. "That sounded like a completely foreign language to me."

"I have no idea. I just got the flow of it—the odd word here and there," Saffron said, glancing nervously over her shoulder back into the shop. "Anyway, you did super."

"Hardly super," I disagreed. "I'm realising that it's one thing to speak Spanish around here and quite another to understand it."

"But they say if you can understand the Sevillanos, you can understand anyone anywhere in Spain," she replied, looking at her watch.

"Yeah, I suppose," I sighed. We waited outside in the hot street without saying anything. I leaned against the shop window, enjoying the sunshine and watching people go about their day. Calle Trabajo was a narrow road on which cars and mopeds raced up and down at breakneck speed. Since my arrival, I'd seen many streets like this, often blocked with delivery van drivers parking wherever they wanted to. This could have been Seville's answer to speed control, I thought, as the traffic could barely get past them, let alone go fast in the narrower adjoining streets. Cars often parked bumper to bumper, but the locals had a system to get out. They would put their hand on the car horn and hold it until someone realised they had to come and unblock you. All this made Triana a noisy neighbourhood and Seville an even noisier city.

While we stood watching the pedestrians and the traffic, Saffron chewed nervously on her bottom lip. I looked over the top of her headband to see Maria exiting the shop with a large bunch of keys in her hand. "She's a bit scary," said Saffron, putting her hands to her face and hiding her mouth. I found this gesture hilarious because if Maria spoke a word of English, it would be one word more than I figured. Hell, the woman didn't even seem to speak Spanish.

"A bit," I whispered back anyway. "Her bark is probably worse than her bite." In the meantime, Maria brushed past us and shouted,

"¡Venga!" in a loud voice, like she was a member of Franco's militia, and we were captured socialist forces. She then strode across the busy road in a manner that would have given the Green Cross Code man a coronary. At least two cars slammed on their brakes and honked loudly at her—all without her seemingly caring—as she made her way to the other side, occasionally throwing her hands up in the air as if she had the right of way. Turning to look at each other, we nodded in unison and stepped into the road after Maria before she disappeared into the three-storey block of flats opposite.

We followed her through a metal gated door and up two flights of concrete stairs to the second floor. At the top, she switched on a small landing light and then turned right before knocking on the opposite door. After waiting a minute, presumably for an answer that would never come, she produced a key, turned the lock, and entered the apartment.

The flat was a real find. Any gut feelings I'd had about Saffron earlier were disregarded at the point of entering. It was spotlessly clean and well-equipped. Saffron was beaming as we walked in. Maria seemed very proud of the flat, and for the duration of our visit, she pointed at objects and named them in Spanish like a game show hostess telling a pair of idiots what they could win if they weren't such a pair of idiots. The highlight, for me, was when she pointed at the small black and white TV on the sideboard and said very slowly to us, 'la tele' like it was the Spanish technological equivalent of the space shuttle. She then opened the doors to two bedrooms on the left, both of which were spacious and bright. It was a no-brainer, and we hadn't even seen the roomy kitchen or third bedroom by this point.

"Ask her how much the deposit is and how she wants us to pay," I said to Saffron, who hadn't left my side since we entered and was following me around like a puppy that had recently been removed from the litter.

"No, you do it," she whispered. "She scares me." I opened my mouth and gave it my best shot.

"¿Qué es la fianza y cómo quiere usted que le paguemos?" Not brilliant, but not that bad either. On hearing this, Maria launched into a tirade of Spanish, the upshot of which, well, it seemed to me in translation anyway, was that the place was dirty. I turned to Saffron, who was now bent over and hiding behind me. "Did you get any of that?" I asked her. "Please tell me you got some of that?"

"Only that the deposit is already paid by something or someone called Sueco."

"Who or what is Sueco?" I asked her, looking at Maria, who was now pointing to the window and saying very slowly, "La Ventana."

"I don't know and I don't have my dictionary with me to find out," she replied testily, and a little stressed. "It would be really super, Andy, if you could sort this out." I sighed, turned back to Maria, and asked her the relevant question.

"¿Sueco? ¿Qué es Sueco?"

"Sueco, Sueco," she shouted, in the way that the Spanish do when they think that only by shouting the word a little louder will you somehow miraculously come to understand it. Looking blankly back at her, I plucked up the courage to shrug my shoulders. At this, she tossed her hands up in an extravagant gesture whilst tossing back her head and looking up at the ceiling. After another minute of repeatedly shouting the word at us, she promptly trooped over to the bedroom we hadn't yet seen and pushed the door open. There, lying on the bed facedown, clad in yellow trainers, knee-length yellow shorts and a yellow shirt, was a tubby, spiky blond-haired figure more than the worse for wear.

"Sueco," repeated Maria. She then pointed at him with two outstretched hands and, gave a toothless grin. It was at the point of observing the figure's somewhat exuberant fashion sense that the penny finally dropped:

Sueco: meaning Swedish person of the male variety.

"I don't like the look of him, and I don't want to share with him either," Saffron protested after Maria had left. The figure on the bed had rolled onto his back but was doing nothing more than making his chest go slowly in and out and letting us know he was, at least for the moment, still alive.

"Well, you don't have much option considering he's paid for the flat three months in advance," I told her, a little sharply. "Anyway, I like it, and it's in a perfect location for classes. I'm going to hang around until he wakes up and ask him if he'll share with me. Do you want in or not?" I was hoping it was a no at this point. She wriggled her freckled nose and tilted her head over as if she was thinking about it.

"I guess so," she replied glumly, crossing her arms and bending her hip into a sulky pose. "But this flat was supposed to be ours by rights, according to Roger. If anything, we should agree that he can share with us."

"Why don't you take that up with Maria then?" I asked, knowing she wouldn't want to pursue that line of questioning. "She seems a pretty reasonable woman for a psycho," I said, laughing. She looked down at the floor and shuffled her feet.

"Well, I don't like the look of him," she mumbled.

"You said that already. Look, you haven't met him yet," I reasoned, sticking my head through the bathroom door and seeing what appeared to be a nice new shower with no hint of mould. "He's probably a good laugh. At least judging by his clothes, he must be." She giggled at that, and we went into the kitchen to wait for him to come round.

When he eventually appeared, about two hours later, he didn't seem in the slightest bit perturbed to find two strangers drinking coffee in his kitchen. He was a sight to behold, with hair sticking up in every direction and more wrinkled clothes than an old bull elephant's goolies. He slumped into a chair, gave a comical salute, and introduced himself as Johan. Johan Anderson. He was twenty-two years old, going on forty, and a graduate of philosophy at Uppsala University. His family owned a timber business that he would work in after taking a year out. He'd enrolled in a few classes at the university but didn't know whether he'd attend any of them. He spoke impeccable English, like many Swedes do, and was very proud of this as he'd never even been to England in his life. "How is it, Johan, that your English is so good?" I enquired, passing him a robust cup of coffee.

"My family used to watch Monty Python re-runs, and we picked it up from the TV, old bean," was his studied reply. "To be honest, my French is better than my English." This made me wonder how that could be, considering how good his English was. When I asked him about sharing the flat with the two of us, he was delighted to share with two Brits. "A good Christian country like my own! And, all the better, with a reputation for enjoying the odd alcoholic beverage, much as I do myself," he said, lifting the steaming mug of strong coffee to his lips and slurping it with little dignity. "Have you noticed how cheap the alcohol is here? I must admit I have."

"Well, I don't drink alcohol," Saffron scoffed from the safe distance of the fridge. "So don't think I'll be going on any drunken binges with you because I won't."

"That's perfectly fine, my dear girl, each to his own," he said, taking another rather loud slurp. "I don't expect I shall be sober enough to notice your absence. But you are a fine-looking young lady, and if you change your mind, I would be delighted to buy you a drink." Saffron pulled a nasty little face behind his back as he turned away, but she didn't see his response. He winked and grinned at me. I decided there and then that I liked Johan Anderson very much.

He'd given Maria three months' rent in advance because "I always lose my money. So this way, she has it, my money is banked, and you can give me the rent back in stages."

It also turned out that Maria had taken a shine to him and had named him El Sueco Loco or the Mad Swede. Johan had discovered the flat through Maria's son Antonio, who he'd had the good fortune to bump into at a bar in the bus station soon after arriving. Antonio and Johan had hit it off, and after the two of them had painted the town red, he had brought Johan back to see the flat. Antonio was very much the apple of his mum's eye, and she agreed to let Johan rent it even though some people — us —were coming over to view it. Johan's Spanish was also, depressingly, excellent. This explained how he'd been able to charm the formidable Maria, who'd let him have a room before we'd even seen the flat.

Ten minutes later, I shook hands with him over the table, and Saffron reluctantly muttered an "Okay, I suppose so" from the fridge. We were all officially flatmates.

6 GET READY FOR THIS.

Extract from a letter sent to the Orkney Islands on the 24th of September, 1991

'...in a really nice flat. Saffron is nice enough but a little bit odd at times. Johan is as mad as a hatter, and I like him a lot. I'm all settled, and the course begins this week, so that'll be good for me to get into a proper routine.

In reply to your advice about going up there 'when it doesn't work out', don't take this the wrong way, but I'm never moving back there. I was only four when we left, so I don't even remember it. I understand why you returned, but that was right for you, not me. To be truthful, I feel more at home here than I have anywhere for some time.

Got to go now; there's a bit of a row going on. Don't worry though, it's just my flatmates!

Love,

Andrew xxx'

Two days later, I'd checked out of the awful hotel and moved into the flat. It was homely, with lots of space and light, which contrasted well with the small, grubby hotel room. It was also nice to have flatmates. I'm not sure Johan and Saffron were typical flatmates, but we quickly settled into a regime where I was the middleman, generally seeing Saffron and Johan separately. They rarely saw each other because they kept very different social hours. Saffron was up and about early and the same to bed; Johan never went to bed early. At times, I thought he might actually be a vampire.

I got caught up in some of his late-night binges in the early days, which wasn't so bad before the university classes started. But when the term began in earnest, it meant I missed more classes than I should have. During this bedding-in period, I decided I needed to meet more Spanish people and spend time around them if I was going to improve my Spanish. Johan and Saffron were natural linguists, but I needed some help.

I woke early one Saturday morning with a plan to do my own thing. Avoiding Johan's attempts to drag me to the nearest bar wasn't that tricky as he didn't get out of bed until three. He would try to persuade me to drink cold Cruzcampos late into the day, which, admittedly, did not require all of his coercive skills.

Avoiding Saffron was a much more difficult task. She always tried to tag along with me unless I was in Johan's company, and then she would fire disapproving looks. I was thankful that she'd already gone out, probably shopping for groceries, as Johan kept eating all of our food. I didn't mind Johan's petty pilfering; it was Saffron's constant complaining about it that got me down. "My cheese has gone from the fridge again," she would moan.

"Why are you telling me?" I would ask. "I haven't eaten your cheese."

"Because you're his friend."

"Well, eat his food. Get him back."

"He doesn't buy any. He just eats mine."

"He doesn't, you know; he eats mine as well."

I showered, dressed, and stepped out of the front door into the glorious sunshine. One of the great things about Seville, in the residential areas, is that you are never more than a minute's walk from a cafe/bar. Our local was two doors down from Maria's shop. It was a small cafe/bar that hugged the corner and had four tables outside on the street. Johan had named it 'Unfriendly's' because of how rude the staff were to us when we went in. Instead of putting us off, though, we were resolved to spend as much time and money in there as it took to make them be nice to us. So I went in, waited twenty minutes before the waiter reluctantly took my order, and wolfed down some chocolate con churros (strips of sugar-coated pastry dipped in hot chocolate) and an espresso. Then, I made the twenty-five-minute walk to the university. I had always previously disliked the concept of walking, but I realised that was because I'd never walked in the sun or in Seville. Besides, I had seen enough of the traffic to realise that driving around the city was not a viable option for anything other than possible organ donation.

At the university's main entrance, lots of people were milling around. Students, both local and foreign, were still attaching themselves to classes or using the university as a meeting place. I wandered through the stone archway into the notice board area on the downstairs level; it was full of 'Intercambios.' These were Spanish students of English who were looking for English students to help improve their language skills. There were hundreds of small cards on the board, and many of them would never get a call. It dawned on me that I was in a unique position. Most of these students would be incredibly lucky to 'bag' a native English speaker. This was good because it meant I was in demand.

I cast an eye over the board, flipping through the cards in the hope that something, or someone, would catch my eye. Some of the cards from girls seemed very appealing, but as I had sworn off them, I decided that it might be better if my first couple of intercambios were men. After a few minutes of reading through the cards, one caught my eye.

'Hello, my name is Sergio. I am twenty-one years old, and although I speak English well, I am very keen to improve my English. I prefer to meet after nine as I have a job after class. You can call me on the following number any time after ten at night.'

Good. The guy was a night owl like myself and already fairly proficient in English. I didn't want someone whose English was as bad as my Spanish, as it might lead to communication problems. I scanned through the others, but nothing stood out, so I decided one would be enough for now. I needed to be able to walk before running. I started to write the number down on the small pad in my hand. "Hello, Andy, how are you settling in?" asked a rumbling voice from behind me. I turned away from the board to see Prof. Johnson. He was holding a large file under his arm, with papers protruding from it in every direction. He looked like he'd just come from his office.

"Great, thanks! Just thinking about an intercambio," I told him. "Are you working on Saturdays? I thought that was illegal here."

"No, I'm forgetting things as usual. My wife says I would forget my head—"

"If it wasn't screwed on?"

"Exactly. How are things in the flat?" he asked, shuffling the file from one arm to the other and pushing papers back in haphazardly. "All working out okay?"

"Err…okay, I guess," I told him. "We're sharing with some mad Swedish guy. I like him, but I'm not sure Saffron does."

"Ah! Saffron. Nice girl but can be a tad difficult to get along with. We were colleagues in the early eighties, her mother and I, you know?" I didn't know where this was going but decided, as he was an old family friend, it might be prudent to say nowt—as my mother used to say.

"We get along okay," I edged. "Just the usual flat-sharing problems, the kind of thing you'd expect between two guys and a girl living together."

"That's good. Splendid. It's good to know everyone's getting along fine. Well, I must be off. See you Monday in class?" The way he said this may have indicated he'd already noticed one or two of my Johan-induced absences.

"Looking forward to it," I told him positively. He smiled at me and turned off towards the Plaza de España. I finished writing the number from the card down onto the pad and put it into my shirt pocket.

Back at the flat, Johan was in the living room eating some of my bread in the form of toast and downing what was likely to be coffee number three or four. It was pretty early for him. "And where have you been, old bean?" he smiled, not in the least bit perturbed that he was eating my bread.

"Don't you ever buy your own food, Johan?" I asked, sitting opposite him. "You're driving Saffron up the wall, and I can't say I'm wild about it either."

"Fancy nipping to Unfriendly's for a beer? My treat," he

replied, skilfully changing the subject whilst munching on the toast.

"You're still intent on making them like us," I groaned, picking up his scrunched copy of yesterday's El País. "Despite the fact we have no chance of actually succeeding."

"I am intent. No matter how much it costs."

"Ah well, I'm game if you are."

Needless to say, they were very rude to us.

After three hours of an alcohol-induced siesta—Johan's 'beer' turned into three or four—I got up, showered, and crossed the road to the phone box on the corner. As usual, it was busy. There was a tall girl in a trilby hat chatting away and apparently in no hurry to get off the phone, despite the fact that my presence made a queue of three people waiting to use it. When she eventually decided to vacate the phone, she approached me and asked, "¿Tienes fuego?" I shook my head and wondered what it was about me that made me look like a smoker.

After half an hour of queuing, I finally made my call. It was after ten, and I dialled, hoping for an answer. It rang a few times and just when I was about to hang up a voice said:

'Dígame?' I didn't reply in Spanish. I wanted to see if his English matched what he'd written on the card.

"Hello, is Sergio there?"

"This is Sergio," came the reply in a very monotone voice.

"Hello. My name is Andy. I got your number from the university message board."

Silence. I wasn't expecting that, but I went on anyway. "I was wondering if you wanted to meet up for a drink." I waited for a while as he appeared to consider this. Then, the penny seemed to drop.

"Oh! The university message board. You are an intercambio. Yes, that would be very good." I could see some people shuffling their feet in the queue behind me.

"Well, if you want to meet up, that's great. You name the time and the place as you know the city better than me. I can make it pretty much any day at the moment." He again considered this for a moment.

"Do you know the San Telmo bridge? We could meet near the Torre del Oro side on Wednesday at about nine as I finish work early?"

"Yes, I think so. I'll see you there then," I said, glancing over my shoulder as the queue behind me started to stretch around the block. "I'll have black jeans and a black T-shirt on so I'll be easy to spot. I have to go as I'm at a phone booth, and your countrymen are starting to look a little impatient."

"Okay then. I will look for a man in black. See you on Wednesday."

"Adiós," I said, throwing my only word of Spanish into the whole conversation.

"Adiós." I put the phone down. The guy standing next in line reached past me to pick the phone up and started to dial. I moved out of his way and looked down towards Unfriendly's, where Johan gestured wildly for me to come over. My mouth was dry, and I pondered what to do. At that moment, I saw Saffron in her purple kaftan walking on the other side of the street towards the flat. I ducked behind the booth, waited until she was inside the stairwell, and then went to join Johan for another beer.

I didn't make the next couple of lit. classes for Johan-induced reasons. Part of the problem was that no one seemed bothered whenever I didn't turn up. As I was paying for the classes, the lecturers evidently thought, correctly: more fool you. Whenever I bumped into Johnson, as was the case from time to time, he was more than happy to give me any work I'd missed. He set me a couple of extensive essays on Magical Realism and the Aragonese novels of Ramón J Sender, which he wanted in March. Though that was five months away, I knew I would have to rapidly improve to do them to any significant standard.

So, after one of the language classes I managed to attend, I called into the bookshop that he recommended in the Centro and bought five or six of the novels on the book list. I just prayed Johan couldn't find a use for them. I would never see them again if he did. His bedroom was like some cosmological black hole sucking any consumer goods and food into its bowels and another dimension.

When I got in later, I took out my Spanish dictionary, closed my bedroom door, and attempted to read Crónica Del Alba, my first-ever Spanish language novel.

The Wednesday of my meeting with Sergio arrived, and as I left the flat heading out onto Calle Trabajo (the name meant Work street—an irony there, I thought), I realised I was feeling a little nervous, which probably went back to my childhood days when my mum told me to be careful of strange men, and here I was meeting one near the San Telmo bridge after dark.

When I got to the Plaza de Cuba a little before the bridge, a fine light rain began to fall. It was the first rain I had encountered since arriving in the city. I looked around to see the Sevillanos scurrying about, looking for cafes and bars that would allow them to escape the shower. It became a little heavier as I strode onto the bridge, holding a newspaper I'd snatched from an empty cafe table over my head. By the time I got to the other side near the tower, the rain had begun to subside. But there was no sign of my intercambio. Looking down at my watch, I saw that it was only ten to nine. Finally, the rain stopped, and I looked once more along the bridge as traffic flowed past me. There were perhaps forty people walking my way. He could be any of them. I turned and looked down into the waters of the Guadalquivir when a voice to the side of me said in very good English, "Hola! I guess that you are Andy?" I turned, surprised. In front of me was a striking, dark-haired man with a lean, muscular frame. He was dressed very smartly in a brown leather jacket and blue jeans. His eyes were almost black, like deep, tranquil pools that you couldn't fathom. "That makes you Sergio," I said, a little flustered by his height and bearing.

"You are surprised I am so tall, no?" he asked, holding his hand out and guessing correctly that I was floundering.

"A little," I replied, taking it. "But I'm not heightist or anything."

"This is because I am not Spanish," he said, ignoring my ridiculous comment. "I am Basque, from near San Sebastian in the north."

"Oh, right! Errm…shall we go and get a drink?" I asked. "I know a bar near Constitución, around the back of the Cathedral. Johan, my flatmate, showed it to me."

"Okay, if you like," he said less than enthusiastically. "But I have to tell you, I do not drink alcohol."

Great.

The walk to the bar was done mostly in silence; we sort of ambled side by side, not knowing what to say to each other. I was disappointed by the initial meeting; it was evidently not going to work out with this guy. This impression was only furthered when we reached the bar, where they were showing the Real Madrid match live. "I'll get us a drink, and we can watch a bit of that if you'd like," I suggested, hoping to find some common ground and a subject we could talk about for the rest of the night. I reached into my pocket for a thousand-peseta note. "Do you think they'll win the title this year or suffer the heartache of last?"

"I don't like football," he told me, whilst looking around the bar like he was caught in the middle of a bank holdup. I regretted what I said next, not for the first time.

"You don't drink and you don't like football? Are you gay or something?" I asked in what I hoped was a jokey voice. It turned out to be another one of those smart-mouthed comments that always got me into trouble. He raised his dark eyes and peered into mine. After ten seconds that stretched into eternity, he finally said,

"Yes, I am." That was a bit of a conversation-stopper, to be honest. Then followed the mother of all uncomfortable silences. "Is this a problem for you?" he asked, searching my face for an answer.

"Err...no. I don't think so," I said, trying my best to backpedal furiously. "It's just that I don't really know many gay people. Except for this guy with a dodgy haircut who, it turns out, wasn't having sex with my ex-girlfriend after all, despite what Doug said." As anyone would, he looked a little confused at this point, maybe even wondering if I was a bit mad. But I pushed on. "I've lived a fairly sheltered life, although I turned my ex into a lesbian if that's any help." I couldn't have rambled any more than if I'd joined the ramblers and become their head rambler. Meanwhile, this earnest guy was eyeing me intently, trying to work out the inflections in my voice. Was I being humorous, or was I being a complete moron? I myself would have strayed towards the latter. Thankfully, he went for the former.

"You are making a joke?" he asked, crossing his legs and clasping his hand over his knee.

"Look," I said, "as far as I know, I have nothing against anyone. Not unless you're a Liverpool fan, and as you don't like football, that's highly unlikely. What would you like to drink?"

"Zumo de Naranja." Doug always said that orange juice was a gay drink, but I didn't think it was best to expound that particular theory to my new Spanish friend. Instead, I hurried off to the bar for a brief respite.

Three lagers and three Zumo de Naranja's later, and it was going as badly as only the worst blind date can. He told me that he was an engineering university student living in a flat near the Plaza de Toros. Like nearly all the local students, he worked. In his case, he held a part-time job at a nearby bakery. I'd told him my back story, with the obvious exception of the painful fact that attractive women kept dumping me.

After another twenty minutes of awkward conversation, we discovered all of the things we didn't have in common. That was when he said he had to go. There was a palpable feeling of relief on my part when he said it. We paid the waiter and got up together. I noticed on the clock in the square that it was half ten. Half ten on a Thursday, and the city was quiet. I walked with him back to Constitución when he stopped. "People at the university do not know," he said, somewhat randomly. "I think it is best if they do not know."

"I'm sorry," I said, not entirely following.

"Thank you," he replied, not understanding that I was not following. "I only told you because you asked. If you did not ask, I would not have said anything. Your question, it took me by surprise."

"Not as much as it did me. My mum always said my mouth was too smart. I'm always getting myself into trouble with it," I confessed. "I'm sorry. I didn't mean to offend you. I know how to keep my mouth shut, though." He studied me carefully for a second or two.

"If you would like to call again, please do. Besides, we have only spoken in English tonight, so we can talk in Spanish next time." Whatever language we used, it didn't sound like this guy knew too much about the language of fun. He held his hand out again. I took it.

"I'll call sometime next week, and we'll meet up," I said, not knowing if I was lying or not. "Adiós Sergio."

"Adiós Andy."

He turned, put his hands into his jacket pockets, and headed towards the Plaza de Toros. I looked around and decided to walk down to the Puente de Isabel 11 (Queen Elizabeth the Second Bridge) to pass some time. If I crossed there, it would be a little longer before I got back to the flat, and I would be sure to avoid Johan. That way, I might have a chance of making my early class. I looked over the river to where the bright lights of Calle Betís were blazing and where Johan was sure to be searching for a late bar and smiled.

It was a great city.

7 CAN'T STOP THIS THING WE STARTED.

Extract from a letter sent to Seville from the Orkney Islands on the 30th of September, 1991.

'I would never have left if it had been up to me, but your dad needed that job. Regardless of what you remember, you were happy here, and I should have brought you back when you were still young.

As for feeling at home in that foreign Spanish country, there's no accounting for taste. Anyway, remember what I told you when you were young: keep away from strange men, son. Because I do worry about you and the company you keep sometimes.

Love, Mum'

I missed my lit. class in the morning but made the language class in the evening. After my lecture, I went for an espresso and tapas with a couple of guys with whom I'd become friendly.

It was around nine o'clock when I returned to the flat. Saffron's leather sandals were on the wooden shoe stand in the hallway. Each sandal was perfectly aligned, a ritual that made me smile. She was fastidious about removing her shoes upon entering the flat, partly because she was scared of Maria, who had a habit of making spot checks. In stark contrast, Johan kicked his shoes off wherever he happened to be when the mood took him. It wasn't unusual to sink down onto the sofa and find one of his yellow flip-flops poking out from underneath a cushion. I had even come across the odd pair in the shower cubicle. It was no wonder they didn't get on. They were poles apart in nearly everything they did. Johan was simple enough, but Saffron was complicated. I couldn't figure her out, and that bothered me. The only thing I could work out at that moment was that she was home.

Apart from the odd car beeping its horn outside, the place was completely silent. This told me that Johan had either gone somewhere and was getting drunk or had already been out, returned drunk, and was now sleeping it off in bed.

I found Saffron sprawled across the chair in the living room. Her slim, lightly freckled, suntanned legs were dangling over the arm, swinging up and down. She was holding a Spanish thesaurus on her stomach and appearing to be completely engrossed in it despite it being upside down. From the barely audible grunt that she uttered when I said hello to the non-existent eye contact, I decided it was probably best not to question her on upside-down reading techniques. It was clear that she was giving me the cold shoulder. Having had three exes, I was well versed in the cold shoulder treatment and able to spot it regardless of any female insistence that everything was 'fine.' I told myself that whilst it might go with the territory in a relationship, I wasn't going to sweat about it as far as Saffron was concerned.

Ignoring her in much the same way she ignored me, I went into the kitchen and peered into the fridge. The tapas I'd eaten a couple of hours ago hadn't assuaged my hunger pangs very much. One measly chicken burger remained from my last visit to the local supermarket. There had been three left when I'd looked the previous morning and as Saffron was a veggie, it didn't take much working out where the other two had gone. I found two pieces of bread that Johan had somehow missed and began heating some extra virgin olive oil in the frying pan. As the oil began to sizzle and spit, Saffron appeared at the door. She leaned over to the fridge, opened it slowly, and stared intently at the contents. In truth, there were only three bottles of water and two slices of Manchego cheese that were hard around the edges and well past their sell-by date. Taking out one of the cold bottles of water, she held it against her face, then removed the cap and took a long drink. When she finished, she stared at me while holding the bottle loosely by the side of her hip. She seemed to be thinking about what to say. "Why didn't you go to literature class today?" she asked me. So that was why she was cold-shouldering me.

"I didn't get up until eleven," I replied cooly, removing the wrapping from the burger and placing it on a plate beside me. "The alarm didn't go off."

"Well, I shouted you at nine, and I knocked on your door," she said petulantly. When I didn't reply, she continued her lecture. "You know, lit. class is important for developing vocabulary, and it's an insight into the complexity of the Spanish mind." She looked at me expectantly as if I should apologise for not knowing this.

"Saffron, I am quite aware of how important lit. class is. But you're not my mother, and it's not your job to look after me," I said stiffly. Her face winced, and I immediately felt mean. "Look, I know I shouldn't miss class, but I'm an adult, and I can make my own decisions. Besides, I was reading Ramón J. Sender today for Johnson's essay, and I'm on the case. You shouldn't be worrying about me; I'm not a child, you know?" This seemed to brighten her spirits a little.

"Isn't he just marvellous?" she beamed.

"Who, Johnson?"

"No silly, Sender," she replied, missing the joke entirely. "He's just so amazing. His Réquiem novel is an indicting critique of the Civil War." There was that annoying enthusiasm again.

"I don't know if it is, or if it isn't, an indicting critique," I said, flipping the burger in the now crackling oil. "It's really slow going for me as I have to keep looking up all the vocab."

"Oh, I could help you with that," she said brightly, moving closer into my personal space. Her face was lit up like a Christmas tree with a dodgy light connection. The bright kitchen strip light illuminated every freckle on her face in a very unfavourable way.

"That's really nice of you, Saffron," I replied, flipping the burger like it was about to be served at the new El Bulli. "But it's probably better if I do it myself; otherwise, how will I learn?"

"Oh, okay," she sighed in a disappointed tone and took a step back. "I suppose it makes sense." I looked down at the bread and noticed that there were tiny specks of light green mould on the crusts of both pieces. I was so hungry I weighed up whether to just eat it anyway. I looked at my food and cursed Johan under my breath for scoffing all of the fresh bread I'd bought earlier. My chicken burger sandwich had become a sandwich without the bread bit. Preoccupied with the food situation, I hadn't noticed that Saffron was lightly pressing her very firm side against me. I felt an urgent need to switch the conversation.

"I've just been on an intercambio," I said, stepping around her to find a clean plate.

"Really?" she shrieked and gave a little excited bounce while clapping her hands together. She often reminded me of Tigger. "That's so cool. I've been meaning to arrange one myself. I haven't had time with all the classes." Another dig. I ignored it.

"Yeah, I went on one with this bloke who turned out to be gay, would you believe?" I announced this like I had actually discovered gay people and would eventually be awarded the Nobel Prize for having done so.

"No way, you're kidding?" she gasped, clapping her hands together again, hardly able to contain herself. "Wow! There are gay people in Spain. Of course, I knew there were and everything, but that's just so amazing. I hardly know anyone who's gay. I wish I did know lots of gay people. I'd love to know them. It would be incredibly interesting. I think gay people are fascinating, don't you? Do you think that I could meet him?" I thought about this for a moment.

"I'm not sure if I'm going to meet him again," I said, flipping the burger for the last time with a plastic spatula. "I might phone him next week. If I do, maybe you can come along."

"Wow, super!" she beamed. "I imagine he and I could be terrific friends."

"I have to warn you," I cautioned, putting the burger onto the empty plate and scanning the kitchen for any possible tomato ketchup. "He's not exactly what I would call a barrel of laughs."

"Well, perhaps he was nervous," she said, grinning like a

Cheshire cat. "I'll bet he's incredibly interesting when you get to know him. I can't wait to meet him." I tried to return the smile, but I was pretty sure it had come out as a grimace. Meanwhile, she sashayed off into her room, happy as the proverbial Larry. I felt a palpable relief to be left alone. I could never put my finger on it, but being in her company invariably left me exhausted. I tried to push her out of my mind when I remembered that I'd hidden some fresh bread in the top cupboard. I opened the door. It was gone.

And Saffron only eats brown.

The following day, I had a late afternoon lecture and arrived about twenty minutes early. I looked around. There were a few small groups of people, but I couldn't see anybody I knew, so I decided to kill some time in the bar.

There were no familiar faces, so I bought myself an espresso and sat at one of the small wooden tables. Pulling out Sender's *Crónica del Alba* from my bag, I tried to focus. My Spanish vocabulary increased daily, and recognising new words meant I could make more sense of what I was reading.

My head was buried in the book when I heard a small but loud group of people enter the bar. Four guys were causing a commotion, and I was surprised to see Sergio. I was even more surprised to see that he was the loudest member of the group. I watched him with interest as he laughed and joked with his friends. His behaviour was radically different to when we'd met. As I observed him, it only occurred to me that he had probably been as anxious and nervous as I had been.

They ordered espressos at the bar, and after some friendly banter with the waiter, they carried their drinks over to an empty table. Sergio caught sight of me and nodded curtly. He pulled out a wooden chair, scraping it across the marble floor and sat facing the window with his back towards me.

I didn't quite know what to make of his body language. I glanced up occasionally from my book, but he didn't give the impression that he wanted to talk to me anytime soon. After a few minutes, he said something to his friends, and they looked in my direction. He stood up and ambled over to me.

"Anything interesting?" he asked in Spanish, with his hands in his jacket pockets.

"Sender," I replied, showing him the book cover. I stuck my hand out. "Nice to see you again, Sergio." He hesitated momentarily, then took my hand and shook it briefly.

"Yes, you too," he said.

"I wasn't sure if I should call," I said awkwardly. "Should I call?" He paused as if he was giving the question some serious thought, then said,

"Yes, I would like that." Turning to walk back towards his group, he smiled and reiterated, "I would like that a lot."

I waited a few days before phoning Sergio. I had decided to give it another go partly because my observations of him in the bar convinced me he was more fun than he was letting on and also because one of the reasons for coming to Seville was to do new things and meet new people.

This time, he sounded relaxed on the phone and suggested we meet near the cathedral at nine-thirty on Wednesday. One of the things I was getting used to in Seville was that everything happened later than it ever would in England. The Sevillanos don't even think about going out until nine, and then they only think about it. Most hit the tapas bars and restaurants about ten at the weekend. "I have a good idea for a night out," he told me. "I think that maybe you will really like it." Whatever he had in mind, I neglected to mention it to Saffron. I didn't think it would be fair to subject Sergio to her wide-eyed enthusiasm when we were just getting to know each other.

When Wednesday arrived, there was a tricky moment shaking Saffron off the scent. I'd stepped out of my room when she appeared from nowhere and accosted me, asking where I was going. "I'm going to meet Johan in La Moneda. Want to come?" I asked, feeling bad about the lie but not enough to redress it. She scrunched the freckles on her nose at the thought of it, just as I knew she would. She would rather have her manicured fingernails pulled out with a pair of rusty pliers than spend an evening in Johan's company.

"I don't think so," she scoffed, turning her back on me and entering the bathroom. "And when you see him, will you ask if he knows where my Walkman is? I can't find it anywhere."

"Err…yeah, course I will," I said, recalling that he'd left the flat an hour earlier in a pair of my cargo shorts while humming INXS very loudly. On top of his oversized blonde locks, he wore the very same Walkman earphones that Saffron had been looking for.

After she disappeared, I ventured out of the downstairs door and onto the street. The barrio of Triana stretched out before me with energy and vibrancy as the traffic razzed around, car horns sounded, and Spanish voices shouted at each other. There was an exuberance and vitality about Spanish people that I loved. I made my way through the cacophony and headed towards the city centre and the cathedral area.

The cathedral is Seville's centrepiece. It's a wondrous, gothic masterpiece encapsulating Seville's religious and architectural history. Imposing in its grandeur, it towers over the main street and adds an almost arrogant resonance to the city. It is made all the more striking as it stands alongside the Moorish Giralda tower. This former minaret was converted into a bell tower, an example of Christian and Muslim culture working in wonderful harmony not always evident elsewhere in the world.

Strolling down the main drag of Constitución, I was once again captivated by the cathedral looming above the road, almost erasing the night sky above. When I reached the impressive entrance to the cathedral, Sergio was already there, an unusual trait for a Spaniard, but as he'd already reminded me, he wasn't really a Spaniard.

He cut a Harry Lime figure in The Third Man as he stepped out of the shadowed doorway, and the early streetlight lit up his face. He offered me his large hand with a 'Qué tal?' I was conscious of his size. Sergio must have been six-three, as he had at least three inches on me. I shook his hand and replied,

"Bien, y tú?"

"I am very glad that you have called," he said, switching back to English and zipping up his grey windcheater, even though it must have been over twenty degrees. "I didn't think you would do so. I thought that perhaps you have a problem with gay men."

I thought about the bloke from the wine bar.

"No, only if they have dodgy haircuts," I replied, holding his gaze with a straight poker face. He peered at me through dark Basque eyes.

"I do not understand this, but it is a joke. Is that correct?"

"Not a very good one," I laughed.

"This is the truth," he smiled broadly, and for the first time, I saw warmth and humour in his eyes that had been previously hidden from me. "Vamos. I take you to La Carbonería. My friend is playing there, and he is very good."

"What's La Carbonería?" I asked uneasily.

"You will see," he grinned at my apprehension. "Don't worry." With that, he began to walk with long, loping strides as I followed at his side, trying to keep up. We crossed to the back of the cathedral, taking the left up the Calle Santo Tomás and continued towards the Barrio Santa Cruz, the old Jewish area of the city.

As we took a sharp right, we suddenly found ourselves in the middle of picture-postcard Spain. We were surrounded by quaint, whitewashed houses with exotic fauna tumbling over balconies and cascading down the walls like exquisite floral waterfalls. We made our way down narrow cobbled alleys, which led into vibrant squares full of bustling restaurants and bars. The crowds sat outside in the warm autumn air, enjoying a drink, tapas, or both. Their chatter flowed, along with the light haze of cigarette smoke that always seemed to accompany middle-class Sevillanos. Many wore multi-coloured jumpers draped around their necks in the US college style. Some Spanish guys in uni referred to them unflatteringly as pijos, which is a difficult word to translate, but the sentiment is one of a sort of over-privileged toff. I had been told that the barrio was one of the more expensive parts of the city. "Come on Sergio, what's La Carbonería?" I asked again, pulling my eyes away from the beauty of the barrio.

"It is what you might call a Flamenco bar," he said, looking sideways at me. "It has too many tourists for the real Sevillanos to call it Flamenco, but my friend plays there because the tourists have money." Having observed Sergio with his friends, I wondered why he was so serious about everything around me and was beginning to question if he would ever lighten up.

When we got there, and I swear it's not an easy place to find, I discovered that it had previously been an old coal bunker, hence its name. It had been lovingly converted into a beautiful bar with a flower-filled garden and outdoor candle-lit seating. Though the hour was early by Seville standards and especially early by Flamenco standards, the place was crammed with a tourist crowd. A group of Japanese girls in their twenties were buzzing around and photographing everything that moved or didn't, and a few antipodean backpackers were dotted about. Occasionally, the odd American voice rose above the crowded tables and cut through the air; the bar had drawn a mixed international crowd, and it wasn't hard to see why.

As we approached the narrow door, a company of old men with dark leather skin played guitars that were seemingly attached to their fingers. They were seated in an alcove, tapping their hands rapidly against the guitar body in between effortless strumming. Their fingers moved so fast that your eyes couldn't take in what they were doing. A chorus of gravelly, smoke-strained voices cried in melancholic rhythms, which you could feel in your very soul. It was beautiful and haunting. I followed Sergio as he weaved amongst the crowds of people and down into the cellars, the bowels of the old warehouse. Rapid clapping filled the air, and feet banged in glorious time to the music.

We pushed through to the bar area, where I bought drinks. Then, following Sergio, he led us to a long table full of

Australians, where he pulled out a couple of free seats at the end.

"We will stay here until my friend plays, okay?" said Sergio, looking at the stage where the current performance was finishing.

"Sure," I replied, pleased we had a good view. He took a drink from his glass and gestured towards the toilet. I nodded, and he disappeared in that direction. As I watched the people on stage getting ready, I felt a tap on my shoulder, and a voice behind me asked,

"Is it safe to stand this close, or am I at risk of having your drink thrown all over me?" I turned to see the girl from the university bar, Maggie, standing behind me, holding a glass of red wine.

"Hello again!" I replied, surprised to see her there. She wore a lime green cut-off top tied across hipster jeans, revealing a slightly protruding stomach and a piercing. It should have been an unflattering look, but somehow, on her, it wasn't.

"No, not this time. Well, not if I can help it. It's a crime to spill beer, and if it isn't, it should be."

"Have you been here before?" she asked me, sitting down.

"No. It's the first time for me. It's a great place, though, isn't it?" I replied.

"It's fantastic," she agreed. "Well worth the half an hour we spent trying to find it. How did you get here?"

"I'm here with an intercambio," I told her. "His friend's playing here tonight, so I'm out practising my Spanish. What about you?"

"I'm out with my flatmates," she said, pulling a face and looking over her shoulder. Lowering her voice, she confided, "To be honest, they're both a bit...how shall I say it...boring?"

"Oh dear," I laughed. "That's not something that can be levelled very easily at my flatmates, at least."

"Are you still living with that Saffron girl?" she asked me, glancing around. "I only met her briefly, but she seems like an odd character. Is she always rude to people she meets for the first time, or was I an exception?" I saw a glint in Maggie's eyes and wondered how many glasses of wine she'd had. I suppressed an urge to laugh. This was mainly at her directness but also at her use of the word 'that,' which is always a giveaway as to what someone thinks without actually saying it. I lost count of all the times my mother said: 'Are you still going out with that Rachel?' 'Are you still friends with that Doug?'

"She's a bit different, that's for sure," I said, putting my empty glass on the table beside her. "She can be a bit self-obsessed, but she's okay. Our other flatmate is a mad Swede. He's great, even if he does nick everything in sight. We're sharing a flat in Triana."

"I'm in La Macarena," she told me, taking a drink from the glass she was holding. She pressed her hand against her mouth to suppress a hiccup. She swallowed and grimaced. "My flat's not that nice, and my flatmates are okay, just incredibly boring…" She tailed off, and I noticed Sergio approaching from behind her.

"Here's my friend," I said. "Let me introduce you." Maggie turned as Sergio arrived.

"Hello," she said. "I'm Maggie, a sort of friend of…Andy, isn't it?" I felt a little miffed that she hadn't recalled my name easily when she remembered Saffron's without much difficulty.

"Sergio," he replied, extending his hand. "Encantado." Maggie shook it and then broke out into what sounded like native-tongue-sounding Spanish. I didn't grasp much of what she said, but she and Sergio spoke to each other animatedly, as if they'd known each other for years. Their conversation was so rapid I could barely follow, let alone join in; I watched them, feeling like a spare part. They were so caught up in whatever they were talking about that they didn't even glance at me as they laughed and joked together.

"Anyway," she said, breaking away from her conversation with Sergio and finally noticing me. "I'd better go and see where the two bores have got to and what their plans are. They wanted to get away early and are probably hanging around waiting for me to go home with them. It was very nice to meet you, Sergio, and it was nice not having you throw a drink at me, Andy," she said with a mischievous grin. Sergio took her hand and, in an exaggerated gesture, bent over and kissed it. "Why, thank you," said Maggie, placing the back of her hand against her forehead and playing along gamely. Then she gave me a wink, turned toward the entrance, and was soon lost amongst the crowd.

"She's a very nice girl, no?" said Sergio, breaking my concentration.

"Yeah, great personality," I muttered, straining my neck to see if I could see her. "And her Spanish is pretty good by the sound of it."

"She told me her grandmother is Spanish and has been coming to Spain every year since she was a little girl. So it does not surprise me. You are interested in her?" he asked, with a glint in those dark brown eyes.

"Me?" I exclaimed, caught a little off guard, "No. She's not my type. I mean, she's nice and everything. It's just that I usually go for someone a little less...err—."

"Gorda?" I was horrified by his use of the Spanish word 'fat.'

"No, no! Not that at all," I protested strongly. "I'm not that shallow. And besides, Maggie's not...she's only...err...well, a tiny bit overweight, that's all." Sergio scanned my face before smiling.

"I think we are all, how you say, shallow, at times, no? Come, my friend is about to play." We pushed our way through the growing crowd to get closer to the small stage. The people on it began to play, sing, and dance. It was incredible. Watching Sergio's friend Emilio play Flamenco guitar was an extraordinary thing to behold, and I was mesmerised. It seemed as if the guitar was an extension of the self, with hands and fingers moving at breakneck speed around the neck, touching chords and notes I never knew existed. All the while, the Sevillanos on stage and the very few in the audience clapped in perfect unison to the beat of the music. This was while the foreigners, such as myself, found the rhythm almost impossible to replicate despite our best efforts.

During the twenty minutes that Emilio played, two gorgeous young girls attired in full gypsy regalia wove intricate patterns and tapped out their rhythms in a performance that would have made any hot-blooded male sweaty under the collar. This was accompanied by an excruciatingly thin, old gitano (gypsy male) wailing beautifully in a language that was nothing like the Spanish Johnson was introducing us to on the rare occasions I'd made class.

Later that evening, when Emilio had finished, he joined us, and it became clear he was more than a friend to Sergio. We chatted for a while in Spanish, well, as much as I could, while Sergio kept leaning forward and putting his hand on Emilio's knee.

When I left La Carbonería, it was around two in the morning and still very lively. Sergio had returned with Emilio to his flat, and I wandered the thirty-five-minute stroll back to my piso. All the while, I kept thinking about the wink that the girl Maggie had given me and what a pity it was that she wasn't my type.

8 LOVE TO HATE YOU.

Extract from a letter sent to Southern England on the 15th of October, 1991

'....not really that super. He keeps taking my things, and he's perfectly beastly. Worse, he seems to get on with the hideous troll who keeps coming in and shouting in Spanish at me. I do like my other flatmate, though. He's very good-looking, and I'm sure he likes me too because he keeps looking at me in a funny way....'

Five weeks into my Sevillian adventure, clear patterns had emerged in my relations with my new flatmates. In common was the fact the two of them had some very annoying habits. However, a palpable difference had become evident to me: whereas I could live with Johan's annoying habits, I wasn't sure that I could live as easily with Saffron's.

To summarise, Johan snored, drank too much, and took anything that wasn't nailed down as his own personal property. I often found him walking around the flat in anything from one of my T-shirts to a pair of my undies. Not only did food go missing when he was alone in the flat, but he would have little problem eating it in front of you. He was just as likely to pilfer your CDs, books, or Walkman if he had a mind to.

On the positive side, he was extremely likeable and personable; everywhere he went, people were drawn to him. His dry sense of humour and easy-going nature made him attractive to both men and women alike. He was also much more intelligent than he cared to project and as liable to say something profound as he was something stupid. I noticed he was happy enough to play the affable fool when it suited him, especially around Saffron. I took him with me to meet Sergio, and by the end of the evening, he was laughing uncontrollably at Johan's antics. Johan somehow managed to 'borrow' Sergio's new hat at the end of the evening. "Aren't you going to give it back?" I asked when he appeared for a late breakfast, wearing it and very little else the next day.

"Why ever should I, dear boy?" he replied. "It looks so much better on me than on him."

"Johan," I rolled my eyes. "You live in Cloud Cuckoo Land. He's like a male model, and you're...well...not."

"Yes," he agreed. "That's true. All the more remarkable that it should look so much better on me."

Whereas Johan's crimes were many, Saffron's could be reduced to two. The less serious one was that she had a bad habit of talking incessantly about her bowel habits. I don't know why it bothered me so much other than my mother had raised me to think that not only did ladies not talk about the toilet, but also to believe that they actually didn't go. In the whole time that I was with Rachel, I don't think I ever heard her so much as accidentally break wind. So to hear Saffron exit a toilet while you were buttering the toast with whatever bit of bread and butter Johan hadn't used and say, 'Well, that was mostly wind' or 'My word, the veggie diet is super for passing, but that was a little smelly,' was something I didn't appreciate.

But far and away, her worst crime was that she never had anything positive to say about anyone except me. This meant that everyone around me was reduced to a bitchy comment or snide remark. The two girls in the flat opposite us were 'the German lesbians.' Johan became 'The dreadful Swede.' Maria was referred to as 'the troll' and so on. It wasn't just annoying but highly tedious. I began to dread being alone with her. The funny thing was, though, no matter how horrible Saffron was to Johan —and she was pretty rude to him most of the time—Johan never said a bad word about her to me and was always very polite when he spoke to her.

By the time autumn arrived, I was avoiding Saffron as much as possible. One way I achieved this was to skip the odd class that we shared. This was less of a tactical manoeuvre on my part and more to do with Johan's extraordinary persuasive powers. I mean, he never went to any classes. What I found remarkable was that even though he didn't go to class, his level of Spanish conversation was moving well beyond mine and Saffron's. Saffron was a good linguist, but Johan was gifted. Whenever Maria came charging into the flat to complain about something we'd done, which was quite frequent in those early weeks, Johan would disarm her with controlled ease. Within minutes, the human tornado would be laughing and shaking her finger at him as though he were a favourite son that she couldn't be angry at for very long. Then he would send her away with kisses on both cheeks, leaving a warm, affectionate smile on her face. This was contrasted with the fact that Saffron was absolutely terrified of her, and I couldn't understand anything she said. If Johan wasn't around, I would look at Maria with an expression on my face that was as empty as a politician's promise. Eventually, she would give up and, exasperated with my lack of understanding, would march off, jabbering in a loud voice all the way back to her shop.

Then, there were the constant petty flatmate arguments between Johan and Saffron. I'd been in student digs in Leeds when I did my degree, so it wasn't as if I wasn't used to them. But these were on a whole new level, with the most childish disagreements over Johan stealing Saffron's chocolate stash. There is something about the theory that women who don't drink alcohol substitute chocolate for it, although Johan was like quite a few women I'd met who enjoyed a fair quantity of both. I was more often than not on Johan's side, even though he was the instigator of most of the arguments. I saw more than a bit of my mother in Saffron; she was what I would call a stasher, whereas Johan reminded me a little of myself as a young boy, where the fun lay less in eating my mum's chocolate stash than proving to myself, and in turn to her, that I could find it. What added to all the calamity was that Saffron refused to keep her stash in her room, which she could lock with a key if she wanted to. 'I shouldn't have to,' she would argue pointlessly.

"But you do have to, as he keeps finding it and eating it," I would tell her, exasperated. "And then you're stressed about it and make a big fuss."

It made no difference where she hid the stash. Johan had an unnerving psychic ability to sniff it out. He'd find it behind the bread bin, in the linen cupboard, tucked under old newspapers in the magazine rack, and even inside the small electric cupboard in the hallway we never used. It was rarely there when she came to find it. What made the whole thing worse was when he left evidence of the discarded stash wrappings around the flat for Saffron to find when she got home.

The arguments that followed were of the same pattern, with Saffron becoming overdramatic, screaming theft, and threatening to get the police. Meanwhile, Johan would look contrite and talk her around by promising never to do it again. Despite the fact he was clearly in the wrong, he always came out of these arguments ahead in my eyes as Saffron's behaviour was petty and spiteful.

It all kicked off one afternoon.

Johan discovered a bar of chocolate that had been concealed inside a pillowcase. Saffron must have been convinced he'd never find it as she'd hidden it at the bottom of an ironing pile. Johan hadn't gone near an iron since I'd been there, and even I thought that would have been a safe enough bet. Saffron stormed through the door as he was seated on the settee eating the chocolate. "You hideous Swede!" she screamed at him, running over and snatching the empty wrapper out of his hand. "That's theft. I could report you to the police."

"But, my dear girl," he replied calmly, "however, would I know it was yours when I found it in the ironing?" She turned to me.

"Andy, will you not tell him? Just for once, won't you stop taking his side?" I sighed and put down the paper I'd been reading.

"Look, I'm not taking sides. But you leave stuff where he can find it. Why don't you just keep it in your room? You wouldn't go in her room, would you, Johan?"

"Certainly not, old chap. A lady must have her privacy," he said, with a mock solemn face. Saffron stamped her feet, gave out a loud scream, and stormed out of the flat, slamming the door so loudly behind her that the walls shook. I looked pointedly at Johan, and he shrugged, giving me the wryest of smiles.

"I don't know why you do it! Can't you buy your own chocolate?" I asked despairingly.

"And what would be the fun in that?" he replied with a devious smile. "I think she enjoys the mental challenge." I tried not to laugh.

"Johan, you're unbelievable," I told him, shaking my head. I had to give it to him; he was incorrigible.

"Thank you. I will take that as a compliment," he said, taking his glasses off and wiping them on his T-shirt. He lifted them up towards the light at the window and peered through the glass lens, "Are you coming out for a few drinks?"

"No, I need to do a bit more reading."

"Okay, we'll be in La Moneda if you change your mind," he said. Then, licking his thumb, he wiped it across the lens and gave it another vigorous rub with his T-shirt.

I went to my room, opened my book, and lay on the bed, enjoying the warmth of the late afternoon sun shining through the window. Three hours later, I was fast asleep.

I was abruptly woken up at about two in the morning to the sound of the front door banging shut and an obviously drunk Johan bumbling about in the living room. Cursing him under my breath, I got up to tell him to keep the noise down before he woke Saffron up and really set things off. I got to the door in my boxers and switched the living room light on. There was a figure picking itself up from a drunken fall. To my horror, it wasn't Johan, the useless tosspot, but Saffron. "Saffron? Are you okay?" I asked in a concerned voice. I reached across to grab her elbow as she wobbled, precariously close to knocking over the floor lamp.

"I've had a wittle drinky," she slurred, now standing up with my assistance. "Shorry for any noishe."

"But you don't drink," I said stupidly because it was pretty clear that she was trollied.

"Incorrect. Incorrect becaush I ham drunk," she giggled manically, clawing without success at a light switch to her right, which I'd already switched on. "Sho, incorrect." She looked like she was going to fall again, so I grabbed her around the waist. "I'm shorry, Andy, but I need to go to bed now." She leaned her head against my shoulder, and her knees began to give way again. "You could put me into bed and shake avantage shof me if you wanted to." Then she pressed herself against me, and I realised that, as I had been expecting Johan with Saffron long in bed, I only had my boxers on. I couldn't let go of her as she'd fallen, but she was pressing hard against me now. Things took a downward spiral, and it became one of those unfortunate occasions when the sexual organ begins to operate completely separately from the mind. For my own part, I didn't want 'to shake advantage' of Saffron. Not because I didn't fancy her, attractive as she was. I wouldn't have dreamt of doing anything to Saffron in that state. Regardless of that fact, though, Mr Organ was telling her something to the contrary, and she was picking up on his fairly obvious signals. "Mmmmmmmm, Andy," she slurred. "I love you. Do you love me?" This was bad. No, wait, this was very bad.

"You're a little bit drunk, Saffron," I said, moving my hips into a less tactile position. "Let me help you to bed." In retrospect, that was probably not the best thing to have said at that particular moment.

"I like the shound of that, Andy. It shounds shouper." She followed this with a very loud hiccup and said, "I'm not a virgin, you know." Her unfocused eyes wandered over my face for a response, which I determined she wasn't getting. I ignored the comment and turned her around gently but firmly. Guiding her towards the bedroom, I pushed her lightly from behind with my hands resting on her shoulders, the way you can with drunk people. I eventually got her inside the door and fumbled for her light as she propelled herself towards the bed. Dropping facedown into her pillow, she mumbled something about needing to remove her dress.

"I'll get you some water. You need to drink something, or else you'll have a massive hangover in the morning." I went to the kitchen and poured a glass of cold water from a bottle in the fridge.

I returned to her room with the water only to find she'd done a faster disappearing act than Houdini. Wondering where on earth she'd got to in her state, I heard a flushing noise behind me in the bathroom. In the time it had taken me to get the water, she'd upped and gone to the sanctity of the sacred place for drunks.

I knocked, then pushed the door softly to see whether she had locked it. It swung open, and she was doing the old toilet bowl cuddle. Having stripped off her sundress, she was down to her pink knickers and bra in what must have constituted record time. I felt uncomfortable seeing her half-naked. I wasn't sure if it was an invasion of privacy. I asked myself if I should leave or stay and look after her. It looked like she'd finished for the moment without being sick, so I stepped into the bathroom and sat her up. I put the glass of water into her shaking hands, and she lifted it gingerly towards her mouth to take a sip. Saffron's face looked a little pallid as she raised it towards the ceiling and gurgled. Then she swirled the water around her mouth, making her cheeks suck in and out like miniature bellows before swallowing. After a while, she leaned back against the wall with a deep breath. She placed the glass to one side and closed her eyes. I pulled away a strip of toilet paper from the loo roll on the wall to wipe her chin where some water had spilt. Pushing her damp hair away from her face, I noticed how pretty she looked. She opened her eyes to look up at me pathetically while I took hold of her hand like you might a small, helpless child. "Come on. Up you get," I said, dropping the tissue into the bowl and heaving her up from the floor. I put her arm around my shoulders, and she slumped against me, unsteady on her feet.

"I love you, Andy," she slurred. "Really love you." I tried to pay no heed and, sliding my arm under her armpit, I pulled her towards the living room. She seemed docile enough until we passed the couch, where she suddenly sprang to life like one of those zombies in the films that had been hit with a shovel and that you were convinced was finally dead. She flung her arms around my neck and began pulling my head down. Caught completely unawares by the sudden zombie-like lease of life, I staggered backwards onto the couch, where we rolled over and toppled onto the floor. She was now on top of me and kissing me hard. For a moment, I'd responded without thinking, and my arms found their way around her slim waist. I caressed the nape of her back. "Oh, Andy. Yes," she said, breaking away from the kiss and pulling both bra straps down her arms to expose a very pert pair of breasts. Suddenly, I realised what I was doing and started to pull her straps back up over her shoulders, saying,

"No, No! We can't do this, Saffron." As we lay there in a heap in nothing but our underwear, our body parts entangled, her bra at half-mast, the door opened, and a very drunk Johan stumbled in.

"Is this a private party, or can anyone join in?" he asked before sliding down the wall onto the floor.

"You, my dear friend, are a sly old dog," he said the next day, winking at me across the breakfast table and reaching over to take some of my toast.

"It wasn't what it looked like," I said wearily. "I was trying to extricate myself. He waved a half-eaten piece of toast at the grammar book I was studying and declared,

"Not very successfully from where I was standing."

"Seriously, she was nearly as drunk as you were," I protested. "And I was helping her into bed. Like a gentleman. You do have them in Sweden, don't you?"

"I'm sure you were the perfect gentleman. I would definitely help her into bed myself if I were in the same situation. Except she prefers your help in this department, I am thinking."

"Don't go there. I prefer not to think about it," I said,

massaging my throbbing temples. The only sound in the apartment was the hum of the fridge and the odd passing car outside. I was tired and not in the mood for his jibes. With a sigh, I picked my book back up and pretended to look at the usage of the verb conocer. He reached over to take the last piece of my toast, and I slapped his hand away.

"Where is the lovely lady now?" he enquired, picking remnants of food from his teeth.

"Gone to the supermarket, I imagine," I said, putting the book down again. "Probably to replace the food and chocolate you nicked. It's going to be embarrassing when she gets back."

"Why don't you come out for a few beers with your uncle Johan then?"

"Don't you ever go to classes?"

"Not if I can avoid them," he laughed, swatting his hand at an annoying fly that had joined our company. "Anyway, I wanted to show you the bar behind the cathedral. They do the best gambas al ajillo I have ever tasted. Come on. My treat." It was tempting, but I was going to have to face the music with Saffron one way or another, and I preferred to get it over and done with.

"Nah, I'll pass and take a rain check," I said, getting up to go to the bathroom.

"Your loss," he smiled at me. As I rose from the table, he reached over for the toast. I entered the bathroom and pulled the cord for the light. I was immediately hit by the smell.

"Johan!" I shouted back down the corridor. "It stinks in here."

"I haven't used it today, old chum."

The combined veggie and alcohol diet didn't bear thinking about.

When Saffron returned a few hours later, it was not the awkward, sheepish young lady I had expected. "I'm going," she told me, matter-of-factly putting two full shopping bags on the table.

"Going where?" I asked, puzzled, putting the TV remote down.

"I'm leaving the flat," she replied as if to an idiot. "I'm going to live with a group of girls who are all really nice in La Macarena. It will be super. Unlike here. Where it really is not very super at all. Not with you and the dreadful Swede."

"If this is about last night, you don't have to—"

"It's not about last night," she snarled at me with an attitude usually reserved for Johan. She picked up a book, waved it around in frustration, and then let rip. "It's about you and him. You've left me for him, and I'm unhappy here. Does that surprise you?"

Whilst this 'you left me for him' was a bit dramatic, I saw a grain of truth in it. Johan and I were close, but Saffron wasn't close to either of us. In some ways, she'd been pushed out by our laddish behaviour, not purposely, but pushed out all the same. I was at a loss for words. She turned away, dropped the book into a bag and began to haphazardly stuff the rest of her belongings into it with fury. I got up and walked awkwardly towards her. This behaviour was so out of character that I began to feel concerned.

"Look, if there's anything I can—"

"Don't," she growled. Then she breathed in deeply through her nose like she did when she was in one of her yoga positions and calmly pushed her palm flat out towards me, "Come any closer! My mind's made up. If you could keep out of my way, Andy, now that would be super."

"That's going to be difficult, considering we share one or two classes."

"Maybe not for long."

Then she turned away gracefully, leaving me slightly perplexed and feeling more than a little disconcerted by what had just happened.

There was no point in talking to Johan when he got back as it was a) two in the morning and b) a very drunk Johan who was 'singing' what I imagined were lewd Swedish football chants.

That caused one of Maria's visits the next day. She bustled in through the door without knocking and started the hand waving and shouting that always accompanied these visits. I caught a couple of words which sounded like 'noise' and 'last night.' Saffron had already left for an early class, thankfully. I told Maria in my best Spanish that any noise last night had nothing to do with me, and then I went to fetch Johan from his room. It was one of those moments when the useless toast-stealing git had his uses. After shouting at him for five minutes, I eventually resorted to throwing water on him to get a response. He opened a bleary red eye and asked what all the commotion was about. When I explained that a very irate Maria was in the lounge waiting for him, he staggered out of bed, wearing only my boxer shorts, to talk to her.

Five minutes later, she'd left, laughing like a little girl who'd just had her first fairground ride. Johan had told her some story about Saffron's new boyfriend coming around drunk and kicking his head in and being an absolute hero. "Nice," I told him. "Good job, Saffron's leaving."

"Sad, my dear boy, but now we must get someone who is a little more fun. A little more like us," he said, looking into the mirror side-on and pulling his stomach in. He then started to do squats whilst I tried to reason with him.

"I'm not sure getting someone like us is that good an idea," I suggested. "We need a little tempering. Another one of you or me could see Maria throwing us out. And talking of Maria, we need the rent next week, and we'll be short of Saffron's thirty thousand for the next rent."

"You make a good point," he said, the bones in his knees cracking as he got up from his final squat. "I myself am paid up but broken, as you say."

"Broke, Johan. You mean broke."

"Yes, broke. I cannot believe I was grammatically incorrect there," he chided himself. "Do you have the money?"

"I could swing sixty thousand for this month, but not again," I said, unable to take my eyes away from his Swedish version of the sit-up. He jerked himself up and down like a maniac for about ten seconds before flopping onto his back, panting.

"Besides, if I stick with you, I'll be broke before Christmas. I'm well over budget as Unfriendly's has been taking far too many of my hard-extorted pesetas, and they've still not been nice to us. We need another flatmate, and we need one quickly."

I went off to class, and he went off to bed, presumably worn out from his 'exercise.' My analysis of the situation wasn't positive. Most students would have found somewhere by now, but who would want to share it with two reprobates like Johan and me?

When I got to the flat later that evening, I was relieved to find Saffron had gone and without any awkward goodbyes. There was no note either unless Johan had eaten it. I breathed a sigh of relief, went into my bedroom and lay down on the bed, wondering how we could find someone at such short notice to pay a share of the rent.

9 WIND OF CHANGE.

Extract from a letter sent to Seville on the 20th of October, 1991

'...due out next month, and the word in the mags is that it will blow you away. I agree. Rattle and Hum wasn't their best, but this one is gonna be a totally new sound and put them back where they belong. I sent for my Nirvana tickets today. They're playing here on the 5th of December, and it's going to be mint.

Okay, I've been avoiding this, so before I sign off, I have a bit of an apology to make. You'll never guess who I bumped into the other day…'

I woke up the following day to the realisation that Saffron was no longer living with us, and it felt strange, sort of liberating. Until she'd left, I hadn't realised how claustrophobic I'd begun to feel being around her. This was intertwined with a weird feeling that I might actually miss her. Then there was the immediate concern about the fact that Maria's rent was due the next week and we couldn't keep paying the full rent between us indefinitely. We needed another flatmate and quickly.

I lay there wondering how to find someone to share the rent. It wasn't long before an urgent need to go to the bathroom interrupted my thoughts. I got out of bed and felt my way in the dark. On Maria's orders, Johan had pulled all the shutters down. The neighbours had recently made complaints to Maria. They'd been privy to watching the hideous Swede lollop about whilst attired in only a pair of Everton undies on his way to the bathroom or kitchen. As I got there, I pulled on the thin cord to hit the light and lifted the seat. I froze in horror.

What awaited me was a vegetarian present from Saffron. I took in a couple of deep breaths, aimed the point of the brush downwards, and hit the flush, where it was sucked below the stormy ocean, never to be seen again.

A couple of minutes later, I exited the bathroom. At that moment, the door to Johan's room opened, and he staggered out dressed only in a pair of yellow Winnie the Pooh boxer shorts. "Has it gone?" he asked, holding his dick with both hands. "Has it gone?"

"You knew it was in there?"

"Yes, that's why I haven't taken a leak all night," he said, pushing past me, lifting the toilet lid and taking out his Swedish trouser snake. "But I knew you could get rid of it. I had every confidence in you, old chap." I rolled my eyes and left him to it. When he got back into the lounge, relief was written all over his face. He went over to my tape and shoved a U2 bootleg Doug had sent me from the upcoming new album in the deck.

"Don't play it too loud, or you'll have the German girls over," I warned him, trying to figure out from the grammar book when the Spanish used the imperfect tense. "And anyway, you should be out searching for a flatmate, or we're knackered."

"Do not worry, good sir," he said, turning the music up. "Something will happen; it always does."

"Not if you just stand there in your Winnie the Pooh shorts, it won't!" I said over the music. "Turn that down, will you? It's not even your tape."

"What did you say?" he grinned, clearly enjoying himself. Then, all of a sudden, he reached for the dial and lowered the volume. "Shhhh! What is that noise?"

He was right. There was a noise. It was the doorbell.

I opened the door, and the last person in the world I expected to see was standing there. With one hand on her hip and an elbow on the doorway frame, she stood in a pose that Marilyn Monroe would be proud of. It was Maggie. "Hello," she said, grinning brightly. I'd never noticed before, but her green eyes were quite striking against her fair skin. She was wearing a tight, black spaghetti-strap top, which made her big boobs look enormous. She'd eschewed the jeans I'd seen her wear previously for even tighter ones, which clearly stated she cared even less than ever. I was glad Saffron had gone, as I don't think I could have coped with her bitchy remarks. "Well, are you going to leave me standing here, or can I come in?" she pressed.

"Sorry! Come in, please," I said, caught off guard. "Go through; the lounge is there." She brushed past me and into the tiny hall. Her jeans didn't cover everything, not that she cared. When she entered the lounge, Johan was still wearing his Winnie the Pooh boxers and two odd socks he'd probably found under one of the cushions. Obviously, on hearing the doorbell, he'd decided to dress for company. Not that he gave a toss, either. You might have seen it as an extraordinary general meeting of the couldn't-give-a-toss society.

"Hello, and who are you, my dear?" he asked, getting up and shaking her hand.

"I'm Maggie," she replied, not looking in the slightest bit perturbed as the mad Swede shook her hand, let go, and gave his crotch a ball scratch.

"And to what do we owe this unexpected pleasure?" Johan enquired. He sat back down but continued to rake ignominiously away at his nether region.

"I bumped into Saffron a couple of hours ago at the uni," Maggie replied, switching her head back and forth between the two of us. My heart sank a little at the mention of Saffron's name. I was still feeling guilty about how it had all ended.

"She told me that she had left the flat in Triana, that she couldn't stand living with a pair of losers any longer, and that she was better off out of there because it was simply dreadful. I'd met Andy briefly before," she said, by way of a very brief explanation to Johan. "And apart from the fact that he was with an odd bird like Saffron, he seemed okay," she laughed. "Anyway, I figured you might be in the market for a new flatmate?" She sat down uninvited and conversed exclusively with Johan as though I wasn't in the room.

"Do you like drinking, and do you have the rent?" Johan asked, cutting to the chase whilst staring at her cleavage.

"Yes to the first part and yes to the second part," she replied, crossing her legs, stretching her arms back, and lounging on the sofa like she already owned the place. I remember thinking how attractive that gesture might have been if she was someone I could have fancied.

"What do you say, Andy?" Johan asked as he finally tore his gaze away from her chest and looked at me with a big grin like Christmas had come early.

"Oh, after Saffron, I'm sure Andy's in," Maggie said, waving her hands at him and giggling. "Anyway, he'd better be, as he owes me laundry costs from pouring a drink all over my new blouse and jeans." I was lost for words when Johan stepped in with an invitation.

"Unfriendly's it is, then." He got up, had a final scratch, and sloped off to his room to put some more of my clothes on.

"Unfriendly's?" Maggie smiled quizzically at me.

"You'll see soon enough," I said, feeling bewildered at the speed with which a new female flatmate had been thrust upon me.

Two amazing things happened when we got to the bar. The first was that Maggie asked us what we'd like to drink and then went to the bar to get the order. Johan was very impressed, as you might have imagined. He sat down at a corner table on the outside terrace and hid under the sunshade to shield himself from the surprisingly strong October rays. Being Swedish, his skin burnt if he went too near the toaster in the flat. We took our seats, and he leaned in towards me. "I like her," he said, resting his chin on the heel of his hand and tilting his head sideways as he watched her at the bar. "I like her a great deal."

"I can tell. Yeah, she's nice," I agreed and also turned to watch her chat with the worst of Unfriendly's barmen, a tall, rude ogre Johan had christened the Dark Lord. I thought about how unpleasant he must have been to poor Maggie as I saw her walking back towards us without any drinks.

"Don't worry," I consoled her as she reached the table. "There's a knack to getting served in this place, and that guy is probably the worst of them all. The trick is not to take it personally. I'll go and get them."

"He's bringing the drinks over," she said, looking at me as if I'd lost my mind.

"The Dark Lord is bringing the drinks over!" Johan shouted a little too loudly, almost falling off his chair.

"Yeah, Juan's bringing the drinks over," she repeated, as though she was addressing two dimwits. Ignoring our gaping mouths, she put her canvas handbag down on the table and rooted around inside it.

"He has a name, and it is Juan," Johan said, tilting his head backwards and stretching his arms up to the sky. "The Dark Lord is Juan." We heard a noise behind us, and the Dark Lord of rudeness dropped his silver tray and put three paper beer mats, followed by three Cruzcampos, on the table and said,

"Buenos días" in the chirpiest of chirpy voices. Maggie put her bag back down on the floor and reached for her drink. She held it out to him, smiling.

"Salud!"

I swear Juan gave a smile that was sweeter than chocolate con churros.

10 EVERYBODY DANCE NOW.

Extract from a letter sent to Northern England on the 27th of October, 1991

"...can't believe you bumped into her. I always knew he'd never leave his wife, so what you said doesn't surprise me. He really is a slimeball, and if there is such a thing as karma, he's got it coming to him. Don't worry about 'accidentally' giving her my address. I (of all people) know how persuasive she can be when she wants something. Although I haven't got a clue what she might want it for. Maybe she's going to write me a letter and beg me to take her back! If she is, she can forget it. I've moved on, literally.

You look after yourself and I'll catch you for a drink when I'm back in July if you can't get out here.

Take it easy, Doug, and thanks again for writing.

Andy.'

The following Wednesday, I met Sergio for a drink at the university. He was attending a late English class, and we'd previously agreed to meet in one of the upstairs bars near the English department afterwards. "How are you?" he asked in English, taking his coat and hat off and folding them neatly on the table in front of him.

"Good," I replied, taking out a five hundred peseta coin from my pocket. "And you?"

"I am well," he told me, ignoring the coin. "I buy you the drink. Beer?"

"Oh, go on then," I said, rolling my eyes. When he returned with the drinks, we chatted about nothing in particular for ten minutes when he asked me a question that stopped me in my tracks. "Would you like to go to a club with me this Friday?"

"I thought you went to...erm..." I smiled apologetically. "You know? Your sort of clubs on a Friday?"

"I do," he said, flashing his white teeth in a wide grin. "Do you want to come? I think you might find it *interesante*." Find it interesting? I had to sit back to think about that. A gay club? Me go to a gay club? What if I got hit on? I wouldn't know how to handle it in more ways than one.

On the other hand, if I said no, Sergio might be offended and wasn't my coming to Seville all about doing things I'd never done before? Not to mention, I was a little curious. Sergio sat patiently, watching me with interest as I pondered the question for a few seconds longer. I hesitated and then, on impulse, made a decision. What was the worst thing that could happen?

"Err...okay. That would be great," I said, trying to sound positive.

"Good," he smiled. I will write you some directions to the area you need to go to. We can meet in the square there."

"It's a date then," I said, without thinking. "Well, not a date, date. Not that kind of date, obviously." He lifted his eyebrow and then winked at me. I couldn't help but laugh.

On the way home, I wondered whether I'd made the right decision. What would Doug say if he found out? Never mind about Doug. He wasn't the most immediate of my worries. What if Johan found out? It was probably for the best if Johan did not find out. And then there was Maggie. It would also be better if I didn't mention it to her either. By the time I got to the flat, my head was spinning. I decided to go straight to bed and not say anything to anyone.

Friday rolled around quickly enough. A couple of Unfriendly's visits, a night out at the cinema with Maggie to see an old Almódavar film, and before I knew it, I was about to check out Seville's gay scene.

After my last lecture of the day, I confined myself to quarters with a book to pass the time, but it was impossible to concentrate; I realised that I was nervous. Johan returned from his quest to visit every bar in Seville, banged around in the kitchen for a while, and finally went to bed. In next to no time, waves of soft snoring could be heard from his room. It was early evening and time to get ready, which I did quietly so I wouldn't disturb him. However, disturbing Johan was virtually impossible. On several occasions, I was convinced he could have slept through a major Krakatoa eruption.

Choosing appropriate clothing for a first visit to a gay club turned out to require more thinking than I would have imagined. I didn't want to look too gay, although I had no idea, other than putting one of Maggie's dresses on, how I could achieve that particular status. I also didn't want to look too hetero and, therefore, look completely out of place.

After half an hour of agonising, I had a different perspective of what Rachel went through whenever I used to take her out. She would drive me demented, wittering on about having nothing to wear, even though she would be standing in front of a wardrobe full of clothes. I found an old eighties pink shirt and agonised about it being too stereotypical. I realised I would never get out of the flat if I didn't choose something, and quickly. I went with the pink shirt, black jeans, and faithful Converse.

I left an hour earlier than I needed to but an hour later than planned due to what my mother calls faffing. I then stopped at a bar that I knew Johan didn't frequent. After a couple of beers, I relaxed and sat there trying to analyse why I had put myself through all this. I wondered if perhaps I should have said no.

In retrospect, I had been curious for a while about the world that Sergio inhabited. From what he had told me about his world, it seemed exciting and a little bit more dangerous than the one I'd inhabited. I was sometimes envious of how easy and often he seemed to get laid. The way Sergio described it, casual sex came without any strings attached. It wasn't a world I could easily imagine as, in my experience, any attempts at casual sex came with as many strings attached as the Berlin Philharmonic Orchestra.

The nerves were slowly building as I crossed the San Telmo bridge and down the river towards the Plaza de Toros area.

Sergio had told me that the bars and clubs, which were a fifteen-minute walk behind it, constituted the main gay district of Seville. I had never lived anywhere that had a gay district. There certainly wasn't one back in my old town, not unless you counted the men's toilets in the local park.

I was a little anxious that someone would hit on me, and I'd have to explain to them that I was straight despite the shirt. I decided that if it happened, I should be polite but firm, then wondered why everything I was saying to myself was becoming a double-entendre.

I arrived at the place Sergio had told me to meet him. Loud pulsing beats blasted from the bars and clubs in the vicinity. That whole year in Seville was characterised by a song that lingered long in the memory. It was played in whatever club or bar, straight or gay, you went into. It was playing when I spotted Sergio. He had his arms folded in his best James Dean pose and stood in the square, talking to what was, presumably, another of his many 'friends.' The thrilling beat to the song booming out everywhere that year in Seville was Ce Ce Peniston's 'Finally.'

It was playing in the distance as Sergio waved to me. He pointed towards a club near the square and gave me a hand gesture to indicate he'd be over shortly. As I stood waiting by the doorway, I saw it was a predominantly male environment. There was a distinct absence of pretty girls that you saw everywhere else in the city.

Sergio came over after a minute. I was apprehensive and wondered whether I should have worn the pink shirt after all. The yellow Fred Perry that Doug bought me for my birthday, dodgy but not outright gay, might have been better. But Johan had already worn it, and I hadn't seen it for weeks. "You have not changed your mind?" he asked, combing his hair back, still in James Dean mode. He had told me that a big poster of Jimmy adorned his bedroom wall, taking pride of place there. Mind you, to the left of it, he had one of Madonna, so I guess there's no accounting for taste.

"No, I haven't changed my mind," I laughed. "I'm up for it, as we say in the UK." Another double-entendre.

"Okay then, vamos."

We walked across the square towards a brightly lit neon sign with the unimaginative name Chicos emblazoned upon it.

On reaching the entrance, Sergio gave the doorman two mil peseta notes, and we stepped downstairs into the dark bowels of the club.

The first thing I noticed when we got downstairs was the sheer energy and fun taking place, which I hadn't seen in a club before. There was also no sense of any menace in the air. I had been schooled in the nightclubs of northern England where you were always just one wrong glance or one stray word from some drunk taking a dislike to you and providing a good reason to visit the local dentist. Here, there was no sense of that danger, and it felt liberating. Looking around, people were mostly out on the floor, shaking it in grand fashion.

Suddenly, Sergio shouted loudly in my ear, "Let's dance; I love this song!" I barely heard him above the deafening sound system as the DJ spun 'Finally.'

"Okay," I replied, nodding, but I could see that not being gay could be a hindrance on the dance floor, where everyone seemed to be superb dancers. I'd heard the stereotype that gay men could dance. Well, multiply this because gay Spanish men could really dance.

We hit the floor running and to the beat of Ce Ce's great song. I'm not that bad a dancer—well, for a straight, northern guy. But I looked like a one-legged duck with a crutch compared to some of the guys laying down their moves. Sergio was one of them, making me look bad by comparison as he lost himself in the song and produced a few sharp turns and moves that frankly made me want to get off the dance floor. What's more, he quickly had about three guys around him competing for attention. I also needn't have worried about the shirt at all since the number of guys dancing around with pecs of steel on show and wearing only vests was legion.

As Ce Ce faded into the next track, I saw how easy it really was in his world to get laid. Sergio had not been making any of it up. He was already up close with one lucky guy, well, the lucky guy for the next hour at least. He was a tall blonde who looked more Scandinavian than Sevillano. That's when I noticed:

I was alone.

Sergio held up his hand to me with his fingers splayed out, indicating he'd be gone for a few minutes. Then, he walked in the direction of the exit with his newfound love. Meanwhile, not one guy was anywhere near me; a big space had opened up in my general vicinity. The gay police had thrown a massive cordon around me. At first, I thought it must be my dancing, but then I began to figure it was my looks. As much as I'd had some success with women over the years, I was a no-no with the gay community. As the track ended, I moved off the floor and slunk away to the bar. Considering how packed the club was, the carpeted bar area was surprisingly quiet, and its carpet was non-squelchy.

I ordered a beer from the camp barman, when he put it down on a small paper mat, I attempted a smile and he turned away with yawning disinterest. I stood there for half an hour like Britain's famous nineteenth-century foreign policy—in splendid isolation.

When Sergio returned from wherever he'd been, he was all smiles. "Well, what do you think? Are you enjoying yourself?" he asked, putting his hand on my shoulder.

"Not really," I said, pushing my thumb into the top of the beer bottle. "I mean, there are guys out there hitting on each other, and no one's even bothered to come near me." I laughed.

"Ah," he said, laughing loudly and shaking his head. "The Americans have a word for this—gaydar."

"Gaydar?" I parroted back.

"Yes, it means that they recognise you are not gay," he told me, removing his hand from my shoulder and lifting it to flick his hair back. "They do not want to waste time on you because you are not gay, and so this is why no one is approaching you. You are not used to this, yes?"

"Well, it's just that I thought, you know, someone might—"

"Give you the attention? You like attention, Andy, yes?" he was throwing his head back and laughing loudly. I had to admit, it was a fair point.

"Yeah, I suppose so, doesn't everyone?" I said, fumbling in my back pocket to check I hadn't lost any mil peseta notes, a favourite party trick of mine.

"See, you are good-looking, but you are not gay. Gay guys go mostly for gay guys. Sí, some would like to, how do you say? Turning a straight man, but it would have to be a gay, straight man."

"I'm sorry, I don't understand," I said, watching two young men dressed in white Freddie Mercury vests who were busy exchanging tonsils ten feet away from me.

"You are too straight, Andy," he shouted, throwing a mock punch to my arm. "It is not so simple as to wear the pink."

"Is this like a gay lesson?" I asked, "I wondered when you'd mention the shirt!"

"Okay, when the next track comes on," he smiled, putting his arm around my shoulder. "Go on to the floor and let the music take over you. Don't think about the music, be the music. Don't be shy."

For no particular reason that I can explain, I decided I was going to go for it. It might have been the three Cruzcampos I had drunk in the short time I'd been standing by myself and the beers I'd had before I got there. The music faded, and The Farm's 'Altogether Now' came on. "I'm going to do it!" I announced to him, putting my beer bottle on a nearby table. Then I hit the dance floor and began to gyrate, paying no attention to anyone. I tried to let the music take over me. I started to bang my hands up and down like I was being electrocuted by a faulty kettle and then took to twirling about and grinding my crotch. The whole effect was likely to have resembled one of those geriatric discos the local authority holds at Christmas. In particular, that moment when one of the old blokes who's being shepherded back to his secure dorm breaks free from the nurses and heads onto the dance floor before being forcibly restrained for his own good.

When I looked up, I saw a tall, muscular guy around my age approaching me. He was gyrating in front of me. Cracked it! I can do gay! I turned to his side and then inexplicably began to grind against his legs. This time the effect must have been remarkably similar to watching your auntie's naughty Chihuahua trying to dry hump your leg.

That was the moment I saw Maggie. She was stood at the edge of the dance floor and looking at me wide-eyed. Panic-stricken, I broke away from a now very confused guy, who seemed like he had actually been enjoying getting dry-humped. "Lo siento," I told him and burst straight over to her. "What are you doing here?" I gasped.

"I had no idea," she smiled, chewing on some gum and crossing her arms. Her face was exhibiting stifled amusement and curiosity.

"No idea of what?" I asked, feeling defensive and a little embarrassed. She said nothing but raised her eyebrows at me. "I'm not gay if that's what you mean," I said.

"You're not gay?" she replied, frowning. "Well, if you're not gay, that was a stellar impression."

"Yeah, well," I shouted above the music. "It's funny you should say that because that's exactly what it was: an impression. You can ask Sergio if you don't believe me." I realised that I sounded about twelve years old. Nevertheless, I turned around to find him. But, of course, he'd gone; he'd probably copped off again.

"Well, I'd heard you guys in the closet will do a lot to protect your secrets," she shouted over the music. "But this is ridiculous."

"What are you doing here anyway?" I asked, trying to change the subject.

"I'm with a couple of intercambios," she replied, fiddling with her earring. "They both have jealous boyfriends, and if they want to go clubbing, they go to a gay club. We were just leaving when I thought I saw you and came back to check. Don't worry,

I've had my laugh now. Not least at that shirt. See you later, sweetie." At this, she pecked me on the cheek, turned away in a swirl, and started up the stairs. I don't know why I was bothered because it had nothing to do with her, but I followed her outside. After a few strides, I managed to get alongside her in the square.

"Maggie, please!" I shouted, to the apparent amusement of a couple of passersby. I reached for her elbow and pulled her around. "I'm not gay." She turned around and was grinning from ear to ear. I finally got the wind-up. "You had me going there."

"Not as much as you had that bloke going," she snorted, sitting on the steps of a small monument. She was creased up and holding her stomach from laughing. The tears rolling uncontrollably down her face. I stood waiting for her to pull herself together. "Oh, Andy, that was priceless. What the hell were you doing?"

"It's a long story," I sighed, putting my hands in my pockets and swinging a kick at a discarded cigarette packet on the pavement. "Let's go and get a drink."

I left Sergio to the night while Maggie and I went to a quiet bar that was still open near the cathedral, where I told her the story of how I'd come to be there. "So there you go," I finished, leaning back into the chair and drumming my fingers on the table. "I'm not gay."

"Of course not," she smiled, pulling out a small compact mirror from her bag and examining her face for God only knew what. "Anyway, you're far too interested in me to be gay." That took me aback. I couldn't believe the cheek of it. Interested in her? She had to be kidding.

"No offence, Maggie," I said in what I hoped was a firm but kind tone. "But I'm not interested in you in any way other than as a friend."

"Why not?" she asked, with her now familiar directness. "Why wouldn't you be interested in me?" I didn't reply straight away. I didn't want to touch on issues she might be sensitive about.

"You're not my type," I said, concentrating on tearing a small paper napkin into little pieces.

"From what I've just seen in that club, you have no idea what your type is," she retorted, flicking a bit of the napkin back at me with her finger. "In fact, from what I've seen of you in general, you have no idea about most things." She said in a voice that was remarkably calm and assured.

"That's a bit harsh," I protested. "I was only messing about in the club. I wanted to broaden my horizons and experience something different, that's all. There's nothing wrong with that."

"No, there's nothing wrong with that, but tell me, Andy," she asked, leaning forward and revealing her ample cleavage into my eyeline. "Why did you come to Seville? It's a big step to take for someone your age." The way she said 'someone your age' made me feel like I was Shirley Bassey without the makeup on.

"I came to learn Spanish, obviously," I said tetchily, sitting back in my chair and getting out of the way of her cleavage. "And to broaden my horizons. To experience new things through the medium of education."

"Then why on earth don't you go to any classes?" I was so shocked I couldn't reply.

What the hell did it have to do with her if I went to classes or not? How dare she question me and how I was living my life here? I walked over to the bar, pushed a mil note at the barman, and then stood at the door waiting for her. It was late, and I didn't want her to walk about the streets on her own.

She must have realised that she had spoken out of turn as she picked her bag up and came over. I was expecting an apology, but instead, she asked with an impish grin, "I take it that's your final word on the matter?"

We walked back to Triana together without speaking.

I made my eight thirty lit. class the next day, though, and every day after that.

11 THESE ARE THE DAYS OF OUR LIVES.

Extract from a letter sent to Newcastle on the 7th of November, 1991.

'... to hear that you're feeling a bit under the weather, Mum. I hope it's nothing to worry about, but I'll call next week sometime to see how you are.

I'm all settled now and much happier here. My new flatmates are very different to my previous ones. Andy is very interesting, and he's got 'potential', as you used to say. Though at the moment he's doing a bit of sulking, but he's still sort of cute despite that.'

When I bumped into Maggie at the breakfast table two days later, she mercifully acted like nothing had happened. It was another of her many good sides. From what I had discerned of her, she didn't carry things on for ages like other women I'd known. Rachel could go three days or longer without uttering a word if I'd upset her. There was one time she lost her voice, and I didn't even notice for two days. "Johan was legless last night," she said before gulping down a large mug of tea and watching me pull up a chair. "He made a play for me and then fell over."

"He does that a lot," I said, picking up an old copy of El País to read and turning to the sports at the back.

"What? He's made a play for you as well?" she goaded me, putting the mug down. "You'd have enjoyed that, I imagine. In light of what I saw the other night, I mean."

"Don't you ever give up?" I sighed, turning the newspaper page to read about FC Barcelona's exploits. "You're relentless."

"Sorry, no more gay jokes. I promise I'm finished. Can we be friends at least?" she started to bat her eyelashes in a ridiculous manner. "Even though I'm not your type, and you definitely don't fancy me?" I couldn't help laughing despite wanting to be annoyed at her.

"Yeah, anyway, moving on," I said, taking a deep breath and blowing out hard. "I thought a lot about what you said, you know, about attending classes, and I might have sulked a little—"

"A little?"

"Okay, a lot. But it got me thinking about why I came here and what you said was right; I haven't taken it seriously enough."

"That goes without saying," she said, putting her feet up on the chair next to her. "I'm always right. It's an annoying habit of mine that you'll need to get used to."

"In my experience," I said, leaning over and playfully pushing her feet off the chair, "that's an annoying habit most women have." Suddenly, Johan's door flew open and banged loudly against the wall, making us jump. He staggered into the living room light with his mouth wide open and gave a yawn, which sounded like a sick hippo. Through the kitchen door, we watched, with amusement, as he stretched his arms up to the ceiling and then squinted around the sunlit room like Mr Magoo without his glasses. He wore my Stone Roses t-shirt and absolutely nothing else whilst displaying most of his tackle. The fact he'd been sleeping in it was lost on me for the moment as my eyes were drawn to his extremities.

"For the sake of fuck," he said when his unfocussed eyes eventually located us in the kitchen. "What is all the noise at this unchristian hour of the morning? Some of us are trying to get some sleep." His hand had reached down and scratched his aforementioned Swedish fishing tackle, then he turned his back to us, revealing a round, hairy arse. He went back into his room and slammed the door shut. Maggie started to laugh helplessly, and so did I.

As November arrived, I began to meet up with Sergio twice a week. On Wednesdays, we had our chat meetings, as we called them, and Maggie sometimes came along. She was great fun to hang out with, intelligent, amusing, and never boring. We covered a wide range of topics over the following weeks, and my admiration for her increased as she effortlessly dispensed wit and sensitivity. Sergio was very keen on discussing research into what made people gay. He could talk for hours on the whole nurture/nature debate and was firmly on the side of nature. He would constantly allude to articles he'd read in newspapers or magazines that claimed to have discovered a gay gene in rats or something else that I didn't always agree with. Maggie was clearly on the side of nurture but handled his arguments with compassion and understanding while managing to get her points across, something she never did with me. Our conversations sometimes felt like the equivalent of being hit with a sledgehammer.

The other good thing about her coming along to our chats was that being around her and Sergio was leading to rapid improvements in my Spanish. Sergio told me he didn't often connect with women, but Maggie was different. "There is something of the man about her, no? I say this in a good way."

I guess she was bloke-ish, but I quite liked that about her. She wasn't overly sensitive either, although she could be very combative when the mood took her. Most of all, I liked that she was smart and sassy. When I mentioned this to Sergio, he asked me to translate the word sassy or explain it to him and I couldn't. After ten minutes of trying, he said, 'Descarada!'

On Fridays, I occasionally went to a club with Sergio. When I did go, I resolved to abandon my needy, attention-seeking behaviour and just enjoyed myself. This led to me being more relaxed and occasionally getting hit on. If this happened and I told the guy I was straight, they would use the moment to practise their English on me. In Seville, it seemed everyone wanted to practise their English.

It could be a bit irritating going into clubs with Sergio and having him disappear for an hour at a time, but I was more worried about his promiscuity in light of the HIV situation. I raised this with him one night after he'd disappeared. "Don't worry, Andy," he told me after returning from an encounter so brief that Noel Coward wouldn't have bothered writing about it,

"I am always very careful."

"I hope so because you don't want to be putting yourself at risk," I said, sounding like his mother. "I've read a lot of scary stuff about it lately, as I'm sure you have."

"I don't take risks, Andy. I am not stupid. Anyway, I don't like to be penetrated, and if it's necessary, I always have protection."

Whooaaaaa! Too much information.

Later that month, we got the news that Freddie had died.

Being a fan of Queen in the seventies it shook me pretty badly. I couldn't believe he was gone and felt numb with the shock. As a teenager, I'd bought Bohemian Rhapsody and their early albums. I didn't even know he was gay back then. Come to think of it, I didn't know anyone was gay back then. My teenage years were fully immersed in the insular world of a small northern town where the idea of being gay didn't exist in my consciousness. Sure, there was always the one boy in your class who wouldn't get a shower with everyone or play football, but I'm not sure we knew what he was outside of the bullies calling him a pansy. Proof, if ever it was needed, that ignorance is not bliss.

What affected me the most about Freddie's death was the fact that I hadn't even known he was ill. I'd been so immersed in my own life that the news came as a massive shock. Doug had sent me tapes of Nirvana and U2, but outside of that, I wasn't in touch with what was happening in the pop world.

I found out on my way to the university on a glorious late November day. I'd stopped in my favourite little newsagents on the corner and read all about it inside one of the Spanish papers I rarely bought but often read. As chance would decree, when I got to the university, I bumped into Sergio, which didn't usually happen without pre-arrangement as our class times and study areas were very separate. He was sitting forlornly on one of the large staircases, and a number of students were forced to walk around him. When I approached, I could see he was visibly shaken and clearly taking Freddie's death as a prelude to his own mortality. "Hey! You okay, Serge?" I asked, sitting beside him and blocking even more of the stairway.

"Have you heard the news? I can't believe it," he replied, rubbing his hands across his damp eyes and shaking his head. "Freddie Mercury."

"Me neither," I answered while moving myself to let a couple of guys squeeze past. "I was a big fan."

"I was not a fan of his music," he admitted. "But he was a leader in many ways and someone people looked up to because he was always himself, and that is important in life, is it not?"

"Freddie was always Freddie," I agreed, then put my satchel between my feet and a consoling hand on his shoulder. "I remember him best at Live Aid, where his was easily the best performance. Everyone said so, even bands that didn't like him."

Sergio started to cry harder. I didn't know why he was taking it THAT badly. I squeezed his shoulder with my arm, then, on impulse, turned him towards me and hugged him. I guess we looked like a couple of Queens ourselves on those stairs with his sobbing head on my shoulder, but I didn't care. A few people made their way up a couple of the stairs and, faced with the sight of us, went back down and walked back to the next ones. I couldn't say I blamed them.

I eventually got him moving and walked him through the city until we were about halfway to his flat. On the way, I even gave him a rendition of *'Killer Queen'* that brought a reluctant smile to his drawn face and attracted a few strange looks from the locals. When we said goodbye, he was visibly brighter and promised he was feeling better and would try to snap out of it. As I had only one class that day, which I'd now missed, I decided to return to the flat.

When I got back, Maggie was seated in a chair in front of the living room window, taking in the weak rays of the late morning sun. She was reading a Wilbur Smith novel in Spanish and dressed in the most unflattering dressing gown I think I have ever seen. It was a shocking, blue, hairy thing that appeared to have come from an emu. I'd seen it before, and Johan had christened it 'the Blue Duck Egg' because she looked like one in it. That said, Maggie still wore it in that couldn't-care-less trademark way of hers. "You heard?" she asked, looking up as I closed the door. "About poor Freddie?"

"Yeah," I sighed, putting my satchel on the table and sitting next to her on the arm of the chair. Even though she was wearing the Blue Duck Egg, and it should have been impossible to tell, she seemed to have lost a little weight. I nearly congratulated her on the fact before remembering that women were sometimes sensitive on issues of weight, even when you said something positive like: 'Well done on your weight loss; you fit into that dress much better now.' So I didn't mention it. Anyway, if she had lost weight, it was likely down to Johan stealing all of her food. I put it to the back of my mind and continued on the topic of Freddie. "It's bad news. Sergio's really shaken up about it. I've just had an emotional moment with him at the uni."

"I'll bet," she said, unable to resist the dig. She put a bookmarker in the page she was on and looked up at me with a straight face. "How did you find out?"

"Oh, I read it in the newsagents on the way in," I told her. "What about you?"

"The same, only I bought it, unlike you," she grinned. I ignored the jibe.

"I didn't even know he was ill," I said, getting up and sitting on the sofa. "Hadn't got a clue."

"Come on!" she gasped. "You must have seen the later videos. In that last one he did, he was so gaunt. It was a real shame to see him like that."

"I didn't pay much attention to them. And in those I saw him in, I thought he might have had bulimia or something." I trailed off and shrugged my shoulders. I felt guilty admitting my ignorance but couldn't work out why for the life of me.

"Do me a favour," she scoffed, sounding irritated, and returned to her book. Ignoring the body language that signified my dismissal, I pressed on and voiced something that had bothered me since I read the news.

"Why didn't he make it public, do you think? You know, let people know he was ill."

"Why should he?" she asked me in surprise. She drew her knees up under her chin and into the unfathomable depths of the Blue Duck Egg whilst giving me a full-frontal view of matching slippers.

"Well, because he was a public figure," I reasoned. "He owed it to people to warn them, don't you think? He might have saved lives." She took a little time to consider this.

"Err...privacy is important," she eventually stated, scrunching her face at the idea. "And perhaps he was thinking about his own family. Anyway, I don't get your point. It was nobody's business but his own. Perhaps he didn't want to die in public with all those vultures from the press sniffing around."

She'd made a good point. I was learning that Maggie always made good points, which annoyed me. Perhaps that's why she didn't have a boyfriend because she was always annoying potential boyfriends by constantly making good points around them. "Well, I think he had some responsibilities," I blustered back at her. "It goes with the territory if you're a public figure. He could have warned people. It might have saved a few lives in the process. That's all I'm saying." I was now up a few octaves from where I'd started. Maggie pressed her lips together and rocked forward a little.

"Warned people about what?" she asked, her face tilted to one side and looking at me with a curious expression.

"You know?" I went on and widened my eyes. "That."

"As far as I know, we don't know what the cause of death is," she said, almost whispering in stark contrast to the increasing volume beside her. "And a bit of news for you in your futile attempts to become part of the gay glitterati of Seville: not everyone who's gay has AIDS, and not everyone who has AIDS is gay." I thought long and hard about my studied reply.

"Oh fuck off, Maggie, you know-all!" I snapped and stormed

off to my room. I banged the door loudly behind me so she could hear it, and that way, she would know that her good point had annoyed me, and maybe that's why she didn't have a boyfriend.

I lay on the bed and tried to understand why Maggie infuriated me as much as she did. What was it about her? Sitting there in that stupid Blue Duck Egg like she was…was…I had no idea what she thought she was.

It was pathetic.

I eventually fell asleep, but before I did, I vowed to question Maggie about her unexplained weight loss. Let's see if she could talk herself out of that with one of her good points.

Instead of questioning Maggie, I brought it up with Johan the next afternoon after returning from my lecture. He'd caught up with me in the Plaza del Cuba on my way back from university and persuaded me to go to Unfriendly's for the hair of the dog that didn't simply bite but savaged me like one of those rottweilers that are always in the English newspapers.'

It was only two o'clock in the afternoon, and very few people were around. Johan liked it that way as it gave little excuse for the three waiters on show to ignore us. Since Maggie's arrival, they were more civil but the red-carpet treatment of actually getting served quickly, attentively, and with good humour only appeared when she accompanied us.

After Unfriendly's waiting staff rustled up two San Jacobos (a thin fried chicken strip tapa) and two Cruzcampos, I was keen to question Johan about his thoughts on the weight loss issue. "Listen," I said, accosting him as soon as he started to drink his beer. "Don't you think Maggie has lost some weight lately? What do you reckon that's about?" He yawned and bent down to pick the soles of his very silly-looking green sandals. No wonder he wore my clothes when those sandals were the best that Swedish sartorial elegance could muster. Johan was one of those guys where you could fashion no sense from his fashion sense. "Hello? Did you hear me?" I continued. "I asked you a question."

"Oh, I heard you," he replied, sitting back up and reaching for his fork. "I heard you. Maggie is what you might call a plump English rose. She is a beauty but not a delicate beauty. And in my opinion, she is neither plumper nor less plumper than when I first met her." I wasn't sure if I liked his usage of the adjective plump, but I left it alone for the moment.

"Are you sure about that because—"

"Drink your beer and eat your food," he commanded, picking up a classic Unfriendly's fork. Classic in the sense that it first needed to be cleaned before you could eat with it. Not that Johan was doing much eating. He started waving it around in the air like it was a lightsabre. "You don't see Maggie because you look at her too much. You don't know Maggie because you think about her too much. Now eat your food before I do." With this, he buried the fork deep into the middle of his San Jacobo, lifted it to his mouth, and forced it in.

"So," I asked, ignoring his faux Swedish philosophy and trying hard not to stare as he made the kind of throat movements a seagull would make whilst swallowing a live eel struggling for its life. "Let's get this straight so we understand each other: she's not lost any weight then, in your opinion?" He made a final disgusting gulp, stuck his fork into the second piece, and leaned forward, putting his hand on my arm.

"Are you aware of the famous quote of your bard, 'Beauty is in the eye of the beholder'? Because if you are not, you are an arsehole." I thought about this as I looked down at my San Jacobo. He couldn't be suggesting that, could he? I mean, could he?

"Surely you can't be suggesting that I fancy her?" As he began chewing, he held his hand up and showed me his palm. He carried on for about another minute, unable to speak, before picking up his napkin and wiping the sides of his mouth like he was at some cocktail party for interior designers.

"I am," he said, finally. "I am. And don't call me Shirley."

We started to giggle. Five minutes later, the waiters watched the two of us doubled up, crying helplessly with laughter in an otherwise empty bar.

12 TOO BLIND TO SEE IT.

Extract from a letter sent to the Orkney Islands on the 1st of December, 1991.

'...so I'm working hard on the essays. The weather here has turned a bit nippier than I expected, as November was really warm. I've decided to stay here for Christmas and New Year but thanks for the invite. I hope you're not disappointed, but getting up there and back would cost a fortune. I don't remember the family Christmases you talked about. It's another memory of Dad I don't have anymore.

I appreciate your offer to pay for the flights, but I can't take your money. Take care of yourself.

Love,

Andrew xxx'

In early December, the temperature dropped, and an unusual cold snap settled over the country. Johan went back to Sweden for the whole month as he wanted to spend Christmas with his family. On a positive note, my Spanish was improving by the day. I knew this because whenever I went to Maria's shop to buy milk or bread, I could almost hold a decent conversation with her despite her thick Sevillian accent. I didn't always understand everything she said, but the tone in her voice sometimes made me think that that was not always a bad thing.

In the first week of December, I popped into her shop for some things that Maggie and I needed. Maria told me that the radio predicted it could get as low as zero in Seville for the first time in twenty years. "It's okay, Maria," I told her, scooping the milk off the glass counter and putting it into a VIPS carrier bag. "I'm from the north of England. It's always cold there."

"But, son, the cold in Seville is like no other," she said, wiping the counter down with a cloth and then throwing her hands up in the air, making the usual Sevillian grand gesture. "It eats into the bones."

Later in the week, as the thermometer in the kitchen plummeted towards zero, I realised she was right. It was a different sort of cold, one that got inside your bones, like she said, and made you shiver. I'd been up to Orkney to visit my mother in wintertime, and it was below minus with a biting wind chill, but it didn't feel as cold as it did in Seville that December.

As the cold snap set in, it was the perfect time for the radiators to break. I went to the shop and told Maria about it. She said that Spanish homes were built for heat and not for cold. It was probably because the heating was hardly used, but she'd send someone over to fix it. Maggie got in from a late class just before nine while I was seated in the living room watching El Día Después, a Spanish football programme. I must have cut a fine figure of Northern manhood dressed as I was in two pairs of jogging pants and socks. "Brrr...It's a bit nippy out there," she said, putting her small bag down. "Not very southern Spainy."

"I know," I replied, more intent on watching Barcelona net their third than having a conversation. "It's worse than Northern England."

"Very fetching," she said, spying my rigout and flinging her coat over a chair. "Do we have to watch this garbage?" Now frowning at the TV and Michael Robinson's beaming face.

"It's nearly finished," I told her, stuffing the last of a packet of patatas fritas into my mouth in the hope that the action of chewing might warm me up. "Anyway, I wouldn't take your coat off; the heating's broke."

"You're kidding me," she muttered, reaching for her coat on the chair. "I thought you'd turned it down or something to save money. It's brass monkeys in here."

"I've already spoken to Maria, and she said she'd send someone over to fix the boiler, but so far, nobody has shown up," I told her, getting up to turn the TV off as the credits began to roll.

"I suppose it will be mañana," she answered glumly, tugging

the zipper up to her chin and reaching for her gloves in the pocket. "It's always mañana here when it comes to fixing things."

"Mañana, if we're lucky," I replied, watching her pull a cream-coloured woollen hat firmly over her head. She looked very cute, I thought. "Good day?"

"It was okay," she said. "Want to go down to Unfriendly's? They'll have the heating on inside on a night like this."

"Can't," I replied, slumping back onto the couch. "Maria said someone was coming round today. She didn't say if they had a key or not. If we're out when they come, we could be freezing all month."

"This won't last more than a few days," she said confidently. "It never does here."

"Well, I hope you're right," I grumbled. "Or I might have to set fire to Johan's bed for warmth."

"You don't need to set fire to stuff to get warm," she said in a mock sultry voice, wiggling her hips suggestively as she walked towards her bedroom. She'd certainly got my attention. "There's lots of ways to keep warm." I watched her, feeling vaguely uncomfortable, as she lingered by the open door.

"Such as?" I was feeling warmer even as I said it.

"Well, there's..." she said, now holding my look and provocatively licking the corner of her mouth as she paused. She broke out into a smile "...taking an electric shower. Which is what I intend to do." She twirled around and shut the door with a giggle. I couldn't help noticing the temperature had briefly risen a few degrees in the flat.

About an hour later, the buzzer went. I was shivering as I got out of bed, which was the only place I could think of to keep warm. To my dismay, when I opened the door, Maria's son Antonio was standing there. He was a tall, rangy, bearded guy in his late twenties. Whenever I saw him, he seemed to be strolling around the street doing nothing particularly constructive with his life other than sticking his hands down the front of his Velour tracksuit bottoms and his head into car windows. The cars he stuck his head into usually had attractive women in them. He wore his coloured shirts tighter than tight and had more cheap jewellery on his hands than Rackner's had sold in the previous twenty years. Johan got on like a house on fire with him and assured me that he was okay, but he always seemed a bit of a knob to me.

I invited him in and he said nothing other than assenting to give me a curt nod. He had a tool bag, the sure sign of a man's man. I had never had a tool bag in my life. It was no wonder I was prone to going to gay clubs.

Maggie was in the kitchen where she'd gone after her shower to make herself the staple food of the flat—a chicken burger sans pan. Ignoring the reason he was in the flat in the first place, which was to fix the heating, he put his bulging tool bag down and wandered in to talk to her. What hacked me off was that he had the nerve to close the door behind him, probably so I couldn't hear what they were saying. When I pressed my ear against it, I could follow eighty per cent of what was being said, which was about eighty per cent more than I liked.

He was flirting with her.

This irritated me immensely. Firstly, he was skinny and good-looking in an emancipated Emilio Estevez way. That in itself annoyed me. Also, Maria had told me he had a stunning girlfriend, yet he constantly flirted with some of the best-looking women in Seville; that was when he wasn't lazing around, pretending to be between jobs. He was one of those guys who always seemed to have money even though he didn't work. And now here he was, flirting with Maggie. What for? He couldn't fancy her; she wasn't his type. He was using her for some despicable flirting practice. I almost felt like I should punch him in the nose to protect Maggie's honour from this stick insect Lothario, who was nothing more than a dirty flirt user.

After a minute or two of their nonsense, I opened the door to find them standing close together, their shoulders virtually touching as they leaned side by side against the countertop. I marched in and pushed my arm between them to open a cupboard and remove a glass. They stepped back as I reached in and then ignored me as I poured some water into it from the fridge. I wasn't even thirsty. Other than a cursory glance, they ignored me as I stood leaning against the cooker, taking little sips of water. If that wasn't demeaning enough, it wasn't half as bad as seeing Maggie play along with the flirt user. She was twirling a strand of hair around her finger, laughing loudly at his pathetic jokes, and touching his arm lightly when he joked about something I couldn't understand but was bound to be crude. The charade irritated me so much that I banged my half-empty glass onto the worktop. This little tantrum stopped them in mid-conversation. They looked at me with raised eyebrows and an expression of mild amusement. For the second time that day, I felt my face flush and barged past them without excusing myself and went to my room. I sat in bed trying to get warm while listening to the news in Spanish on the bedside radio, but it was impossible to concentrate when they were laughing so loudly.

I endured it for an hour before he finally left. After he'd gone, I heard a light knock on my door, and Maggie said very softly, "Andy? Are you asleep? Andy?" I didn't answer. She went back into her room, and I heard the door close lightly. I waited for about forty-five minutes, but the heating still didn't come on. The muppet hadn't fixed the heating, despite having a tool bag.

After putting on another layer of clothes, I got back into bed and somehow got some sleep even though I was unbelievably cold. When I woke, I had no idea what time it was. The shutters on the windows in the flat blocked out all of the light, making it impossible to tell. I reached for the alarm and flicked on the lamp. It was three a.m., and had the band KLF been here, they might not have found it so eternal but more freezing. Not feeling remotely tired, I decided to get up and have a cup of tea. I was surprised to find Maggie in the living room. I wasn't expecting to see her at that early hour. She was sitting on the sofa, her head buried in an enormous duvet and a book. "Cup of tea?" I asked, feeling hacked off with her, although I couldn't figure out why for the life of me. "I'm freezing; I thought it might warm me up." She shook her head but didn't look up. "You okay?" I asked, feeling very much like someone who had done something wrong rather than someone who had been wronged.

"I was just wondering," she replied, with her head still firmly buried in the book, "why you sneaked off to bed in another of your now legendary sulks." She raised her clear green eyes to meet mine, and I realised there was little point in lying to Maggie. She was like that poker player who you can't beat because they have a read on you.

"Oh, it's just Antonio, he annoys me with his, 'Oh look how handsome I am' routine. I'm going to flirt with anyone because I'm so handsome. It's pathetic." She put the book down.

"Not a routine you're familiar with?" she asked, pulling the duvet around her tightly. "But more to the point, are you inferring I'm just anyone? Is that what your sulk was about because he was flirting with me?"

"No, of course not," I spluttered and, faking a move towards the kitchen. "You're free to do whatever you want with who you want; just watch him. He's not your type anyway."

"Wow!" she exclaimed, her eyes flashing at me in anger as she ditched the book to her side. "You know so much about types, don't you? You know I'm not your type, and you know he's not my type. Anything else I should know?"

"No," I said defensively, "I was only umm…saying." I escaped to make myself a cup of tea. When I returned, she'd put the TV on and scrolled through the five Spanish TV channels. I felt colder than ever. I sat on the sofa beside her and stared at an Almódovar film on channel two she'd found. "It's freezing," I moaned, holding my hot mug with both hands and lifting it up to my mouth. "I can't believe it gets this cold here."

"It's quite warm under here," she replied in a smug voice with the hint of a smile tugging at her mouth. She nestled into it and watched Carmen Maura give it her all with some guy on the bed.

"Well, I don't have a big duvet like you," I lamented, wishing I'd brought one with me like she had.

"That's too bad," she replied, turning to me with a knowing smile. "If I were your type, you might be tempted to get under here and snuggle up…enjoy all of this lovely warmth." I looked back into her eyes, which no longer looked cold and angry but warm and inviting. Then I saw a glimpse of her sleeve and saw she was wearing the Blue Duck Egg underneath. It reminded me that although she was witty, sharp, and full of personality, I wasn't attracted to her.

"I might at that," I said, slowly getting up until I was standing in front of her. I rubbed the back of my neck, "If you were my type."

I went to my room, flicked the light off, and clambered into the bed. I didn't sleep a wink the rest of that night.

It must have been the cold.

13 EVEN BETTER THAN
THE REAL THING.

Extract from a letter sent to Seville on the 12th of December, 1991.

'...can't really say too much about it all, Andy, other than to say I don't know how it's all going to work out. Things don't look good at the moment, and the future seems really uncertain. As for your offer, I would love to come over, but I'll have to see. Christmas isn't something I'm looking forward to and I wouldn't be much fun to have around anyway.

P.S. On a happier note, have you heard the new U2 album? Get ready to eat your words because it's amazing like I said it would be!! I'll do a copy for you and will send a tape over next week.

Cheers mate,

Doug.'

On the last Sunday before Christmas, I had arranged a meeting with Sergio in the Plaza de España. The Plaza had quickly become one of my favourite spots in Seville. It was built for the 1929 Ibero-American exposition and was near the university. As I entered on the riverside of the park, it was a comfortable thirteen on the large electronic board outside the entrance. I smiled contentedly and walked up the ornate red brick road, flanked as it was by huge palm trees on either side. In the distance, I could see the stunning baroque buildings and the pavilions that harked back to the great Moorish style. The beautiful blue and white ceramic tiles reflected the clear winter light into my vista. The park was full of people enjoying the simple pleasure of a Sunday afternoon stroll. As it was mid-December, for once, there were more Sevillanos milling about than tourists.

I reached the pavilions and sat down on a wall, where I

people-watched for a while. Thankfully, the cold snap had lifted this last week and as a lad from the north of England, I found the temperature quite comfortable. I was attired in nothing more than a long-sleeved T-shirt and gilet. It amused me to see the locals wrapped up in heavy-duty coats. Sergio, being from the north—but the north of Spain, so it was all relative—arrived after a few minutes dressed in a light grey jacket with a contrasting charcoal scarf expertly draped around his neck and shoulders as though he'd just stepped off a catwalk. As we walked to the nearest cafe, we passed a couple of pretty girls who stole glances at us and grinned at each other as they walked by. Of course, Sergio was oblivious to the attention he was attracting from the opposite sex, even if I wasn't.

We sat down and ordered two espressos. Sergio began to tell me about his swimming coach, who claimed to have a girlfriend but kept giving him deep, and, so Sergio thought, erotic massages after every swim session. "I tell you, Andy, you have to see this guy," Sergio said in Spanish, taking out his comb and brushing through jet-black hair that most men would have killed for. "He has an incredible body, and he's so good-looking he could be a film star. Yet he says he has a girlfriend and that he's straight, but he also insists on massaging me every time we finish the session."

"Sounds like he might have a few issues," I said, looking around distractedly and realising that Sergio's world was full of straight men who were, in reality, gay. I was always surprised at just how exciting straight men were to him. The idea of turning a straight man was, for some reason, to him anyway, some gay El Dorado. "But what do you think?" he pressed, stretching round to put the comb in his back pocket. "Would you give a guy you know massages?"

"I can't say it's the straightest behaviour I've ever encountered," I replied and shuddered as I imagined a bottle of oil in my hands and Doug sprawled out before me on one of those massage beds. "No, I wouldn't massage a guy."

At that moment, I turned my head and saw her. As soon as I

saw her, I knew. She was the reason I had come to Seville. She was the most beautiful girl I had ever seen. She was standing near one of the pavilions, her left hand on her hip, her right hand hanging down, holding a cigarette, and talking to a girl who might have looked stunning enough, except she had the misfortune to be standing next to this goddess. Her hair was as black as coal; curly ringlets framed the sides of a perfectly formed dusky face. She was wearing a red riding hood coat and a short leather skirt. Her shapely legs were covered with woollen tights and black, knee-length boots. She looked about five foot six or seven, with a slender figure that couldn't have been bigger than a size ten. "Did you hear what I said, Andy? I asked you a question," Sergio repeated, leaning over and breaking through my trance.

"Erm…I'm sorry," I replied, glancing back at him briefly before turning back towards the girl. She'd gone. In the brief second of looking at Sergio, she'd gotten lost in the Spartan crowd. I felt an anxiety spread through my body. "Did you see that girl?" I asked him in a voice that fully reflected the panic I was feeling.

"What girl?" he asked, swinging his head around to look behind him to where I was frantically searching. "What girl do you mean?"

"That amazing girl. The most beautiful girl I've ever seen. You must have seen her. She was just there." I was now out of my chair, standing up, and trying to get a better view of the pavilions. Sergio remained seated.

"I didn't see anyone. As you know, looking at girls is not really my thing."

"No, I suppose not," I said, sitting back down after having failed to locate her. "She was so beautiful, and now she's gone."

"I wouldn't worry," he told me as the waiter turned up and put our coffees on the table. "There are thousands of beautiful girls in Seville, Andy. Even if you don't see her again, you'll see another one soon enough."

But I had a feeling I would see her again. After all, she was the reason destiny had brought me to Seville.

Christmas was a quiet affair at the flat, with Maggie cooking a Christmas dinner, with all the trimmings, for Sergio and me. It was good, even though it couldn't hold a candle to one of my mum's Christmas dinners.

After washing up, Maggie, Serge, and I sat around the table, Maggie and I drinking beer and Serge his OJ. Whenever Maggie and Sergio got together, they tended to talk about serious issues. I say talk, but often, it was a good-humoured debate. "I don't agree that it's nature," she replied to Sergio's favourite topic. "All the evidence suggests that nurture is more important in these things."

"Not all the evidence, Maggie," Sergio said. "I have read in El País only the last week that scientists from the US have found that the gay men's brains are different to the straight. This may mean that you are born gay." Maggie poured the rest of her beer into a glass and contemplated this.

"I think that's a stretch. Everybody's born with the same brain. It simply gets different stimuli in the womb and during life—or nurture, to put it another way." At this, she put her hands behind her neck and rocked back on her chair, a sure sign she felt she'd made a good point.

"So how come men and women use their brains differently?" I asked, sensing that we might get her on the back foot for once.

"Who rattled your cage?" she grinned at me.

"Well," I said, glancing at Sergio, "it's been proven that women use the right hemisphere while men use the left more. Stands to reason that if brain usage is not the same, it might explain someone's sexuality, which is bound to be brain-related anyway." Sergio laughed.

"He has a point, Maggie."

"No, he doesn't," she said, rocking forward on her chair and clearly relishing the debate now that I was in it. "If that were true, it would indicate that men or women would be better than each other at certain intellectual things. And correct me if I'm wrong, but as far as I'm aware, men can't do anything with their brains better than women."

"Chess," said Sergio, holding up a finger to indicate he'd scored a point. "No woman has ever been world chess champion."

"That's because it's a stupid man's game," said Maggie, banging her hand on the table and laughing. "Look at normal intellectual pursuits such as writing novels or speaking languages. Women are every bit as good as men."

"Playwrights," I dropped into the conversation.

"Eh?" she asked with a quizzical expression.

"Shakespeare, Wilde, Miller, Bennett, O'Casey; name me a brilliant, world-famous woman playwright?"

"Well…"

"Ah," Sergio clapped his hands together in glee. "He makes the good point." Maggie's face scrunched as she sat thinking. She broke out into a smile, then stood up, holding her glass in the air. "Andy McLeod, I will probably think of one later, but for the moment, you have me, and as you know, that's not an easy thing to do. Salud!" Sergio stood up, too, and tipped his orange juice my way.

"Salud, Andy!"

I waved at them to sit down and laughed. It was a fun moment, and I might have enjoyed it all the more if Maggie's gracious action hadn't contrasted so sharply with mine over the last couple of months.

Maggie went to a friend's house in the country for a few days after that. Serge and I went out a couple of times, but for some reason, the holidays lacked any excitement after Maggie left.

She returned on the thirtieth, and we went out to watch *Tacones Lejanos* (High Heels), an Almódovar film showing at a small cinema across the city. During the film, I'm sure I felt Maggie's leg press against mine, even though her eyes never left the screen. I felt a bit weird because part of me wanted to push back, and another part that won out wanted to pull away and not get involved, but the whole thing ruined the film for me. Even more so because she kept laughing at bits I couldn't translate, and I felt a bit stupid.

When we returned home, we stood awkwardly before finally agreeing it was late, and we were tired and should probably go to bed. We said goodnight in the hallway at our respective doors, and for no reason I could explain, there was an odd tension between us, a lingering look that was hard to break away from. I had a fitful sleep while dreaming about Maggie in high heels.

Maggie went out to a New Year's Eve party at the flat of some Irish girls she knew. I didn't feel like going, even though she tried to persuade me. I didn't know what was wrong with me, but I felt restless, and my mood was low. So I stayed at home and went to bed early. It was my first sober New Year since I was fourteen.

Johan returned on the third of January, and I was very pleased to see him. His return signalled the end of the holidays and the recommencement of normality. The first thing he did was drag me out to a bar on our side of the river. With Johan around, normality was more fun than the holidays. He wanted a belated Christmas celebration, but Maggie had to meet a couple of students she was teaching English to and was keen to earn some extra cash. She had lessons booked that night and went to those despite Johan's protestations that she was being a bore.

Fate works in mysterious ways. I hadn't wanted to go initially and had planned to work on an essay. But Johan, being his usual persuasive self, told me it was for my benefit and that I needed some post-Christmas cheering up. It turned out, that destiny was putting in back-to-back shifts for me.

When we arrived, it was a quiet affair. The city was much like any other European city in early January—dead. There were a few hardy Swedes Johan knew and two Irish girls who'd had the New Year's Eve party that Maggie had gone to. We sat around the large table in a group, generally having a laugh. At least it was a laugh until Antonio walked in holding a crash helmet under his right arm like he was some kind of Hell's Angel on a Harley-Davidson instead of a mummy's boy on a moped. He strutted in like a preening peacock in tight trousers. He was wearing a shirt so loud that had he worn it in a built-up area, he could have been arrested for disturbing the peace. One of Johan's friends, a guy called Sven, got up, and they shook hands. I could see the Swedish guy beckoning him over to our table to join us, an idea I was not very keen on.

I then noticed a slimmer figure wearing a motorcycle helmet. The figure lifted its arms and began tugging at the helmet. As soon as it was off, I recognised her instantly—it was the girl from the park. She put the helmet on a nearby table, tugged at her gloves, and shook her long black curls into place. The hypnotic effect of the headshake reminded me of the Harmony hairspray adverts in the seventies, where the girl woos the whole room as her hair tumbles around her shoulders in slow motion. When she'd finished shaking the ebony mane out, I watched Antonio lean over to whisper something into her ear, and she nodded back at him.

They bought two Cokes at the bar and came over to our table, squeezing in where they could. As usual, Antonio and I didn't speak a word to each other. But my eyes were drawn to his companion's face all night. Although the main language had been English, everyone switched to Spanish to accommodate them as they sat down. I was sat just about as far away from her on the table as it was possible to be. The Swedish guy introduced them as Antonio and his girlfriend, Mariló.

During the next half an hour, she seemed to fall into everyone's conversation except mine. I tried hard not to keep staring, but she was gorgeous, and my stomach turned over with every stolen glance. Johan kept looking over at me, then at her, and raising his eyebrows. I tried to tell him that she was the girl I'd told him about, but he shrugged his shoulders as if he didn't understand. Eventually, Antonio nodded towards me and, to my surprise, said in Spanish, "You're the guy from the flat, no? Johan's friend?"

"Well spotted, Sherlock," I said dryly in English. He gave me a puzzled look, and Johan kicked me hard under the table.

"Do you like football?" he asked enthusiastically and told me he was a big fan of Manchester Utd. I was very close to saying, 'Of course you are. You're not from Manchester, but Johan was scowling fiercely at me to be nice. My dislike for him had grown exponentially after seeing his girlfriend. I mean, if he had a stunning girlfriend like that, why was he flirting with Maggie?

When they got up to go, Mariló didn't give me a second glance. I watched, slightly surprised, as she pulled the helmet over her head again and fastened the strap. The Spanish had one of the worst road safety records in Europe but some of the safest elbows, as this was where most Spaniards wore their helmets. As I gawped at her exit, Johan leaned towards me and said, "That, young Andrew, is a fine example of the Spanish ladyhood."

"You never told me he had such a stunning girlfriend," I said accusingly. "How come you never said anything?"

"This is the first time I have ever seen her," he replied.

"I don't understand. You're out with him all the time." I replied, frowning. He winked at me.

"Let me say that whenever he and I go off to the Flamenco clubs, he hasn't yet brought her along, and there are good reasons for that." I turned my head away to the exit and muttered a Spanish swear word under my breath,

"Gilipolla."

During the rest of January and early February, temperatures dropped to low single digits again. I spent most of my time grafting hard, going out less, drinking less, and working longer on my essays. Some of this was due to my rapidly diminishing funds, but more importantly, I was enjoying the work and could see my efforts paying off. My Spanish was improving rapidly, and I could even understand Maria during my frequent visits to the shop.

In mid-February, I met Sergio for our Wednesday night intercambio, and he was unusually subdued. We'd met on my side of the river, just a few bars away from Unfriendly's. He sounded hesitant and distant on the phone, reminiscent of his demeanour before we became friends. I knew that something was wrong. When I got to the bar, he was inside, seated with a juice, as always. "Hey," I said, taking my coat off and hanging it over the chair."

"Cómo estás?" he asked, indicating he preferred to talk in Spanish, something he rarely wanted to do.

"I'm fine," I replied in Spanish. "Are you okay, Serge?" I asked, searching his face and wondering what could be wrong.

"No, not really," he replied, hunching forward and looking down at his hands clasped tightly between his knees. I waited silently for him to tell me whatever it was that was troubling him. He lifted his gaze to the window, looking out into the dark sky, and blew out a deep breath.

"Andy, I have done a very stupid thing," he said, letting out another small but painful sigh. "A really stupid thing."

"Serge," I told him. "I've done hundreds of stupid things. Show me someone who hasn't. Surely it can't be that bad?" He lifted his gaze up to my eyes and seemed to be thinking about where to start.

"Okay. Last Saturday night, I met this guy who I've liked for a long time. He's an instructor at one of the local gyms. He was flirting with me, and we went to his flat. He asked me to have unprotected sex. He said he just couldn't do protection, so I agreed because I wanted him. I wanted him so much. And this guy must have slept with hundreds of guys, Andy. I mean, he is so good-looking. Hundreds of guys..." He was now holding his head in his hands and scraping his hands down the side of his face. He sat upright and began to flip a Cruzcampo beer mat over and over. Sergio was looking into the dark chasm of his mortality; the visible anguish on his face was palpable, but I couldn't think of anything helpful to say.

"I can see why you would be worried, Serge. Is there anything you can do?" I asked gently.

"I've called the medical centre today and booked in for a test," he replied, catching the mat before discarding it onto the table. "I really do not want to go alone, Andy, and I don't want any of my friends to know I'm going, so I was wondering if..." I could never have picked that sentence up before. Not in Spanish. Not the inflection; the desperation in the voice.

"Hey, of course, I'll come with you, Serge. That's what friends are for," I said. He smiled weakly and, for the first time, looked like the Sergio I had come to know.

At the end of February, I got another visit from destiny. I had a lecture at eleven and was up around nine, which would have constituted a miracle a few months before, but it had now become the norm. Maggie had already left, and I was relieved about that. Johan was still in bed and had broken three plates in the kitchen trying to make a tortilla at three in the morning, which was a difficult task as we didn't have any eggs. Still, he'd be able to talk Maria around when she came for the rent the next week and check the flat for breakages as she often did.

Searching through the cupboards, I found that Johan had drunk all my coffee. I stopped by Unfriendly's and ordered a double espresso. The service was quicker and less rude than usual; I made a mental note to tell the owner that standards were slipping. I arrived at uni twenty minutes early, so I sat on the stairs and pulled out a second-hand copy of *El Reino de este Mundo*. This was the novel that was central to my whole academic year. I had my head firmly buried in it when I heard a sweet voice say, "Hola."

I looked up and saw that she was standing in front of me —Antonio's girlfriend, Mariló. I somehow stumbled to my feet, and before I knew what was happening, she took my hands in hers and kissed me on both cheeks. After the kisses, she stepped back and seemed a little hesitant. I realised why. I was supposed to do the same. I bent forward and kissed her, closing my eyes and inhaling her sweet essence. When I stood back from her, she looked down. I followed her eyes and saw that I was still holding her hands. I blushed and released them. She smiled beautifully. She was a little shorter than I had first imagined and quite petite, probably around eight stone. Her long dark ringlets had been pulled back from her face into a ponytail and tied with a vibrant silk ribbon. Her eyes were almost as black as night, typical of the Moorish genes bequeathed to the Sevillanas, and her face was so beautiful it would make Demi Moore look like the hound of the Baskervilles.

She wore a white, tight-fitting mini dress with matching baseball pumps. Her legs and arms were bare, toned and the colour of caramel that girls back in the UK spent weeks on sunbeds trying to achieve. After a moment of standing and looking at her with a stupid grin on my face, she started to talk to me in Spanish. "It's really nice to meet you again." Amazing, I thought, as I'd never realised we'd ever really met in the first place. "You're the English boy from the bar, no? We met when I was with Antonio on the motorcycle, yes?"

"Err...yes," I stammered, trying not to stare at her. "I didn't think you had noticed me; we didn't get the chance to talk."

"Oh, I noticed you," she said casually and left that piece of information hanging in the air like a glider on a thermal. "What are you doing here?" she continued, fastening a small handbag she had wrapped around her shoulders.

"I have classes," I told her, feeling almost dizzy from the excitement. "I study Spanish here."

"Me too. English classes," she smiled, showing off a perfect set of white teeth. Her dark eyes were twinkling, something I didn't even know dark eyes could do.

"You study English?" I asked, sounding surprised. "Here? I haven't seen you around."

"Yes," she replied, switching into it and speaking very slowly. "I am around. I am not good at the speaking of it, though. It is nice to see you again because I look for practise my English. You would like to practise with me?"

"I don't need to; my English is pretty good," I blurted out. She looked blankly at me for a few seconds while she thought it over before bursting into laughter.

"You make the funny joke, yes?" Hearing her laugh, I couldn't have been glowing more inside if I was a circus fire-eating act that had gone horribly wrong.

"Yes, it was a joke. How funny it was, though..." I shrugged. She reached over and touched my hand. It was only brief, but it felt wonderful.

"I would like that we go out together sometime and talk some more. You do some funny jokes. Would you like?" Even though she was Antonio's girlfriend—no, scratch that... partly because she was Antonio's girlfriend—it was not a question that required a great deal of mulling over on my part.

"Oh, I would like."

When I got home, I shared my news with Maggie and Johan, who were playing cards in the living room. They were strangely unenthusiastic. "So, what do you think?" I asked, taking a can of San Miguel from the fridge and cracking it open in celebratory style. "Can you believe she asked me out? What's that all about? She's so amazing, and she asked me out. I'm sure that this is the destiny thing I've been feeling."

"Are you sure this is why you were meant to come to Seville?" asked Johan, laying a red card down on a black pile before Maggie reached over and slapped his hand. "For this girl who is someone else's girlfriend? Remember, it is Maria's son's girlfriend, and you don't even know her."

"Were you listening to anything I just said?" I asked him and took a slurp from the can. "She's the most gorgeous-looking girl I have ever seen. No one I have ever dated comes close. Not even Rachel, who, despite all her faults, was really attractive."

"So, Antonio's girlfriend is your type?" Maggie butted in before laying a card down and shouting a word in Swedish at Johan. She was scraping all the money from the middle towards her. She looked at me and asked again, "That's who you go for? A girl who's going out with someone else and who you don't even know? But she's beautiful, and that's enough for her to be your type? The disdain in her voice was palpable. I didn't much care for it and neither did I think I owed her any explanation. But she hadn't finished and continued to grill me. So, what's her personality like? Do you know that, at least?"

"Well...she seems really nice with a nice personality," I replied defensively.

"And you were able to deem this from five minutes of chat in a foreign language?" she spat, now putting Johan's losses into her purse. Considering these were my friends and I was happy, they didn't seem pleased for me. Of the two, Maggie seemed particularly hostile, and it was becoming a little clearer as to why.

"What's with you two?" I asked, dropping my empty can into the bin. "I thought you'd be happy for me!"

"You spoke like you have already married her," said an unusually solemn Johan, who, for some reason, seemed like an arsehole for the very first time since we'd met. Maggie snorted in surprise and brought her hand up to her mouth. They looked at each other in a very annoying way.

"Johan, you are a cheat," she told him, deliberately not looking at me and seeing my flushing face.

"I'm only saying that as I am your friend," Johan said, now dealing another hand while Maggie chewed on a matchstick and picked up her dealt cards. "It may be that this girl is your destiny, but I can't agree with what you are doing, Andy. If you do the wrong thing, you will find that the wrong thing happens back."

"Were either of you two even listening? I did nothing wrong," I bleated. "She asked me out, and besides, he cheats on her, you told me yourself."

"Do the wrong thing, and wrong things will happen," he merely reiterated as if that were the final word. He looked over at Maggie, and their eyebrows were raised again. I'd had enough.

"Is that some ancient Swedish proverb?" I asked, getting up and doing my usual storm off, only this time in the direction of the bathroom. "Because if it is, it's...it's...it's utterly shit." As I banged the bathroom door, I heard Maggie say not softly enough.

"He must be on his period."

14 EVERYBODY IN THE PLACE.

Extract from a letter sent to the Orkney Islands on the 14th of March, 1992

'...and thanks for the card and the money, Mum. You really shouldn't have. As usual, I won't be celebrating; no surprises there. It's never felt right since, you know...

As for wasting my life, well, I've met someone! It's early days, and we're not dating yet, but I will let you know how it goes. I'm not saying she's the one, but she seems pretty special.

Anyway, gotta go now and don't worry about me, Mum, I'm doing fine.

Love,

Andrew xxx'

For our first 'date', Mariló had suggested we meet in a small bar across from the university. I'd spent most of the afternoon in the bathroom preening myself. It was like being a teenager again, cleaning your teeth twenty times and searching your face for blemishes. I also agonised over what to wear. In the end, it proved superfluous as Johan had nicked most of my stuff, and a pile of my dirty clothes was lying on his bedroom floor. I had to settle for my black jeans and a casual white shirt.

My class was from five until six, and we were meeting afterwards. I arrived at the small tapas bar and sat at an outside table to wait for her. Despite the rush-hour traffic rumbling down the concourse, the small terrace was pretty and overlooked the university buildings.

It was only a minute or so before a smiling waiter came over. It made me wonder why we went to Unfriendly's so often. I ordered a glass of red wine, and when he returned, we chatted for a moment or two about the weekend's football. Seville had lost again. He shrugged his shoulders at me in resignation as if to say, 'What can you do?' I laughed. He wandered over to serve some Americans who'd just sat down, and I pushed my shirt sleeve up to look at my watch. Mariló was ten minutes late. I took out my Spanish dictionary and pretended to read it so I didn't look like someone I was being stood up.

She was twenty minutes late, and I'd nearly finished the wine. I thought about ordering another one but decided against it. I wondered how long I might sit there before I realised she wasn't coming. A voice from behind me said in almost perfect English, "Are you Andy? Waiting for Mariló?" I turned to see a tall, handsome blonde guy in his early twenties. "Err…yeah," I said, clearly surprised.

"Pascal," he replied, holding out his hand, which I took. "I have classes with her. She sent me over to tell you she's sorry she can't make it. She had to go home. Illness in the family or something, but she asked me to give you this." He handed me a piece of paper. On it was a scrawled note in Spanish, 'I'm sorry. We will meet next Tuesday at 7.30 in the Plaza de Alfalfa.' I couldn't help noticing there was no use of the interrogative in the note. I looked at the tall, grinning Frenchman. "Thanks." I managed to say.

"Okay," he said, still grinning like a baboon. "See you." He turned and left me alone with the feeling that I had just been dumped on by another gorgeous girl.

It was a long walk back to the flat, but when I got in, I was relieved to find there was nobody around. Of course, it was now a matter of self-respect. There was no way I would turn up next week after being messed about like that merely because she was gorgeous.

Was there?

A few days later, I was in a sterile hospital waiting room. I had met Sergio half an hour previously, and we'd walked in silence for ten minutes past the Parque de María Luisa. Sergio was locked in his own world, and my initial attempts to draw him into conversation were fruitless, so I figured that while he might have wanted my physical presence, he preferred his own emotional space to think. He was wearing a long overcoat and dark shades. It wasn't particularly cold, so I wondered if he wanted to be incognito. I didn't know how it could have happened in such a short time, but he seemed diminished in stature and somehow older. The looking older thing was not something I intended to raise with him. Still, worry lines had etched into his face, and he looked like he hadn't slept for days.

On reaching the main reception, we were sent up to the blood area and sat in a room with five other people, some of whom were also likely to be waiting for a blood test. The uncomfortable silence that the white, cold sterility of the place engendered was only compounded by the hostile atmosphere in the room. It was undeniably evident that we were being stared at.

As I'd mentioned previously, staring was practically an art form in Seville. Being trapped in a room with an old granny who appeared to be the Andy Warhol of staring was one of the most unpleasant experiences I had ever encountered. The reason so much art was being chucked our way was obvious: we looked like a gay couple, and people were making a connection at that time that gay equalled La S.I.D.A. Seville was a very safe city usually, but off the beaten track, an occasional mugger had been going around wielding hypodermics and claiming to have the virus. This created tension in the city and the odd outbreak of open hostility like the one we were experiencing.

For my part, I found the scenario really difficult to stomach. It was my first experience of being judged and disliked over a perceived difference. If it got to Sergio, he didn't show it. He was either used to it and had built up a barrier, or he was too worried about the test that was coming to notice it.

In the meantime, I sat next to Sergio, my ankle resting across my knee while my foot twitched up and down. I pulled a pamphlet on blood diseases from a rack on the wall to read and avoid eye contact with two middle-aged men and the old Sevillian granny staring us out. I say us, but the reality was more me because Sergio was ignoring them. He was sitting back in the plastic chair, his long legs straight out in front of him and crossed at the ankles. His hands were loosely clasped together on his middle, and his head rested against the wall. He stared out the window at the clear, blue sky like he was meditating. Meanwhile, I was getting more irritated and had returned their hostile stares with glares of my own.

Things got better, though, when a young nurse sporting a clipboard came in and mercifully hauled the granny away for her appointment. This was not before she wagged a disapproving finger at us on the way out. She said something in a toothless accent, which was undoubtedly offensive but, thankfully, to me, unintelligible. I bit my tongue and swallowed back a sarcastic retort rather than create a scene. It transpired that the granny was the ringleader of Operation Stare Out because once she had gone, both of the middle-aged guys sort of gave up and hid behind magazines.

They departed five minutes later, and we sat quietly in the waiting room, listening to hushed voices from the reception area and the soft footsteps of the staff as their rubber-soled shoes traipsed up and down the corridor. For whatever reason, the silence seemed to trigger Sergio into talking. "I knew I was gay from a young age," he said, staring out into the waiting room space. "Living in a small town with a strict Catholic background, let me tell you, it was not easy." I didn't know what to say, but I felt he just wanted to talk and tell somebody, so I kept quiet. "I was good at school, though. That would be my escape. But you can imagine that being gay and clever at school in a small town did not make me the most popular boy." He turned and looked at me, waiting for a reply.

"No, I suppose not," I agreed, returning his gaze.

"I had to learn to use my fists from a young age. I also grew tall quickly, and the village boys left me alone after a while. In school, I was the best in English. No one can speak English in my family. My father thought that if you could speak English, then you were somebody. So this made my father proud of me."

I got the impression that hadn't always been the case. He

continued, "My father saved and paid for a teacher to give me private lessons. With this, I was able to leave and come as far away from my old life as possible. In Seville, I can be myself. Only now, it seems being yourself is not always a good thing."

"You'll be alright, Serge," I said, touching his arm and squeezing it lightly. He let out a deep sigh.

"I hope so." After a short silence, the young nurse returned with the clipboard and called his name. He got up and smiled at me.

"Good luck," I told him as he left.

When Sergio popped his head back in after the test, I was alone with my thoughts. The afternoon had given me a small insight into a part of the gay world of which I hadn't previously been aware of, and it had affected me. It seemed it wasn't all tripping-the-light-fantastic and hot men. There was a distinct downside, and being judged in that way wasn't something I could have endured regularly.

As Sergio and I exited the fake white light and walked into the watery glow of the Sevillian February sunlight, I couldn't help but ask him about it all. "How do you cope with that?" I asked him as we strolled along the sidewalk.

"What?" he asked vaguely. "What are you talking about?"

"In there. All that… that hatred: that stupid old granny and those two guys."

"Oh, that," he said, laughing, confirming my suspicions. He shook his head slowly. "You get used to it. You learn to ignore it, I suppose. Besides, I was too worried about the test to pay attention to them."

"When do you get the results?" I asked.

"Soon," was all he said. Sergio seemed to be less bothered by the animosity on display in the hospital than I was, and that made me wonder if years of that sort of behaviour forced you to take a detached approach.

For the next week or so, I hung around the university trying to bump into Mariló by 'accident' to tell her I couldn't make the date she'd summoned me to. Of course, I didn't see her, which left me with one of two possibilities. I could either stand her up or go along to the date and lose any sense of dignity I might have. In the end, I chose the latter. This was partly because there was no way I could stand her up but also because, by then, I'd deluded myself into believing that she genuinely couldn't make the first 'date.'

The Plaza de Alfalfa, the location to which I'd been summoned, wasn't in an area of the city with which I was particularly familiar. I only had a vague idea because it was where some German girls Johan knew lived.

As bad luck would have it, I briefly bumped into Maggie on the way out, and she seemed to sense where I was going. This elicited a sarcastic, "Have a lovely evening with dream girl." I didn't dignify her with a response.

When I got to the square, despite everything, my heart was racing like it hadn't since stalking Gaynor Huggins in school paid off with a reluctant date to the pictures. I felt sure she'd turn up this time, and as I waited, my thoughts drifted away to some imaginary point in time where Mariló and I were together. Surely, she was my destiny? I sat down on the ledge by the fountain to compose myself and wait.

I looked at my watch and saw that it was only seven, and I still had half an hour to wait. I passed the time watching tourists and Sevillanos stroll by whilst constantly checking my watch to see how many minutes had passed. The tourists were easy to tell apart. It was funny how I had developed a slight disdain for visitors and, in many ways, considered myself a Sevillano. Hell, I was practically going to get married to one in my head at that moment.

It wasn't difficult to spot her when she turned the corner into the square. She was wearing another white dress, and this one made her look like a divine bride. The contrast with her dark ringlets swept back over her shoulder was stunning. This was all topped off by the obligatory sunglasses.

When she saw me, she waved and hurried over. She wore

small heels, and a tiny bag was swinging from her shoulder. As she drew closer to me, the excitement of being with her was overwhelming, and my heart pounded in my chest. In my head, a scene played out where two lovers embrace and look into each other's eyes, confessing their undying love to each other. She smiled demurely when reaching me, and we did the double kiss thing on both cheeks. "I am sorry I not come last week," she said, in something approximating English. "My papa is not well."

"Don't worry about it. You're here now; that's all that's important," I replied. She then fumbled around her tiny bag to look for her cigarettes and, switching to Spanish, suggested we could go to the cinema. She told me JFK was showing and that as she was studying American history as a subsidiary, she wanted to see the film, but none of her friends would go with her. Although I knew little about the subject matter, the idea of nestling down with her in the stalls to see a film seemed like a very good one at that moment, so I agreed enthusiastically.

As we walked the mile to the small theatre, she chirped like a little bird about her day. She had managed to get a job at the upcoming expo and was very excited about it. She had been nervous about the interview but could not believe it when they told her she could start in March. She immediately phoned her parents, who were very excited, too. She would need to improve her English, though, and maybe I could help.

Could I!

When we reached the cinema, she insisted on paying for my ticket. What an amazing girl, I thought. I could almost imagine Antonio's face when she told him it was over and that she'd met someone new, someone who didn't have a tool bag but who didn't mess around in Flamenco clubs with mad Swedes. Maybe Antonio would move on to Maggie. No, wait, I didn't like that scenario one little bit. Despite the fact that I'd stolen his girlfriend, I still didn't want him to have Maggie. I didn't want anyone to have Maggie. She'd have to stay single in this fantasy world of mine. That would teach her for the sarcasm earlier.

When we got inside, I was slightly disappointed that Mariló

chose an aisle seat near the front, as I was hoping for a canoodle at the back, but what the hell. The film came on. I was looking forward to going for a drink with her after the film, and while the Antonio thing was unfortunate, we'd all have to sort it out and deal with it like adults. It was that simple. I settled down and tried to concentrate on the Spanish emanating from the screen.

Three hours and eight minutes later—yes, I was counting—they were still droning on. I began to hate everyone in the film and everyone associated with it. To my eternal shame, I had even begun to blame Kennedy for getting himself shot at one point. Later years taught me that JFK is hard enough to follow in English, but in a foreign language, sitting next to Seville's answer to Aphrodite, it was impossible.

It was nearly a quarter to twelve when we got outside, and I knew any chances of a drink had long gone. "I did not realise it would be going on for so long," she said in English, looking at her watch. "It was a very long and difficult film, no?"

"It was both those things and less," I agreed, looking around to see that most of the bars had pulled up their umbrellas and shutters. "I don't suppose you have time for a drink?"

"I must go," she told me, searching her small leather purse for something. "But I wanted to make sure of something before I go." My God, could it have been that she, too, saw our destiny together and wanted to make sure?

"What?" I asked, with a smile a game show host would have deemed too cheesy.

"That you understand we are just friends, yes? I have lots of problems with my male friends who are not understanding this." I couldn't think about what she was saying, as it wasn't computing in my head. I had been preparing to tell her she was the most amazing girl I had ever seen. "Because my fiancé did not want me to meet with you," she continued. "But I tell him it is for the English practice only and we are just the friends. But Antonio is telling me you have the girlfriend in the flat, no? And that he does not want that I make her jealous and cause the problem." I suddenly got this weird feeling that I was an even bigger idiot than I'd bargained for. Antonio thought Maggie was my girlfriend. If he did, it never stopped the muppet from flirting with her for one second. This was going very wrong, and my suspicions were confirmed when I heard a car horn beep to my right. I looked around to see Antonio, head hung out of his wreck of a car, pointing at his watch and waving at us both like we were on an open-top bus and parading the FA Cup.

Meanwhile, Mariló stood on tiptoes, leaned forward, and kissed me on the cheek. "Adiós Andy. I go now. I tell Antonio I be here half an hour ago. I am late, and he does not like late," she said before running to the car. When she'd crossed the road, she flung her arms around Antonio and gave him the sort of kiss I'd hoped for. As she climbed in on the passenger side, he stuck his hand out of the window and gave me a beaming smile and a big thumbs up. My head was screaming at me to flick him the V, but my hand let me down as it rose up and then gave them a camp little wave before he sped off, honking what I felt to be his victory horn at me.

I must have cut a solemn figure trudging my way across the Plaza de Cuba that night as it started to rain. Of course, she'd remembered me without even speaking to me; of course, she'd been nice to me; of course, she'd wanted to go out with me. She wanted to practise her English like everyone else in Seville. She had used me, and, let's face it, I was usable.

When I got back in, I was soaked. To my surprise, Johan was sitting in the lounge, wearing my dressing gown and reading a Spanish novel. This was a surprise. Not that he was attired in my dressing gown, but that he was in at that hour, sober and reading a book. He didn't look up, which was just as well. I was hanging my head like the world's biggest idiot. I almost got to my bedroom door before he looked up and spoke. "How did your dream date go, amigo?" he asked, closing the book as an invitation to join him. I slouched over and stood by the couch. I kept my voice down as I knew Maggie was probably asleep, but I also did not want to wake her and give her the opportunity to come in and gloat.

"It was a disaster on so many different levels. It could have been an earthquake hitting a multi-storey car park," I sighed.

"This is a funny line that is not funny, I think," he judged, looking serious.

"No. No, it's not funny at all," I agreed and sat down on the edge of the couch. "I'm funny, though. Well, in the sense that I'm one big joke, that is." He got up and went into the kitchen, returning with two of my cans. He flipped one over to me.

"Tell your uncle Johan all about it."

"Well, Uncle Johan," I said, lifting the can to my lips. "Once upon a time, there was this idiot…"

When I'd finished the can and my story ten minutes later, he gave a smile so wry that it could have been made solely from Jim Beam bourbon, and he shook his head. "Andy," he said, continuing to shake it slowly, "sometimes when we search for the things most difficult to find in life, we learn painfully they are the things that are really the easiest to find—we just look in all the wrong places. And when you look in the wrong places, you find all the wrong things."

"Is that yet another of your shit, ancient Swedish proverbs?" I grinned.

"No, I just made it up. But because I made it up does not mean it is untrue, especially in your case."

"Yeah, well, here's an ancient English proverb. 'Man who lives with woman who isn't his type will get pissed off with Swede who continues to make out she is'." I got up, smiled at him, and he held his can up to me.

"Salud!" he said.

"Salud!" I replied, doing the same before making my way to my room and, for once, doing so without storming off like a child.

Whenever I bumped into Mariló, and it wasn't more than two or three times after the 'date,' I made excuses as to why I couldn't meet her again. She was sometimes a little pushy, which people who want to learn English in Seville can be at times and which really good-looking people can be all the time, but I figured she'd find someone else to use. The agony of being unable to have her faded after a little while; I guess there was a modicum of self-respect kicking in, something I had probably been lacking in the past where attractive girls were concerned.

By this time, I was keeping my head down at uni and, from the feedback I was getting from my tutors, doing well. I was working on the two assignments for the course, and they seemed to be coming along. Maggie had an Amstrad word processor her dad had fit in the car, and she let me borrow it so I could type them up. Johnson had set us ten-thousand-minimum word limits for both; mine were around five and growing. Maggie even consented to read the first one through for me. "Wow," she said, handing it back to me. "That's pretty good. Hidden depths and all that."

"I never know if you're being serious or taking the mickey out of me," I replied, taking it off her and looking down at it like it was the Rosetta Stone of essays. "Are you being serious?"

"On this rare occasion, I am," she smiled, messing about with the printer ribbon. "It's way better than anything I wrote in my second year, and I'm on for a 2:1."

"What? You're on for a 2:1?" I asked, now stroking the polythene A4 holder with my fingers. "You're telling me you have brains as well?"

"Ha-ha!" she said, surfacing from the printer with ink all over her fingers. "I've got it all, as you well know. Anyway, what you've written may not be the best Spanish I've ever seen, but the ideas underpinning it are very clever." With that, she went into the kitchen to wash her hands, and I picked up a copy of the second one.

"Maggie, would you mind reading this one? See if it's any good as well."

"I don't have to," she shouted from the kitchen. "Johan read it last night and gave one of his in-depth, stunning critiques."

"What did he say?"

"What did he say?" she mimicked, coming back into the room. "Let me think. Oh yeah. He said: 'Fuck. It looks like Old Bean is a lot smarter than he's been acting.'"

With that, she entered her bedroom and closed the door behind her.

15 GIVE ME JUST A LITTLE MORE TIME.

Extract from a letter sent to Northern England on the 25th of March, 1992

'...about to hand them in. If my flatmate's comments are anything to go by, I'm an undiscovered genius! Ha ha, I know what you're thinking, mate. There's a first time for everything.

Thanks for the birthday wishes. As you know, I don't really think about celebrations, for obvious reasons.

Anyway, on the serious question of *Achtung Baby* v *Nevermind*, I have to agree with my flatmate Johan, who said last week, '*Nevermind* for the party; *Achtung Baby* for the hangover!' I think he meant they're both amazing.

Cheers, mate. I look forward to hearing from you.

Andy.'

On the 25th of March, I turned thirty. I had no intention of telling anyone, and no one would have been any wiser—except that Maggie read the date on my passport. Johan had found it in my bedside table while he'd been rooting through my stuff, and he brought it out to show Maggie so they could both laugh at my photo. But she noticed that the date of birth made me thirty on that very day. It was a coincidence that I could have done without.

When I returned from my class, they were sat in the living room waiting for me with big, daft grins. "Happy Birthday!" shouted Maggie, jumping up. She put a plastic whistle between her lips and blew out a shrill squeak. She laughed and threw it on the sofa before bounding over to give me a tight squeeze.

"Yes, indeed. Many happy returns of the day," said Johan, who banged me on the shoulder in congratulations and then pushed a can of beer into my hand. "You are a sly old dog! You were not going to say anything."

"Thanks, guys," I said, looking around at them and the small cake with candles they'd bought for me. "But you shouldn't have. I...I didn't really want to make a big deal of it."

"I can't believe you weren't going to say anything," Maggie said incredulously and gave me a little push. "It's your thirtieth, Andy. That is a big deal."

"Not to me, it isn't," I said quietly. I was touched by her concern, so I pecked her lightly on the cheek, which made her blush. "But thanks. It's really nice of you to do this."

"And me. It's really nice of me to do it as well," Johan grinned.

"And you, Johan," I laughed and sat down on the settee with Maggie. "It was very nice of you. Who bought the cake and beer?"

"Who'd ya think?" quipped Maggie, passing me her beer to hold while she used a knife to cut into the cake. As the first piece was cut and placed on a side plate, a large Swedish hand came from nowhere and snatched it away.

"Johan!" she laughed, waving the knife at him like she meant it. "Don't they teach you any manners in Sweden?"

"If they did, dear girl, I have forgotten them," he replied, stuffing the cake into his mouth. "Happy birth—" He began to splutter, spraying cake everywhere as he choked on it. I leaned over, banged him hard on the back, and then passed him a new can. He tilted his head up and took long, deep swallows till nearly all of it had disappeared. He gasped loudly when he came up for air and then belched. "That's better. Can I have some more cake, please, Maggie?"

We started to giggle.

They insisted I had to go out and that I had no choice despite the fact that I didn't want to. I wasn't in the mood for celebrating, but I reluctantly agreed to go to Unfriendly's rather than appear ungrateful for their efforts.

We were getting ready to leave when the buzzer rang, and it was Sergio. I might have thought he'd come to join the celebration, but Maggie had already told me she couldn't reach him all day.

The first strange thing about his visit was that it was

unannounced which was very out of character for Sergio. The second thing was that it was late—not late by Seville standards but late by unannounced standards.

Maggie answered the buzzer and came back with a concerned look on her face. "It's Sergio; he's being a bit odd. I invited him in and told him it's your birthday, but he won't come up. He asked if you would go down as he needs to talk to you in private."

I figured out why he wanted to see me, and grabbing my coat, I asked Maggie and Johan to hang on for a moment. When I reached the bottom, Sergio was standing forlornly with his hands deep inside his leather jacket pockets. He was leaning against the whitewashed wall with a desperate look on his downturned face. "Hey Serge. You okay?" I asked him.

"Andy, I am sorry to spoil your cumpleaños, but I don't know who else I can talk to. Can you come with me to my flat?" His large hand brushed through his thick dark hair, which looked uncharacteristically as if he'd been tampering with a faulty electric socket. "There is something I need to do, and I would like your help to do it." I was pretty sure at that point that it wasn't a bit of internal decorating.

"Just a second, Serge, wait here," I told him and ran back up the stairs to the flat where Johan and Maggie anxiously waited. "I'm not going to be able to make it tonight, guys. I'm sorry, but I have to go somewhere with Serge." They both looked at each other before nodding sympathetically back at me.

"Well, we'll be there until twelve," said Maggie. "If you get back before then, come over and join us for a quick one."

"Okay," I told them, heading out the door. "Thanks for today; it was really thoughtful of you." I went out the door, slapped Sergio playfully on the shoulder, and gave him a 'Vamos' before we took off on the thirty-minute walk to his flat. We spoke very little on the way there. But that was okay; we were now good friends and comfortable in our silence.

An hour later, we were in his dining room and sat on wooden chairs around a large round table. We were both looking at an unopened envelope with Sergio's name on it and a red cross in the top left-hand corner. It had been delivered earlier in the day. "So, you can't open it," I said, picking it up and holding it up to the light. The contents were weightless, but the burden was heavy in my friend's eyes. This letter had the potential to change the rest of Sergio's life.

"Every time I look at it," he told me, gulping his glass of water, "my heart pounds, and I feel like I am going to pass out. I want to know, but I don't want to know. If that makes any sense?"

"It makes perfect sense. Do you want me to open it?" I asked, hesitantly and not wanting to. I also took a drink of water, lamenting it wasn't beer. "I'll open it if you want."

"No," he shook his head vigorously. "I don't think so, but I don't know what I want."

We both continued to look at the letter. "Look, this is silly," I said after another few minutes. "Besides, the suspense is killing me. We have to open it." I reached towards it while he moved his hand from below his chin and got up from the chair.

"No, don't, please," he said. I moved my hand away from the letter and left it there.

"Okay, okay," I said. "But if one of us doesn't open it soon, it might explode." He smiled a little at that. He sat back down, took a deep breath, and pushed it towards me.

"I won't be able to. You do it." I checked with him by raising my eyebrows, and he gave me a determined nod. I picked the letter up with an unsteady hand and prised the flap up quickly with my index finger before he could change his mind. In a matter of moments, the envelope's contents spilt onto the table. Sergio sat back on the stool and searched my face for a sign as I skimmed the letter. Because it was in Spanish, it took me a couple of moments to find the pertinent phrase, but there it was, at the bottom, as clear as day. I looked at him. He was grey and ashen. I gave out a huge sigh and said,

"Negativo." He stared at me like he could hardly believe what I had said. He repeated the word as if to convince himself.

"Negativo." Neither of us broke out into a celebration; the occasion felt too solemn. But in a way, it was the best birthday present I could have asked for. It was great news to receive on a day I had previously associated with bad news.

When I returned home, it was very late; the other two had gone to bed. On the table was a piece of cake and a note in Maggie's handwriting: 'I made Johan promise not to eat this. I saved the last piece for you. Hope you had a good birthday despite everything, and I hope that Sergio's OK. Maggie xx.'

I sat down on the couch and cried. Though I had done this on my birthday many times before, I resolved that this would be the last time.

When I finished, I made a cup of tea and sat in the kitchen eating the cake Maggie had left for me. In the still of the night, I thought about the traumas of the day's events and felt a wave of gratitude for having such great friends. I picked up the note and slipped it into my top pocket, looked around the empty flat, smiled, and went to my room for what I felt was a well-deserved kip.

When I woke up the next day, Maggie was in the kitchen dressed in the Duck Egg and making a cup of tea. "Want one?" she asked as I came in.

"Yeah. Great. Thanks."

"How'd it go with Sergio last night?" she enquired, dropping two bags into the mugs and rummaging for a teaspoon in the drawer. I sat at the table while she filled the cups with water from the kettle.

"Everything was good in the end, but I can't really say more than that. Sorry, I'm not deliberately trying to make it sound all cloak and dagger, but I can't break his confidence." She brought the drinks over and placed them down on the table.

"Sounds intriguing, but I shall leave it there. I'm glad he had you to go to, though; it was clear he needed a friend," she said, plonking herself beside me. "But apart from that, was it a good birthday?"

"Yeah. Thanks for the cake and stuff. It was thoughtful," I told her, encircling the warm cup with my palms. "I'm just sorry I couldn't make it for a drink."

"Don't worry about it," she replied, taking a sip and putting her feet up on the empty chair in trademark fashion. "Anyway, there'll be other times. Besides, we had a few drinks and a good chat. Johan let it slip that it didn't go too well with Dream Girl?" I smiled wryly.

"Well, Johan doesn't appear to have any qualms breaking confidences…but what can I say? I'm an idiot, Maggie. Although I think I might have finally learnt a lesson this time." She locked her eyes onto mine. The late morning sun highlighted the green hue, and they looked like they were smiling right at me.

"And what's the lesson?" I blew out a huge sigh.

"That may be…I've been looking in the wrong places and finding the wrong things. That maybe I should start looking in the right places." She was now steadily holding my gaze.

"Oh, I like the sound of that. Who knows what you might find if you start doing that," she laughed, batting her eyes. I don't know when it happened, but her right foot was resting on the side of my chair. She didn't speak, but we were looking intently at each other. I found that my hand was beginning to move inexplicably towards her foot. It was a very cute foot, and it could have been that my hand going to start stroking it.

But it never reached there.

That was because we suddenly heard Maria shouting out my name. I darted out of the chair with Maggie not that far behind me. It was the tone in Maria's voice that made us move so quickly. It was soft and anxious, not the usual loud and accusatory one. As I got to the living room, she was standing there with concern etched on her face. "Is everything alright, Maria?" I asked her. She nervously jangled the keys in her hand.

"Son, I've just had a phone call," she told me, her hands playing nervously with her set of keys. "Your mother has had an accident."

16 TO BE WITH YOU.

Extract from a letter sent to Newcastle on the 2nd of April, 1992

> '…says: it's better to be safe than sorry. Let me know when the test results are back. I know Dad can be a bit of a worrier, but he's right about this…'

I could see her through a small glass window in the corridor. She was propped up with about six pillows and reading the News of the World. She'd always been a big Labour supporter and was hoping to see the back of Major in the election. So, I had no idea what she was reading that for. Her glasses were sitting near the bottom of her nose so she could peer over the top of them when she wasn't reading. She'd always been fussy about keeping her hair coiffed and, against all odds, had managed to look like she'd just paid a visit to the hairdressers. I smiled at that as it was typical of my mother; her frail frame belied her stoic and determined nature.

At that particular junction in time, the ward sister was proving to be difficult. She was a Scottish bruiser with a thick Glaswegian accent and gave off a Hattie Jacques vibe from the Carry-On films. She was sticking to her guns no matter how much I pleaded with her. "But I've travelled all the way from Seville," I argued. "And tomorrow morning, I have to get a flight back to London and then out to Seville. Can't I see her for ten minutes?"

"Mr McLeod, we have visiting times on these wards for a reason," she reiterated, folding her broad arms across her generous bosom for emphasis. There was nothing soft about her round, chubby face. She had beady eyes that were hard, cold, and unblinking under a starched white paper cap. "If I make an exception for you and your mother, I would have to start making one for everyone. And then what would I have? Why anarchy!" I sighed, and my shoulders slumped in resignation. I doubted the Scarlett Pimpernel would get past her. I was defeated. Through the glass, my mum was oblivious and had picked up a pen to do the crossword by the look of things. I made a final plea.

"So you're telling me I have to wait another three hours until seven?"

"It would appear so, Mr McLeod," she said, with a note of satisfaction in her voice. With that, she double-clicked her pen officiously before writing something on a clipboard she'd taken off the reception desk. She waddled off towards the adjoining ward without another word or a glance in my direction.

I watched her go before turning towards the glass doors leading to the corridor. I figured I'd find a coffee machine and a Sunday paper to pass some time. I was at the point of leaving when a conspiratorial voice stopped me in my tracks. "She's off duty in half an hour." I turned around to see a tired-looking woman in her mid-forties. She was dressed in nurse regalia but had a mop and bucket in her hand. "The other sister's not so much of a stickler. I'm sure she'll let you in. If you want, I'll tell her about the circumstances before I go off my shift."

"That's very kind of you," I said, relieved and smiling gratefully at her.

"It's okay," she replied, shifting the mop bucket into her other hand before starting towards the ward my mum was on. "Go and get a cup of coffee and wait outside in the corridor. Someone will call you into the ward in about half an hour." She stopped and turned back to me. "She's a bit of a character, your mother."

"Oh, she's that alright," I laughed. There was a twinkle in her weary eyes. "And thanks for your help, Nurse…"

"Nurse Smith," she smiled as she moved her hand slowly up to cover her name badge.

Forty minutes later, I pushed the doors back and stepped inside the ward. There were six beds full of older ladies, my mum being one of them. My mum was thirty-seven when she had me, her only son, which was one of the many reasons she worried too much about me. As I approached her bed, she looked briefly startled. She peered over her glasses and saw me. She instantly composed herself, slightly smiled, and crossed her arms. I wasn't expecting anything else. I leaned over and kissed her awkwardly on the cheek, trying to avoid the arm of her spectacles as I did so. She flinched a little at this inappropriate gesture of affection and admonished me, "I told them to tell you I was alright. I told them to tell you not to waste your time coming all this way, but you don't listen. You never listen to anything I say, do you, Andrew McLeod?"

"And I love you too, Mum. Very much," I said, pulling a stool around to her side of the bed and sitting down.

"All that money on flights just wasted," she grumbled, picking up the newspaper and peering down at the crossword. "And it's not even as if you have a job these days, what with having packed in a perfectly decent one to go and live halfway around the world."

"Firstly, Spain's not halfway around the world, Mum. Secondly, the money was not wasted when I was worried about you. You've had a bad fall," I replied, unbuttoning my coat, leaning over like Johan and stealing one of her grapes from a bowl by the side of her bed. "Anyway, what have the doctors said?"

"Oh, them? They don't know anything. The consultant thinks they'll put a new hip in. Might as well, he says. But you should see him. A slip of a lad really, he knows nowt." I smiled as Mum's northern England accent slipped through her newly acquired highland lilt.

"Who's looking after the house?" I asked her.

"Johnny and Cathy. And they're feeding the chickens for me," she said, taking her reading glasses off and putting the paper on her lap. "You look like you've lost weight. All that Spanish rubbish, I should imagine. Are you eating enough? I worry you're not eating enough."

"My flatmate keeps stealing all my food," I grinned at the measure of truth in my joke.

"Tell him I'll bloody steal him if he takes anymore," her face was red and indignant.

"Easy Mum. I'm the same weight I was before I went. I'm fine. Anyway, I love it in Spain."

"Ay," she said, huffing and puffing away, "but you're not staying there, are you? What's your big plan now that you've lost your job? That's the problem with you, Andrew. You weren't careful as a child, and you're still the same now. You lost all your toys as a kid; you couldn't have them for five minutes. Now you've grown up, you haven't learnt very much. Jobs, girlfriends, you can't keep hold of anything." I didn't rise to any of it. It was all just bluster. I looked at her and smiled, which she found disconcerting.

"You finished? Got it all off your chest?" I asked, laughing. "You know what Dr McDermott said about getting stressed."

"Pass me a glass of water, will you?" she ordered, waving her hands at me. "I'm parched." I picked up the cheap plastic jug with lukewarm water and poured some into an even cheaper-looking plastic cup. She took it without saying a word and gulped it all down. When I looked at her, I could see her eyes were moist.

"Oh, Andrew! What are you going to do, son, when you get back? No job, no home, you never got married. What happened to that nice girl? The one that became one of those lesbians. Is she still a lesbian? She was a nice girl."

"She's still a lesbian, Mum, and she only became a nice girl after you met Rachel and you compared them. Before that, you hated her."

"I never," she said crossly, picking up a tissue and wiping it back and forth across her nose.

"You did, Mum. You hated her like she was Thatcher." She blew her nose, and the sound of it rattled through the ward, startling a couple of the old biddies in the other beds. One woke up and began calling out for the nurse.

"None of this would have happened if you hadn't lost your father so young. I blame myself." She was clenching the blanket, her paper-thin skin revealing fragile knuckles beneath.

"None of what? Blame yourself for what? For Dad? That was an accident, how was that your fault? Anyway, I think I've turned out okay. I don't have a job at the moment, but I'll get one when I return, and I'll find the right girl one day. I'm making a new life out there, and something amazing will happen, believe me."

"I wish I could believe you, Andrew. You're such a dreamer, always have been. You get that from your father. He was a romantic at heart. Not that it did him much good in the end." We both sat in silence with our respective memories of my dad. Then she picked up a box of chocolates from the other side of the bed, shook it, and handed it to me. It was a peace offering, so I helped myself to the last caramel, and you know how good that feels.

"Remember how you would hide your chocolates from me when I was a kid?" I asked, popping the caramel into my mouth and squashing it against my back teeth. "But I could always find them?" She nearly smiled at that.

"You were a cheeky so-and-so. Still are," she said, shaking her head at me.

"Mum? Do you still think about Dad? About the accident?"

"Sometimes. Do you, son?" she sighed, letting the air rush out from her mouth.

"Sometimes." I shrugged, looking down at my hands.

"I wished it hadn't happened on your birthday. Not much of a present for a kid's ninth birthday."

"I know. I still feel guilty that he was rushing back because of me," I said, starting to choke up.

"Your father? He never remembered his own birthday, let alone anyone else's. I took care of that sort of thing," she replied in a surprised voice. "And he didn't suffer, Andrew. The police told me that. It would have been instant. They said he wouldn't have even seen the lorry coming, not in all that rain." I looked at her through tears that had begun to well up in my eyes.

"At least that's something," I replied.

A few hours later, I'd said a tearful farewell to Mum—tears

mainly on my side. I spoke with the sister to see if I needed to be aware of anything. Mum was scheduled for the op, and the sister couldn't envisage any problems, though there were always risks with surgery, she told me. A week or so after that, they'd get her back to Orkney with physio and enough support in place for her day-to-day needs. In six to eight weeks, she'd be as right as rain. I looked back through the door, and we waved our final goodbye. Taking a deep breath, I made the first step toward the exit, and the rest that followed were not as difficult.

I stayed overnight at the Columba Hotel in Inverness. It wasn't too expensive and was in a nice spot overlooking the river. The next morning, I took a morning flight to London, and the following day, I flew out of Heathrow and back to Seville. The whole trip had taken a big whack out of my funds, and although Mum had pressed me to take some money off her, I refused, saying, 'I'd only lose it.'

She didn't like the joke, but I was glad I'd gone to see her all the same.

17 COME AS YOU ARE.

Extract from a letter sent to Northern England on the 7th of April, 1992

'...feel pretty down about it all and wondering if I'll ever learn. I can almost hear you saying: 'No, you'll never learn, chasing after the wrong type of women; it's what you do.'

Now it's turned out that Mariló isn't my destiny in Seville, I'm left pondering what or who is. I'll leave that with you and look forward to seeing you when I return towards the end of June.

All the best, mate,

Andy.'

The year was flying by. I had arrived in early September, and it wouldn't be too long before I returned to the UK. March passed in a blur of activity. Apart from the trip to visit my mum, I'd knuckled down to studying and had managed to resist Johan whenever he tried to drag me away from my assignments. Maggie was a massive support in reading and correcting my Spanish assignments. Afterwards, we'd sit in the living room and talk for hours. The subjects were diverse: music, uni, politics. Nothing was off the table; talking with Maggie was engaging and insightful and never dull. I began to realise that after my dad died, I had deliberately distanced the 'vulnerable me' from everyone to avoid getting hurt again. I'd been so devastated by his death that I avoided intimacy, which might explain my relationship with my mum and why I was drawn to beautiful airheads who I only connected with on a physical level.

My relationship with Maggie became less hostile, and we grew closer as friends. Things were going well.

My Spanish had improved so much that I was now dreaming in Spanish. This bizarre phenomenon felt very strange and surreal. In one memorable dream, I was on a double-decker bus with Maggie. She was wearing the Blue Duck Egg and talking dirty to me in Spanish even though I didn't know what she was saying. The whole thing was especially weird because even though I'm not attracted to her when I woke up…

No, best not go into that.

The previous night, Maggie had read through two of my assignments and, handing them back to me, said, "Well, they're no worse than when I last read them. Even the bits I don't understand." I laughed as I took them off her. Putting them in my bag, I wondered if Johnson would think they were as good as my flatmates seemed to believe they were.

A day or two later, before one of my grammar classes, I dropped into Johnson's office to find him searching through a pile of paperwork scattered across his desk. As he rifled through it, he took the assignments from me with a distracted 'Thanks' and pushed them into his briefcase. He told me he had a meeting and waved me a hasty goodbye. I was a huge relief to have finished them and handed them in.

I mulled over how much my attitude towards studying had altered over the last few months. And how, once I'd started applying myself, I enjoyed it far more than when I did my media degree.

A week or so later, I was putting my books into a satchel after a speaking class and chatting to a friend of Johan's when the stand-in teacher called me over. He rummaged around in his pocket for a moment, smiled, and then passed me a note. I looked down at the crumpled paper in my hand. It was from Johnson asking me to call in and see him as soon as I'd got a moment. I didn't have anywhere I needed to be right then, so I went to his office directly, tapped on the door, and stuck my head around it.

Johnson was seated behind his desk, reading some papers. Seeing me at the door, he waved his hands and beckoned me to sit down. "You asked me to come and see you. Is everything okay?" I asked him, closing the door behind me and removing his bulging briefcase from the chair before sitting down. From my new vantage point of the chair, I could see that he was holding my two essays in his hands and reading the top one. "I just got your message."

"Yes, fine," he replied, suddenly dropping them down on the desk in front of him as if they had caught fire and waving his hand over the top of them. "I've called you in about these."

"Oh," I said. "Do I need to redo them or something? I gave it my best shot."

"Do you have to redo them?" he gave a deep belly laugh. "They are two of the best crits I have read in a long time. I need to tell you, and I don't say this lightly: you are doctorate material. I've already shown the one on Sender to Professor Sanchez, an expert in that area. He was very impressed with some of the ideas underpinning the work."

Wow! I remembered thinking—someone is impressed with me, and my ideas underpin stuff. Johnson pulled open a drawer in his desk and found what he was looking for with surprising speed, considering the chaotic state of his filing system. He pulled out a piece of paper, which he slid handed to me.

"What I wanted to see you about is this. A job's coming up in the department," he told me, pointing at the piece of paper that I was now reading. It was, indeed, a job advert. "It's a few hours teaching here in the faculty and visiting England two or three times a year to recruit for our courses. You'd do a doctorate here, probably under my supervision, and there's no doubt you'd find things tight for a couple of years. Most people get by with the small amount the university pays and more from private tuition. But the life here, as I'm sure you're aware, more than compensates. As far as the job goes, I think you'd be perfect. I have another candidate in mind, but you would be my first choice. Interested?" My head was swimming; Johnson was offering me a dream job and the chance to stay in Seville. It all seemed too good to be true.

"I don't know what to say," I replied, my eyes scanning the advert as if it were a missing scroll from the Bible. "Yes, of course, I'm interested, very interested."

"You do have a degree, I take it?" his eyes fixed on me.

"Just a 2:1 in Media Studies."

"Great," he laughed, sliding the two essays over to me. "There's likely to be an interview sometime in early May. It'll be in Spanish, and I think you'll do very well. In the meantime, type up a CV and put it on my desk. Will you do it before next week?" I nodded like one of those toy dogs people have in the back of their cars, without daring to mention that I had no idea how to do a CV.

When I returned to the flat, nobody was there to share my good news with. I had to wait an hour before Maggie showed up from teaching private lessons. She bustled into the flat wearing a light raincoat even though it was twenty degrees outside—very Sevillian, I remember thinking. I shared my news about being called into Johnson's office. She leaned against the kitchen worktop, her coat draped through the crook of her arm, listening intently. I finished and held my breath, waiting expectantly for her reply. She slowly stood up straight and was still for a moment or two.

"Wow! I mean, I suppose, well, that's amazing news, Andy. When will you know for certain?" she asked me, moving back towards the hallway and hooking her coat on the coat stand. She sounded a little less enthusiastic than I'd hoped.

"It's still in the early stages, but there's an interview at the beginning of next month, and they'll let us know the same day," I said, walking into the lounge and flicking the lamp near the tele on. "There's just me and another candidate, but Johnson seems to think it's mine to blow, really." She came over and stood before me as I flopped back onto the couch.

"So that would mean you'd be staying here then?" she asked, lifting her little finger to her mouth and chewing on her fingernail. "Not going home in June like you planned?"

"I guess," I replied, trying hard not to think about how much weight she'd lost lately. "I haven't really had time to take it all in. It's all happened so quickly."

"Well, I'm really happy for you. It's what you wanted," she

said, smiling weakly. I couldn't help noticing her voice breaking a touch. Then she turned, walked towards her room and quietly closed the door behind her. I stared at the closed door and blew out a long sigh. She hadn't even given me the chance to let her laugh at me for needing help with my CV.

When Johan returned an hour and a half later, he was still sober, wearing the Nirvana T-shirt Doug had sent me last week and whistling a very bad version of 'Smells like Teen Spirit' as if he didn't have a care in the world. He took the good news in the way that he took any news, good or bad. "Let's go and celebrate at Unfriendly's," he beamed. The only difference was substituting the word 'celebrate' with 'commiserate' when it was bad news. Either way, it meant a visit to a bar.

"Okay, why not?" I replied, knowing I had nothing better to do and feeling the need for a drink. I picked up my wallet from the dressing room table and had an afterthought. I returned to the kitchen, where Johan was staring into the fridge and clearly eying up my new packet of four chicken burgers. "Shall we see if Maggie wants to come?"

"Of course, the more the merrier," he replied, finding the last of my beers in the fridge, cracking it open, and downing it in one gigantic gulp. I shook my head, went to Maggie's door, and tapped lightly on it.

"Yes," called a low voice from within.

"It's me. Can I come in?" I asked.

"Yeah, sure," she responded. When I pushed the door open, Maggie was sitting on top of the bed with the Blue Duck Egg on, despite it being only half-seven at night. It was obvious that by wearing the Blue Duck Egg, she was going nowhere, but I gave it my best shot anyway.

"Err...Johan and me are going down to Unfriendly's for a small celebration. You know? The job?" I said, edging into the room. "A little something to eat and, of course, the odd drink. Can we tempt you?"

"Mmm, no thanks," she said, with a sad smile, while tightening the belt of the duck egg around her waist. The whole effect made her look like a giant, fluffy hourglass. She swung her legs over the side of the bed and reached over to the dressing table for a book. "I'll give it a miss—wrong time of the month and all that." Ah! That explained her odd behaviour before when I'd told her about the job. To tell you the truth, I was a little bit envious of the 'wrong time of the month'. I had seen how Rachel behaved appallingly, ate masses of carbs, and did all manner of crazy things with complete exemption from consequences. Nevertheless, Maggie looked very down, and I felt sorry for her. I guess being a woman at certain times of the month sucked.

"We could get a tapa takeout and bring it back here," I suggested. "I'll get some of that wine you like from the supermarket. Come on, it'll cheer you up." She looked up and broke into a weak smile, the kind you'd reserve for an unexpected visit from the Mormons.

"That's very sweet, but I'd prefer to stay here alone if you don't mind. You two go out and have a good time," she said, holding my gaze with that sad smile. "Besides, I've got an early class. So I'm going to do some work and then get an early night. I'm really tired." I looked at her for a moment and bowed my head.

"Okay, if you're sure."

"I am," she said, nodding.

"Right, well, I'll see you tomorrow. I'll try and make sure he's not singing lewd Swedish songs when we get back." I turned to go.

"Andy," she called out as I swung the door open.

"Yeah."

"I really am pleased for you. You know that, don't you?"

And this time, she sounded like she was.

At Unfriendly's, we'd drunk a couple of beers and eaten three tapas each before I remembered the CV and asked Johan. "Curriculum Vitae, old chum," he advised me, throwing a pistachio nut into the air and then catching it in his mouth. He never missed, and it was slightly perturbing. "I'll show you how to type one out if you want. I can't see that Maggie would want to help you with that." Before I could ask him why not, he'd spotted Antonio, who appeared with a couple of his mates and went over to speak with him. I kept my head down, not wanting to be humiliated any more than I had been on my sort of date with his beautiful user of a girlfriend. When Johan got back, it was not unexpected news.

"He's going to a Flamenco club. I am going, too, as I have been informed there may be a few Spanish ladies with great promise. Do you want to come?"

"I don't think so," I said, getting out of my chair. "Besides, I want to give women up for the moment, especially gorgeous ones that have anything to do with him. No, you go. And Johan, don't make any noise on the way in and wake Maggie up. She's not feeling too good."

"You need not worry about me, my friend," he assured me. "I will be sleeping at Antonio's flat tonight, hopefully not alone. He has a friend, and she has a friend who has a liking for blonde-haired Norsemen." I shook my head at him and punched him lightly on the arm. I thought about what a tosser Antonio was. With a girlfriend like that, how could he be cheating on her? It seemed some blokes were never happy, no matter what they had.

"That should cover the bill here," I said, flicking three thousand pesetas his way before getting up and stretching my arms wide. "It's on me as I have a job, and you have no prospects for anything other than the hospital the way you carry on. Have a nice evening with Mr Tool Bag." He looked at me blankly, picked the money up off the table, and rolled it under his nose before pretending to smell it. He then gave the most enormous grin possible, stepped over, and gave me a bear hug.

"I intend to, old chap. I intend to."

When I finally convinced him to let me go, I crossed the street, sneaked up the stairs as quietly as possible, and slid my key carefully into the latch. The lights were all off when I got inside, and I stumbled around in the dark, not wanting to wake Maggie. Despite being as black as Maria's cardigans, I found the kitchen, flicked the strip light on and got myself a glass of water. I went into the living room and watched TV with the sound down for an hour or so and then went to bed.

As I was climbing in, the buzzer went loudly and long. 'That idiot Johan,' was my first thought. He would have forgotten his keys as usual, even though he needed them for tomorrow as Maggie and I would be at uni. I was more annoyed than normal because I'd distinctly told him not to wake Maggie up.

I pressed the buzzer to let him in and heard him clambering up the stairs making as much noise as a crippled wildebeest with a couple of lions attached to its back. He tapped loudly on the door. "I'm coming, I'm coming," I hissed before opening it as quietly as possible.

"Charmed, I'm sure," said Doug, walking past me with a suitcase in his right hand.

Five minutes later, Doug was sitting with me in the kitchen with the door firmly shut so that we wouldn't wake Maggie. He was drinking a cold bottle of Cruzcampo. "What are you doing here? Why didn't you write to let me know you were coming?" I asked him.

"Because I didn't know I was coming. I've had problems at work and needed somewhere to go," he told me evasively. He picked up a Spanish Elle magazine that Maggie had left on the kitchen table and thumbed through it even though he couldn't understand a word. "I won't be going back there either."

"You're joking!" I gasped. He didn't say anything and continued to thumb through the mag, avoiding all eye contact with me. "Aren't you at least going to elaborate a little on these 'problems'?" I asked him, snatching the magazine and throwing it back down on the table.

"Right now, I'd rather not if it's all the same to you", he said, finally looking at me and frowning. "I just needed a distraction from all the shit surrounding work and get as far away as possible. I thought of my best friend who was holed up in sunny Spain, so here I am. I can stay for a while, can't I? Without having to explain my every action to you?"

"Okay," I said, throwing my hands up in surrender. "You can have my room for a bit. I'll sleep on the couch or in Johan's room if he's not around. But you need to sort this out, Doug. You have to go back to work eventually. You know you have to."

"That'll be difficult since I'm suspended and will likely be asked to resign, or worse, in the next couple of weeks. So, if it's all the same to you, can we leave it for now?" I looked back at him with surprise and shock. He turned his eyes away and picked the magazine back up in a childish gesture of defiance. I decided it wasn't the time to push things.

"Yeah, yeah. I'll ask the others. I can't see there will be a problem," I told him, but problems were all that I could see.

I slept like a log in Johan's room, probably because I felt very comfortable surrounded by all my stuff. When I got up the following day, it was early. Muffled voices were coming from the kitchen. There was no indication that any of the voices were Swedish so that left Maggie and Doug. I could hear them a little more clearly when I exited my room. To my chagrin, Doug was regaling a seemingly recovered and taking-it-all-in-her-stride Maggie embarrassing stories about me. I went directly to the bathroom and turned on the shower, hoping they'd hear me and be finished by the time I reached the kitchen. They weren't finished, though, by a long chalk.

"….so he's in the toilets, completely drunk, and throwing up. The stripper we paid for is stood outside of the cubicle and banging on the door, shouting, 'You better come out, or I won't get paid.' All we could hear from inside the cubicle was Andy telling her to go away." They were laughing as I entered, but at least they had the decency to stop.

"I take it you two have met then?" I tetchily glared at them both. "And, oh yeah, Doug, that story is so 1983 it's just not funny."

"Maggie thought it was," Doug replied, pouring two cups of tea from the pot and grinning at her.

"I did," agreed Maggie, sitting on the workbench swinging her legs back and forth like a four-year-old who didn't have a care in the world. "I thought it was highly amusing."

"No, you didn't," I said, narrowing my eyes at her and turning to Doug. "Make me a cuppa, you useless lump, or you're out on the street."

"He can stay for as long as he wants. He can even have my room if he has more hilarious stories about you," Maggie laughed.

"Well, he doesn't, do you, Doug?" I replied, turning to him with a hard stare. He looked back at me like butter wouldn't melt in his mouth.

"Nope, none; that's all there is Maggie." His mouth twitched into a small grin.

"That's a pity," said Maggie, vaulting off the workbench onto the floor with no little grace. "Anyway, it's really nice to meet you, Doug. I'll see you around later, hopefully. When Andy's not here," she whispered conspiratorially.

"Don't you have an early class to go to?" I asked, catching her eye on her way out.

"I'm going, I'm going," she replied, waving her arms around. She then grabbed the cuppa from the bench, blew a little kiss at me with her free hand, and exited the door happier than I'd seen her in some time.

When she'd gone, Doug put the kettle on again and started to make another pot of tea. "She's a cracking girl, her," he said, chuckling. "A big girl for her mother, though."

My mother always used to say that. It's a northern expression. So northern that when I asked people from the north what it meant they had no idea. I don't think Doug had any idea either, and even though there was no malicious intent in his voice, he got both barrels of a sawn-off anger shotgun all the same.

"What's that supposed to mean?" I asked, turning and standing right in his face. This was not a pre-planned move because if it came to a fight, I'd be down on my knees faster than an Iron Maiden groupie.

"Steady on, Andy," he said, taking a small step back and

pushing his palms down flat. "I meant it as a compliment."

"A compliment?" I retorted in disbelief. "I wouldn't want to see you insult her then." He was on the back foot and looking as confused as he used to when previous best friend used to lean over and smack him on the head with a ruler in class.

"Look, what I meant to say was: she's a great girl."

"So why didn't you say that then? I know she's a great girl because I've known her a lot longer than you. So I don't need you to tell me that. And it would help if you remembered she's my flatmate," I said, putting my hands on my hips, a gesture that would probably have gotten me a free drink in any of the clubs Sergio frequented. "And by that, I mean, err...that's all she is. That's to say, nothing is going on between us if that's what you're insinuating. It's just, well...a bit of respect, Doug." At this point, I was more than agitated but had very little idea about what he'd done to agitate me so much.

"Understood, mate," he replied, nodding so fast that even Enid Blyton's Noddy would have been in awe of the sheer amount of nodding taking place. "Totally understood."

"Yeah, well, sorry mate, no harm done," I said, stepping back, calming down and lowering my head to look at the tiled floor. "It's just that I'm a bit sensitive about her...her...err—"

"Weight, mate?"

"Oh, for fuck's sake, Doug. Of course, not her weight. What? What? Do you think I'm that shallow or something?"

"Sorry, mate. 'Course not," he said, stepping back again until his lard arse was pushing hard up against the sink.

There then followed five minutes of tea-slurping silence and some avid reading of Elle magazine.

18 LET'S GET ROCKED.

Extract from a letter sent from Inverness Hospital to Seville on the 12th of April, 1992

'... given you the wrong impression that I wasn't pleased to see you because I was. It was very thoughtful of you, Andrew, and I think you get that off your dad. I moan too much, your Aunty Cathy says, and if nothing else, she's a good judge of character.

Anyway, all my moaning is because I care. I'd love you to meet someone like that nice lesbian girl you used to court. I'm sure there's somebody special out there for you, Andrew, and you'll find them when the time's right.

Enough of all that. They're putting the new hip in tomorrow, so I'll be right as rain in a couple of months.

Love,
Mum xx'

There are two amazing weeks in Seville in March/April. The first is Semana Santa or holy week. In English: Easter. In the year of our Lord 1992, it fell in the middle of April. Sergio had offered to show Maggie, Doug, and me the sights. Doug had gotten to Seville only a few days before and seemed in no hurry to return home. Johan was less than enthralled by the festivities.

On the first night, Sergio took us to an area of the city with which we weren't familiar. When we got there, a large crowd was already assembled and lining the streets in anticipation. Hundreds of people were milling about in the square. The still night air seemed to whisper promises of something special, and we were not disappointed. Seemingly without any prompt, the crowd went quiet. In the distance, men's voices raised and carried above the silence. Then clapping broke out sporadically, followed by the sounds of a brass band. Strange-looking figures emerged from the church entrance wearing long white robes and tall, black pointy hats like those worn by the witch in The Wizard of Oz. They were carrying a giant, opulent float elaborately decorated with some of the most extraordinary religious iconography imaginable. Statues and paintings of Christ and the Virgin swayed from side to side as the float was carried through the crowds on the shoulders of men. Candlelight flickered in the soft evening breeze, casting shadows on the walls as it passed. As it wound its way towards us, seemingly of its own volition, the crowd became silent again; only the eerie chanting from the robed figures and accompanying music could be heard. It was mesmeric. Camera flashes twinkled everywhere in the dark, mingling with the candlelight and adding to the heavy atmosphere. In the midst of all the bodies pressing against us, I felt Maggie grab my hand. She squeezed. I smiled at her and said, 'Wow."

For a small-town boy from the north of England, the whole week was an extraordinary spectacle. Sergio guided us through the rest of the week, taking us to the best of almost sixty such parades. The most amazing one took place in the early hours of Good Friday in Triana itself. Strangely, Johan wasn't interested in any of them and spent most of the week in Unfriendly's with Antonio.

He was very interested in the second week, though. This was the famous Feria de Abril de Sevilla (The Seville April Fair). This is always after Easter, and it's a great time to visit Seville. The Feria dates back to 1847 and can only be likened to a giant wedding reception that lasts a week. Various-sized casetas (or large tents) are erected alongside the river, and parties take place inside each of these. The festivities start around eight or nine and continue until six or seven the following day. Each of these tents is owned by an influential family or firm; in some, there's live music and a bar. For the best casetas, tickets or entradas are necessary. And everywhere, and I mean everywhere, people are dressed in traditional Spanish dress and drinking manzanilla, a very dry white sherry. When you first taste it, you wonder why on earth anybody would drink it. But Johan and I became living proof that you can quickly develop a taste for it. Somehow, Johan acquired tickets for the casetas every night of the festival. When I asked him how he managed this when so many Sevillanos couldn't get them every night, he calmly said, "Willpower, my dear boy, sheer willpower."

Fortuitously for us, mere mortals, Johan procured tickets for one of the biggest casetas on the opening night. This is traditionally held on the Monday.

On the opening Monday of the great party, we agreed to meet inside the Feria at ten o'clock. Johan, Maggie, Doug, and I left the flat at around half-nine. Everyone was in good spirits, and we chatted excitedly during the short half-an-hour walk from the flat. The whole city was buzzing with anticipation. It was in the air, and we were breathing it all in.

Mid-April was warm in the evenings, and Maggie was wearing a figure-hugging, black, off-the-shoulder Lycra dress that accentuated her beautiful curves. She'd pinned her hair up and looked incredibly elegant. She looked like she'd maybe dropped another couple of pounds. I loved her shoes, black stilettoes with an ankle strap, but I couldn't see how she would be able to dance in them. "Don't worry," she said, hooking her arm through mine when I asked her. "I won't be. These are for show only. I'll be the Barefoot Contessa once the music starts." I caught myself sneaking the odd look at her shoes and remembering how I would ask Rachel to put hers on after suffering through an episode of Eastenders. I felt a very strange quiver in my stomach as I took another glance at them and then another. In the end, I decided I'd best stop as Maggie would notice and think I was some kind of shoe perve, which I err...wasn't.

When we arrived at the Feria, Sergio had brought a couple of friends. I'd spoken with the taller guy, Ramon, previously at uni and in one or two gay clubs. I didn't recognise the more diminutive guy, but Sergio told me he was living in the flat next door to him and that he'd brought him along because he kept complaining about the music Serge played too loudly. Serge was worried he might be reported to the landlord, so it was a peace offering of sorts. After the introductions, Sergio led us to the caseta for which he'd acquired tickets. Inside was a six-piece band with an attractive female singer. The music was a cross of Spanish/rock, and a crowd was already dancing. It was a fantastic atmosphere, with many of the Sevillanos present oozing sophistication, something the continentals carry off so well.

On the far side of the tent was a bar where they were serving manzanilla. I headed in its direction and gestured at Johan and Maggie to follow. I looked over and saw Doug talking to Sergio and Ramon.

After a couple of drinks, Johan disappeared with some newly acquired friends. Maggie suddenly grabbed hold of my hand and pulled me up to dance. She pulled me onto the floor with both hands and began to twirl around me. The band was playing a particularly appalling cover of 'Como Hemos Cambiado' (How We've Changed). We all knew the words as the song was ubiquitous, and Maggie mouthed the words in Spanish to me while throwing her hands up in the air and shaking her hips. I had observed Maggie dance before and loved watching her vivacious exuberance on the dance floor.

When the song finished, we waited for the next song, but the band's singer announced they were taking a short break. Maggie and I stood looking at each other, and she shrugged at me, disappointed. "There's Maria from my class," she said, breaking up an uncomfortable moment. "I'll go and catch up with her. I won't be long." I walked back to the table where Doug was now seated.

"He's a great bloke that Sergio," he said, holding a manzanilla glass up to his nose and smelling it.

"Good, I'm glad you like him," I said. "How are you enjoying it here?"

"It's amazing. It's much better than I could have imagined. I think I'm going to stay."

"What!!" I replied, surprised by the news. "That's a big step."

"Yeah, I know, but I don't feel like there's anything I want to go back for," Doug said, hunching his shoulders before knocking his drink back in one and getting up without saying another word to get another one at the bar. As I watched him go, to my utter disappointment, I saw Antonio at the bar. Then he swaggered over to Maggie's table while I watched Maggie's face break into a wide smile as she noticed him approaching. He pulled up a chair and sat next to her, and in no time at all, they were getting on like a stupid house on fire. Then the band reappeared at the worst possible moment and struck up a cover of 'Bambaleo'. I couldn't hear what they were saying, but Antonio was making small circular strokes on Maggie's arm, which she didn't seem to object to. I noticed that Doug was now back and droning on in my ear. Something about being able to be himself here, but I wasn't listening.

Eventually, Johan dropped in the seat next to me. "What did you bring that idiot here for?" I asked, turning round sharply. Johan put his arm around my shoulders and squeezed.

"Take it easy, old chap. I did not bring him. He was outside, and he had his own tickets. He was coming here already as he knows the caseta's owner's daughter. What is the matter?" With that, he looked around, and his eyes rested on Maggie. She was virtually cheek-to-cheek with Antonio as he whispered in her ear. "Ah, that is what the matter is," he continued.

"I'm going to the bar," I said, standing up. "And I intend to get very, very drunk. Who's with me?"

"Andrew, that seems like a splendid idea," said Johan, slapping me on the back.

"I'll pass," said Doug, to my surprise. I want to enjoy and remember this. This is very special."

"Up to you," I told him. "You take Johan's keys, as I don't think he'll need them. See you in a bit." When I got to the bar, Johan grabbed my arm and pulled me back.

"Are you sure you want to do this, my friend? Why don't you go over and talk to her?"

"Talk to who?" I asked, waving wildly at the barman to come over. "I don't know what you're talking about." Johan let go of my arm, leaned over to the barman, and asked for two manzanillas.

"Fair enough, old bean," he said. "I cannot help you if you will not help yourself." I looked over at Maggie and Antonio. They were dancing, and Maggie was gyrating her hips in a seductive swirl. Antonio's hands slipped around her waist to the small of her back, pulling her towards him. I picked up my sherry and downed it in one.

"You in, you Swedish lump? Or you out?" He grinned, playfully rubbed both of his hands together, then picked up his glass and did the same.

"It would seem that I am, indeed, in!"

After that, I went into self-destructive mode, and Johan went into Johan mode. We ordered manzanilla after manzanilla. I kept looking at Maggie, hoping she'd come over, but she didn't until it was too late. I was staggeringly drunk when she finally graced me with her presence. "Wow," she said, leaning in. "How much have you had?"

"Wha's it godda do with you?" I asked, turning my back on her. Even in my drunken state, she just ignored me and said to Johan,

"Have a good night, Johan. I'll see you later." Then went back to her table. I shouted after her in a pathetic attempt to get her attention,

"Yeah, see yah, Andy!" At some later point, she must have left, as I lost track of her completely. The others must have come and said goodbye to us, but I don't remember them going. Eventually, I lost Johan, who wandered out of the tent to talk to some Swedish girl and never returned. The last thing I recalled was talking to a pretty blonde girl who worked in a shoe shop in the Centro and arranging a date with her the following Sunday. However, by the following day, I had no recollection of where we'd arranged it for or what her name was. I vaguely remembered stumbling out of the caseta.

When I awoke a few hours later, I was lying in the middle section of the motorway that runs to the south of Seville. I had lost my watch by then, so I guessed from the sun's height that it must have been around seven in the morning. Cars were whizzing past me on their way to work and I had little idea which way the flat was. I looked to the right of me and guessed that it was where the river was. I somehow managed to sit up, and the world swayed sickeningly. The narrow grass divider between the opposing traffic wasn't very wide, and I marvelled at how I hadn't killed myself so far. I scrambled across the two lanes of cars and performed the miracle of not getting myself run over by any of Seville's legion of illegally speeding commuters.

I walked and turned, and walked and turned, through countless streets. Through extreme good fortune, and no real plan, I eventually reached VIPS department store on República de Argentina and was able to home in on the flat from there. My head was thudding with a dull heavy ache, my eyes were stinging from the early morning rays of the sun, and my thirst was raging. I was dehydrated and suffering from the worst hangover I'd ever had in my life.

With shaking hands, I rummaged through my pockets for the keys, and thankfully, they were still there. I pushed the key into the bottom latch and made my way up the stairs, each slow step making my pounding heart feel like it might burst. My head was in so much pain I thought I might pass out. Once inside, I located the paracetamol made for the kitchen and drank copious amounts of water. I began to feel slightly nauseous, but I forced it down while leaning against the sink. My T-shirt was soaked from spilt water and sweat. When the shaking subsided, I figured I'd better go and check on Maggie and make sure things were alright between us before I went to bed. I needed to apologise for my behaviour. I couldn't believe I'd acted like such a prick.

On reaching her door, I knocked lightly and leaned against it while waiting for her answer: nothing, no reply. I pushed the door open, and my eyes tried to adjust to the darkness because she had the shutters down. As the light from the living room filtered in, I could see she had company. The duvet was moving slowly up and down like waves on the sea. The odd sigh and moan could be heard from under the duvet. I felt my nausea rise again. That had to be Antonio. Who could blame her or him? I realised I should get out of there before I made things worse. I turned to go when I heard a voice from the bed. "Eh? Oh fuck, sorry, mate." It was Doug. Doug had been shagging Maggie.

The bastard.

I was furious and humiliated. My so-called best friend had slept with Maggie, even if it had nothing to do with me. Yet somehow, it felt like the incident with previous best friend was happening all over again. All I could think about was humiliating them in return. A red mist descended. I stepped forward and pulled the duvet off them both.

That was when I saw Ramon.

I couldn't go to sleep after that. You might think this was because I'd just discovered my best mate was gay and had been hiding in the closet longer than little Lucy on her way back from Narnia. You'd be wrong, though, because all I was worried about at that moment was: where the fuck had Maggie gotten to? I sat at the kitchen table, wishing I smoked, nursing my headache, and drinking strong cups of back-to-back coffee. I felt like a mother whose teenage daughter had gone clubbing for the first time and still wasn't back at four in the morning.

It was eleven thirty when she finally appeared. By this time, Ramon and Doug had already surfaced. Ramon seemed to be not the slightest bit embarrassed, and his exit was accompanied by a bright smile and a wave. Doug sheepishly left with him without speaking a word to me.

"Hell, you look like my mother sitting there," she said, slinging her bag off her shoulder and dropping it on top of the table. She walked over to the fridge to find some bottled water. "You've not been waiting up for me, have you, tapping the table like that? All you need is a hairnet to complete the picture."

"Don't be silly," I said, my face flushing and pulling my hand off the table. "Did you have a good night?"

"Yeah," she replied and gulped at the bottle. "Very. You?"

"It was okay," I said, noticing my hand was itching to get back to tapping the table. "Well, apart from coming home to find Doug in bed with one of Sergio's mates."

"Eww...messy. But not a massive surprise, I shouldn't have imagined."

"Well, it was, to be honest," I said, scanning her for any possible sign as to whether or not she'd been up to anything. She was right; I was acting very much like her mother. "They were in your room."

"Yeah, I told them they could use it," she said matter-of-factly while screwing the cap on the bottle and putting it back in the fridge. "No one knew where Johan was or what he was doing, and I knew I wouldn't be back until later this morning."

"You told them they could use it?" I gasped, not comprehending.

"Well, they asked at the Feria," she countered evenly, switching the recently boiled kettle back on. "Sergio's family is coming down today to spend a few days at the Feria, but he didn't know what time they would make it. He didn't want Doug and Ramon to be around when they arrived." My head was trying to compute all this with about as much success as a dog with an abacus.

"So you already knew Doug was gay?"

"Yeah, he told me a couple of days ago. You didn't know?" She looked at my gaping mouth, poured milk into her coffee, and stirred. With that, she turned towards her room. "You need to have a conversation with him. Sorry, I'm done in. I'm having this, and then I've gotta get some beauty sleep."

"Look, Maggie!" I shouted after her, as much in panic as anything else. "I'm sorry if I acted like an idiot in the caseta."

"That's okay," she shouted back, but not stopping. "Johan explained it to me. You were jealous. It was sort of sweet, I guess."

"I wasn't jealous!" I shouted, a little more than alarmed. "I just don't like the guy, simple as that." She stopped outside her room, leaned her head sideways against her door, yawned, and smiled.

"Look, Andy, whatever you say. You weren't jealous. I'm not your type, and I'm way too tired to argue with you."

"I'm not arguing with you," I said, getting up and walking towards her. "There's no argument, honest; it's more a misunderstanding. I'd just…well…where did you go last night?"

"Now you do sound like my mother," she sighed, lifted her head off the door, and turned back to me. "If you really want to know, I went with Antonio. He took me back to his flat, and he made love to me all night long. It was brilliant. Is that what you wanted to hear? Is that okay? Got all the details? Can I go to bed now? I just don't have the energy for this." She turned again and used her hip to bump the door open to her room. The way she did it made me feel funny in the nether regions. I don't know why they call them the nether regions. The NOW regions would be more appropriate.

Once in her room, the door banged shut behind her like a jet going through the sound barrier. As she went, it was easy to see she'd been lying about her weight loss, for what reason God only knew. You could tell, though. I could tell. I stood up, marched over, and pushed open her door like I was in a forties Cary Grant movie and just about to put Hepburn in her place. When I got in, Maggie was sat on the bed, pulling at the ankle strap on her heels. "You don't have the energy for me, but you had it for him," I declared, walking over to her. "And leave those on." As I reached her, she looked up at me and slowly took her hands away from her shoes.

"Please," I asked. "Err… because I have a thing about shoes." Her green eyes caught mine like a cat staring at a mouse dangling before it. I swear those babies were sparkling like emeralds in King Solomon's mines.

"Do you now?" she retorted softly, lying back with her arms up behind her head. "It looks like I might have some energy for you after all." I lay down on top of her, and her hand moved to the back of my head and pulled my mouth down onto hers. Her lips felt warm and sweet, and her body pressed with urgency against mine. My hands began to fumble underneath her for the zip on the back of the dress. She sat up to help me, and as I pulled it down, she wiggled expertly out of the dress. She looked amazing; her hair had worked loose and had fallen around her face and shoulders, making her look stunning in the morning sunlight. She wore a black bra that barely contained her breasts. My left hand caressed her beautiful curves as I kissed her and breathed in her scent. She began to sigh and reached for me below. I let out a short and very sharp moan.

"Oh, Andy," she breathed into my ear. "I want to." I needed no second invitation. I pulled my hand down to her briefs and began to slide them down her legs.

That was when the front door banged in the flat. I stopped mid-slide. This was followed by more banging around, and it became apparent that Doug was in the process of packing. My concentration was broken, the moment gone. "I'm really sorry, Maggie, I can't do this now. I need to speak to Doug. I think he's going home. Do you mind if we finish this some other time?"

"Some other time?" her voice straining. "Some other time? You have to be kidding me." She turned to pull the sheets over her to cover herself. It always seemed weird to me that women did that. I mean, earlier, you could be in the most intimate positions with them, and you may have explored every nook and cranny of their body, and then at some random, arbitrary time, they deemed it suddenly inappropriate to see them naked —to see all the bits you'd already seen. She was now holding onto the covers like they were the safety bar on a particularly fast fairground ride. "Is what you have to talk about with Doug infinitely more important than what we were just doing?" I was out of bed, pulling my jeans and T-shirt on. I was more than perplexed by this and didn't really get where she was going, so I switched to agreement, something that had served me well in the past and something else that didn't go down well again.

"No, of course not, and we need to talk. It's just—"

"Need to talk about what, Andy?" she cut in, very aggressively in my opinion. My face looked blank as I considered the question.

It was obvious I didn't have an answer. "Oh fuck off, Andy, will you," she said, grabbing a pillow, putting it over her face, and crashing back onto the bed. "Just fuck off. You're not worth the effort." I stood there looking as much like a lemon as if Vermeer had painted me in a bowl of fruit. I picked my trainers up, walked to the door, and shut it softly behind me.

When I caught up with Doug, he was packing his suitcase in my room. "Where are you off to banging about in such a hurry?" I asked, closing the door behind me.

"I thought it might be best if I got out of your way," he said, clipping the latches down, grabbing the handle, and looking in the general direction of Maggie's room while lowering his voice. "Seems like you have a lot going on anyway."

"Can I be the judge of what's best for me?" I replied, pushing the case back down. "You might have told me."

"Don't be stupid," he replied, flopping onto the bed. "I was police. I couldn't tell anyone. It's frowned upon. They say it isn't, but it is. And, the culture makes it impossible to be openly gay."

"What I don't get is that you were always so macho, going on about shagging this bird and shagging that bird. You even tried it on with Rachel."

"Yeah, well, that's how it gets you when you're stuck in the closet," he told me, staring down at the floor. "You're always forcing it, always trying to be more macho than the next guy. Living the lie. Anyway, it's soon going to be out in the open. The court case will see to that. Local papers and stuff."

"Court case?" I gasped.

"Yeah, court case," he said glumly and put his head into his big hands. "Lewd conduct, they call it. Getting caught in Big Park toilets with a bloke is what the papers will call it. Either way, it's the end of the police for me." I put my hand on his shoulder.

"Shit, Doug. What will you do?"

"Funny thing is," he said, looking up at me. "I'm really not that bothered about the job. It's a relief to get away from it all. I don't even need the money that much. My gran died last year and left me the house. Thing is, it was in a posh part of London, and even though it was a dump, it sold for a fortune. So I don't have any immediate money worries. I'm thinking of staying here. You can be yourself here. Sergio said I can stay with him for a while." He must have noticed my frown at this. "Don't worry, he's not my type." Where had I heard that before?

"Well, I just wished you'd told me. You told Maggie," I said defensively, "And I was your best mate, yet you told her before you told me."

"The emphasis on 'was your best mate' there, I take it?" he asked, studying his shoes. I looked hard at him and fake-punched him on the chin.

"Are my best mate, Doug. You are my best mate."

The next few days were not how I'd expected the Feria to end. Doug left for Sergio's after his parents had gone back home. Sergio had promised to show him the 'scene' in Seville, and Doug was excited about it. It was nice to see Doug excited about anything.

As for Maggie, well, she avoided me wherever possible, and the one time in the kitchen when I bumped into her, I asked her if she wanted to talk and she snapped, "What do we have to talk about?" She went out for one more night at the Feria and that was with some girls she knew from uni.

For my own part, I didn't enjoy the rest of the week. I went a couple of times but on both nights, I only had two glasses of sherry but I was pleased for Doug, who enjoyed it, and was glad when Johan turned up at the end of it still alive and seemingly none the worst.

In the end, I thought it would have been great to spend every night dancing with Maggie.

That was the moment when I finally realised that my type had changed.

19 PLEASE DON'T GO.

Extract from a letter sent to Newcastle on the 1st of May 1992

'...see my tutors and sort it out. I don't know what might have happened between us, but I guess that's something I'm not going to find out now. That's life. As they say...'

At the end of April, I received a letter from the Spanish Department at Seville University inviting me to an interview regarding a post I might be suitable for; at least, that's what I thought it said. Even though my Spanish was pretty fluent, the letter was written in so much convoluted jargon that I needed Sergio to translate half of it for me.

A pressing worry about the upcoming interview was that my frequent visits to Unfriendly's with Johan had sapped my account. Whilst I wasn't facing poverty, I was reluctant to splash out on a suit for the interview.

I decided to speak to Johnson about my dilemma, so I took him to one side after one of my late classes. He reassured me on both counts. The interview would be an informal occasion, and it was highly likely, despite another candidate, that I would get the job. People were very impressed with my essays, he'd told me, tapping the side of his nose in a very odd way.

I rose early on the day of the interview, which turned out to be a scorching May day. A bright haze descended on the city, and the air felt almost too warm to breathe, hitting the back of my throat, making it hot, dry, and uncomfortable. Our flat didn't have air conditioning, and we all suffered from a lack of sleep, as the temperature remained in the twenties throughout the night. The mad Swede had gone to the rooftop or Azotea to sleep. Despite giving it his best shot, he had been unable to convince Maggie to join him. Maybe announcing that he was sleeping blew any slim chance of that happening.

I rummaged through my much-reduced—by budget constraints and Johan's pilfering—wardrobe and finally decided on a Paul Smith shirt and a pair of dark Levi jeans that weren't as faded as my others. I swapped my habitual Converse shoes for a pair of black leather lace-ups from my previous office job in the UK. "How do I look?" I asked Johan, who had returned from the rooftop, thankfully part-dressed and rifling through my drawers to see if he'd missed wearing anything.

"I feel I am looking at the next member of the Spanish department of Seville University."

"Well, you might be if you could be bothered to even look at me," I scolded him, standing sideways to the mirror and sucking in what was a small but decidedly unwelcome, Unfriendly's beer gut. "Anyway, I'm not counting any chickens before they're hatched."

Completely ignoring my old English proverb, Johan pulled a Fred Perry T-shirt out of the drawer, held it up to the light as if he were checking the authenticity of a diamond, and turned to go to his room. I couldn't help but notice that my Ray-Ban sunglasses were tucked neatly into the back pocket of his horrible yellow shorts. "I'll let you know how I get on then, shall I?" I shouted after him.

Rather than wait around in the flat with only my nerves to keep me company, I thought I'd leave for the interview early. Maggie was sitting on the sofa, reading a magazine and eating an apple. She looked up at me, the sun highlighting golden, red hues in her hair from the window behind her. For some reason unknown to me, I wanted to push my fingers through her hair, but she interrupted my thoughts. "You look smart," she said and smiled. She ran her free hand through her curls, unaware of the effect it was having on me.

"Umm, I don't know," I coughed, clearing my throat. I looked down at myself, feeling awkward. "Anyway, I'd better get off for this interview and leave you in peace to read your mag. I'll catch you later."

"Yeah, okay, hope it goes well," she said, shaking her curls and holding my gaze. "Catch you later." I stood looking at her, and our eyes held for what felt like ages. Eventually, I broke away before she did. As I turned to go, she said,

"Oh, by the way. I'm going home in two weeks." I stopped at that and spun around.

"What? I don't understand. You can't be. You're supposed to be here until the end of June," I said, feeling a strange panic rising inside of me.

"My mum's not well," she replied glumly, dropping the magazine at her side. "Really not well. She's being stoic as usual, but my dad's been so worried he's asked me to cut my year short. I checked with my tutors, and they said I'd already passed the year. They've drawn up a certificate of attendance, so I'm done. I've just gotta sort out my flights now."

"Oh," I replied. My head had now become something akin to a giant cabbage at the news. "I'm so sorry to hear about your mum, Maggie. Can we talk about everything when I get back? I've really got to go now."

"We can," she replied, getting up and walking towards the bin with her apple core. "But there's nothing really to talk about. You're staying here, and I'm leaving."

"But I'll see you when I get back home?" I called out, flicking the latch on the front door and opening it.

"Sure. And good luck, Andy," she shouted as I exited into the stairwell.

As soon as I stepped onto the street, I heard a dreadful, wailing noise. At first, I thought it was a passing fire engine or a cat stuck with its paw in a grid. But when I looked to the opposite side of the road, I saw Maria shouting and waving at me to come over. I waved back, dodged a couple of cars, and made my way over to her.

It must have been thirty degrees, and as usual, she was dressed in black with a shawl draped over her heavy cardigan. There wasn't a single bead of perspiration on her hairy, wrinkled face and she looked every inch the black widow. As I approached her, she stood, hands on hips, like there was a fight to be had. I reckoned I could take a few people mano a mano in Seville; it was just that Maria was not one of them. Without any warning, she raised her right hand abruptly. For a brief second, I thought she was going to slap me, having heard about my plan to spirit her future gorgeous daughter-in-law away. Instead of hitting me, though, she smiled and touched me gently on the cheek with her gnarled index finger. "Buena suerte, hijo," (Good luck, son) she said. Then she pinched my cheek lightly before turning around and going back into her shop. She probably didn't hear the sound of my jaw clanking against the pavement.

Once I arrived at uni, I had to locate an office in the administration area. When I found it, Johnson was already in the corridor talking to a tall, thin man and a smartly dressed woman I hadn't seen before.

"Ah, Andy," he said, calling me over. "I'd like you to meet Dr Martinez and Professor Sanchez. They will form the panel with me today."

The woman, Martinez, was fortyish and impeccably dressed in a Gucci trouser suit. Her short dark hair was elegantly cut in a pixie style, revealing small, perfectly shaped ears adorned with small stud earrings. She reminded me very much of the attractive, middle-class señoras who could be regularly seen taking an espresso or strolling with friends around the Parque de María Luisa on Sunday afternoons. She extended her slender arm, and an expensive silver bracelet watch slipped down to her wrist as I shook her hand. We both exchanged an 'Encantado.'

Johnson had told me that Sanchez ran the entire Spanish department. He was a tall, grey-haired man in horn-rimmed glasses who looked like a Spanish version of Christopher Lee. His clear brown eyes were friendly as he held his hand out, and I shook it. His grip was firm and a little warmer than Martinez's. He was probably in his early fifties and conveyed an assurance that put me at ease. "A pleasure. I have heard a lot about you from Doctor Johnson," he said in one of the purest Spanish voices I'd ever heard.

"I hope I can live up to his expectations," I replied with a grin.

Johnson said something to them in Spanish that I didn't catch, and then he ushered me away from them towards a room at the end of the corridor.

"The other candidate's already here, so we'll be ready to go shortly," he told me. "Just wait here until you're called, and good luck." At this, he gave me a silently mouthed 'sorry' to which I returned a puzzled look. He opened the door, grimaced a little, and then guided me by the elbow into the room. The other candidate was sitting on a chair reading a novel. She looked up and met my surprise with a look of disdain.

It was Saffron.

Johnson exited sharply and closed the door behind him before I had a chance to get my bearings. Saffron tossed her head back in contempt and, lifting the book towards her face, ignored me. I looked around the room. It was empty—a typically vacant waiting room stripped of all previous character to enforce its new role. As there was only one other chair in the room, and it was beside her, I was forced to go over and sit in it. She placed both hands underneath her chair and shuffled it away from mine like a pregnant duck. She moved it about three feet away from me. It was a gesture that was as comical as it was painful to observe. We sat silently for what seemed an eternity, but it was probably only about a minute.

"Look, this is silly," I said, folding my hands on my knees and turning towards her.

"What's silly?" she replied, pretending to read the book by flicking over pages and not looking up. "I don't do silly things. Maybe you're mixing me up with somebody you know."

"Saffron, this is silly. Behaving like this. Can't we act like adults?" I pleaded. "I didn't know you were the other candidate. Johnson didn't tell me."

"He couldn't," she said petulantly, finally putting the book on her lap and facing me. She produced a glare that could have withered stone. "I only got the invite yesterday when the other girl dropped out. Roger...Professor Johnson neglected to tell me you were the other candidate. Probably because he knew

I wouldn't have come if I had known." Her shoulders slumped down, and she looked more upset than angry. "Funny thing is, I'd like this job. It would be super to get away from Pinner and meet some of Mum's ridiculously high expectations of me. But now I see that's not going to happen. You're going to ruin this for me like you've ruined everything else here in Seville."

"Steady on. That's a bit dramatic. I understand you don't like me, and you might have good reasons for that, but I'm not ruining anything. It's a job interview, Saffron," I replied, crossing my legs defensively. Then, added as an afterthought. "An interview for a job I'd like to get as well. Anyway, one of us will get it, and one of us won't. If you get it, I'll be pleased for you."

"That's easy for you to say!" she snapped, getting up off the chair and going over to the small window. She looked out onto the streets below and said sulkily, "Because we both know you'll get it. Uncle Roger's told me any number of times how great you are. After I left the flat, I asked him to kick you off the course, but he wouldn't. So I had to change classes just to avoid you. You probably didn't even notice. Anyway, I've only come along for the experience. I'm only here to make up the numbers. And I must admit, truthfully, I won't be pleased for you when you get it."

She didn't look over and continued staring out the window for the duration. After the initial shock of hearing that she had tried to get me thrown off the course, I pushed my indignation to one side. Of course, I'd noticed she wasn't in the same class as me, but I'd only felt relief that I didn't have to see her anymore. It occurred to me, and not for the first time, that she was a very complicated young woman you wouldn't want to be on the wrong side of.

A minute later, against a backdrop of silence and recrimination, Martinez popped her head in, gave a simulated smile, and called my name. I got up and followed her across the corridor and into the interview room.

The next thirty, forty, maybe even fifty minutes were a blur.

Considering Johnson had told me it would be an informal interview, the two Spaniards fired questions at me like I was Davy Crockett and they wanted the Alamo back. Although the spoken Spanish was rapid and complex, their accents were easy to understand as neither sounded like native Sevillanos. Johnson sat to the left of Sanchez, who, naturally, was in the middle. Johnson only asked one or two questions, seeming more than happy to leave all the tricky stuff to the natives. I recall answering a few questions about my essays and trying to explain the ideas behind my thinking. And I was thinking in Spanish, which meant it was more likely I'd explained my ideas clearly. There was a dodgy moment when Martinez asked me a question that got lost in translation. I thought she'd asked, 'Do you like to sin?' I felt this was a bit forward, especially considering I didn't work for her yet, but my very quizzical look and the silence that followed made her clarify the question, which I then translated correctly to mean: 'What would you say your worst faults are?'

Overall, I thought I'd done okay. They assembled their copious notes, we shook hands then I walked back with Martinez to the waiting room where she called Saffron through. She didn't look at me as she walked past, pulling her bright yellow jacket below her hips and flicking her hair back. In the meantime, I had nothing to do but sit down and wait the forty minutes or so for Saffron to return.

I tried to fill the time by attempting to name every member of England's 1966 World Cup-winning team. I kept getting ten of the eleven and, for the life of me, couldn't remember Nobby Stiles. I then tried to picture the faces of my previous girlfriends, but most of them ended up looking like Maggie, which was weird.

When Saffron returned to the waiting room, she ignored me and stood by the window again. It was painful to hear her occasionally mutter. I caught odd phrases such as 'a waste of time' and 'some kind of joke' before I gave up, closed my eyes, and hoped someone would be back in with the verdict sooner rather than later.

It was a very long half-hour, that was on a par with the old granny stare out at the hospital. That was until Martinez re-entered the room and said my name. I'd gotten the job; victory was mine, but it had a bitter taste. I stood up and turned to Saffron to say something consoling, but she beat me to it before I could speak.

"Congratulations," she hissed out of the window.

My walk back through the city was emotional. I couldn't believe I was going to live here permanently. But my mind kept wandering back to my last conversation with Maggie. When I finally got home, I was eager to share the good news, but to my disappointment, no one was there. I had no idea where Johan might be, but then again, it was possible Johan might not know where he was. I only knew that he would be sporting my Fred Perry T-shirt in a bar somewhere. As much as I loved the guy, I was less interested in his whereabouts than I was Maggie's. I don't even know what I wanted to talk to her about. But she consumed a large amount of my thoughts daily, which was ridiculous if I thought about it as I was staying in Seville, and she was leaving.

I took advantage of an empty bathroom, showered, changed and went for a walk rather than hang around the flat and wait for Maggie to return. As it was around five and blisteringly hot, only a few people were out, mainly tourists. The Sevillanos were more inclined to be in their homes at this time of day. I wandered down to the Isobella bridge and up the opposite side of the river to the Torre de Oro. Stopping for a coffee at one of the bars near the bullring and surveying the beauty around me, I pondered how fate had changed the course of my life. In less than one year, it was unrecognisable. Then again, I'd believed I would encounter a woman who was my destiny, but I was mistaken. I crossed the river again, back through the Plaza de Cuba and returned to the flat.

I saw Doug and Johan sitting under one of the large pavement umbrellas at Unfriendly's. Johan waved at me to come over and join them, but I signalled that I was going to the flat. He pulled a face at my reply and gave me a single digit. Johan had recently indoctrinated Doug into getting the staff to like him, and Doug was more than happy to oblige.

I checked inside the flat, but there was still no sign of Maggie, so I went to the bar and filled them in on the day's events.

When the next round of drinks and tapas were served, Doug, Johan, and I cut a gloomy trio, staring down into our glasses of Cruzcampo. "So, I'm confused," said Doug, eventually breaking the silence. "Is it congratulations or not? I haven't got a clue. Am I missing something?"

"Yes, I think you are," Johan answered solemnly. "Andy has his dream job, but Maggie is going back home very soon, and she's not coming back. This puts him in a difficult position."

"What difficult position?" asked Doug, sounding as confused as the previous messages he'd sent out about his sexuality. "I don't understand what Maggie has to do with it all."

"The difficult position, Douglas," said Johan, letting out a long sigh and stretching out on his chair. "Is that Andy is in love with Maggie, and so he is faced with a choice: he can have his dream job or his dream girl, but he cannot, regrettably, have both." Doug spurted his drink out at this.

"Andy's in love with Maggie? I'm sorry, but no way; she's not his type."

"Will you two stop talking about me as if I'm not here!" I said sharply, finally lifting my head from where I had buried it in my drink. "Johan, I think you'll find I'm not in love with Maggie. I like her; I like her a lot. But she's just a good friend, that's all. And I'm sorry she's going. I'm going to miss her, but I'm pretty sure I'm not in love with her. So I can't give up this job for Maggie."

At this, I put my empty glass onto the table and stared at Doug. He hauled himself reluctantly out of his chair and wandered toward the bar, knowing he had zero chance of getting a waiter to serve us. Johan was unfazed at my outburst and merely reached over and took the last piece of tortilla off my plate. "Can I ask you something, Andy?" he enquired, stuffing the tortilla into his mouth. He chewed, and I waited an age for him to gulp.

"Go on," I said.

"Am I your friend?" he asked when he finally finished chewing.

"Of course you are," I replied, not seeing where he was going with the conversation. "A pretty good one as well, with all we've been through this year." Johan nodded as if this was obvious, chewed a bit more, and continued.

"And when I tell you I'm going home soon, do you feel sick in the stomach and need to talk to me about it?"

"No, of course, I—"

"No, of course you don't. Because you are not in love with me," he told me, looking up at Doug, who was shuffling over with three cold beers before snatching his last chicken strip. "At least I pray you are not."

"Are you going home soon?" I asked, realising this was the end of our year.

"All good things come to an end, old bean. I must return to my home country or, more particularly, to my father's timber company. I'm going in the next couple of weeks, so it will be just you then." Doug sat down, plonked three beers on the table, and looked at our downcast faces.

"I got them as fast I could. This is Unfriendly's after all, you know."

20 COMO HEMOS CAMBIADO.

Extract from a letter sent to Seville on the 11th of May, 1992.

'...your mum's really looking forward to seeing you, love. The doctors say she's pretty stable at the moment. She's got a better than 50/50 chance. There's no need to bring the flights forward any more than you have done. You tie up all your loose ends over there first. It will be great to have another woman back in the house, though, because, at times, she only has me to talk to, and I think she misses you.

Anyway, it will be great to see you.

Love,

Dad xxx'

It was ten days before Maggie was due to leave, not that I was counting them down on a calendar in my room with a black marker pen. Somehow, I still hadn't managed to get her alone to talk, to find that exact moment to sort everything out with her. Not that I knew if anything could be sorted out. Part of the problem was that I didn't know how I felt about her. Did I love her, as Johan kept telling me I did?

Finally, on a hot Friday evening, I caught her after a visit to her intercambios. Johan had gone out for the night. I heard the door clunk and Maggie shuffling about in the hallway. I was eating a chicken burger and put it down just as she walked in. "Hi," she said breezily, brushing past me and pouring hot water from the kettle into a mug. "That looks tasty."

"It's all I could find after Johan ate all my cheese and ham," I groaned. "He's like a plague of locusts."

"Yeah, he is, but it's almost endearing in a funny sort of way. I'm going to miss him," she smiled wistfully and sat opposite me.

"How come you never get upset with him?" I asked, lifting a cup of tea to my mouth and gazing at the burger with no appetite whatsoever. "He used to drive Saffron crazy when he ate her food, but I've never heard you complain."

"I've never heard you moan about it either," she replied, raising her eyebrows. "So, if the mystery is in the not moaning, how come you've never moaned?"

"Oh, he annoys me all right, but I like him," I said with a shrug.

"So do I, and there's your answer," she said. I put my cup down and pushed the burger to one side. I needed to get it all out while I had time.

"Maggie, can't you stay? Do you have to go?" I blurted out. Somehow, I'd leaned over, grabbed her hand, and held it in mine.

"I do, Andy," she replied, seemingly unperturbed by the unconscious hand grab and not pulling away from it. Instead, her thumb was running lightly down my wrist. "Believe me, if I could, I would."

"Maggie, I really—" That was when the stupid buzzer rang.

"I'll get it," I told her with a loud sigh and, letting go of her hand, which I might have also been stroking. I got up, and the buzzer went again.

"It's probably Maria about the rent," I said over my shoulder. "She can be so impatient. Alright, alright, I'm coming," I shouted towards the door. There was a loud knock. I walked a little quicker, reached forward, and opened the door.

It was Rachel.

She was another one who pushed herself through without a by-your-leave. "What the hell are you doing here?" was all I could manage as she barged past me with a small suitcase.

"Nice to see you too, Andy," she said coolly, putting her case down, slipping off her thin cardigan, and revealing an even thinner tight top that shouted, 'Look at my amazing cleavage'. "It's so hot here. I love it!" she beamed at me. I stood staring at her.

"Rachel, answer me. What are you doing here?" I repeated in a louder voice. She walked away from me and started to look round the flat.

"If you must know, I needed to get away from it all," she smiled demurely. "I would have phoned, but you don't have one. I only decided to get on a plane yesterday. I thought it would be good to talk. I'm flying back the day after tomorrow, so we don't have much time to straighten things out." Just then, Maggie came out of the kitchen.

"Who is it?" she asked, looking over at us.

"It's err...Rachel, my ex," I said so sheepishly I should have cut out the middle man and just gone baaaaaa! Almost with bated breath, I waited for Maggie to give her both barrels of that wonderfully smart mouth, some amazing put-down to set Rachel in her place. Let her know she was not wanted and that Maggie and I were, sort of, together. Instead, she looked Rachel up and down and said,

"Oh! Okay." Then she turned and walked back towards her room.

"Who's that?" Rachel said, raising her eyebrows and pointing her thumb in the direction of Maggie's room. I was perplexed. I had assumed Maggie would be unhappy at Rachel's appearance, but her reaction didn't indicate that she was. I suddenly felt exhausted.

"You can't stay here, Rachel; there's no room," I blustered. "And, anyway, you still haven't told me what you're doing here."

"Well, having seen the sort of people you're spending time with these days, I would have thought you'd be pleased to see me," she said condescendingly. I sat down on the couch and put my head in my hands.

"I should put you out onto the street right now, Rachel," I groaned. "It's only because I know how bad your finances are and that you can't afford a hotel room that I'm not. My room is there. Take it, but let me tell you, we have nothing to discuss. Understood?" I snatched her bag up and put it in my room. Then I stuffed some money and keys into my pockets and marched outside to buy supplies for breakfast and clear my head.

I considered going to Sergio's for the weekend to avoid her, but it wasn't a problem I could run away from. I needed a plan for

Saturday, and then she'd be gone.

When I returned with some fresh bread, cheese and meat, Rachel had already made herself at home, and was in the shower. I slipped back out and went to the telephone box across the road to phone Sergio. He said he was going to a club with a couple of friends, and there was no problem if we tagged along tomorrow.

Rachel was tired from her travel excursions and went to bed early. Maggie didn't emerge again from her room, and I spent a sleepless night on the sofa. Saturday morning was painful, but in my hour of need, Johan came through for me. He wandered into the kitchen wearing his signature yellow flip-flops, a crumpled T-shirt, and shorts from which his belly hung over slightly.

"What were you doing sleeping on the sofa, old bean? Did you have too much to drink?" he asked before seeing Rachel sitting on a chair, looking radiant if not bemused by the sight of him. "My goodness, I didn't know we had a goddess in our midst, Andy. When did this gorgeous creature arrive?" he asked, bowing before her, taking her hand and kissing it.

Rachel liked nothing more than being adored and was delighted to have so much attention paid to her after the cold shoulder she'd received from me. But even more, she recognised a potential ally and had no qualms about using and manipulating whatever resources she could to get her way. "Oh, I'm Andy's girlfriend. I've come to visit him," she laughed brightly.

"Ex-girlfriend," I quickly interjected, glaring at her, "And you're leaving tomorrow." In a heartbeat, Johan immediately understood and instinctively knew what the situation required.

"Well, I am delighted to meet you, Rachel. Perhaps, as Andy has private tuition already arranged for today, you would allow me to give you a tour of Seville for a few hours?" Rachel's face dropped in disappointment at this.

"You're going out?" she asked. It was news to me as I hadn't organised anything, but Johan had given me an out, which I gratefully accepted.

"Yes. I am Rachel. I hadn't planned to spend the day with my ex-girlfriend as you hadn't told me you were coming. I can't cancel at the last minute." I looked gratefully at Johan, who gave me a wink.

"But we need to talk," she pouted. "I've come all this way to speak to you."

"There's nothing to talk about as far as I'm concerned," I replied, sighing. "But if we have to, we can talk tonight. I've arranged a night out with a friend; we'll talk afterwards if we must." She visibly brightened at this.

"Well, my dear, it seems I am in good fortune. Your beauty will surely match the city of Seville, but first, I need to eat." And with that, he picked up my ham and cheese toastie and started to munch on it.

Shortly after, they left to see the sights of Seville. I hoped to speak with Maggie. She'd been subdued since Rachel arrived and kept herself out of the way all morning. She popped her head into the lounge to say she was meeting with some uni friends and was late. I lay on the sofa and watched TV for the rest of the afternoon, wondering how my life had suddenly become complicated.

When Saturday night finally rolled around, Maggie still hadn't returned, and Johan had gone to meet Doug at Unfriendly's. I was relieved that Maggie was nowhere to be seen when Rachel emerged from my room wearing a black denim mini skirt revealing her long, shapely legs, black leather ankle boots and a military eighties-style jacket. Rachel looked every inch the glamour model she always claimed to despise. On the way to the club, she turned multiple native heads. It was the usual thing I'd gotten used to in England—admiring looks from the males, contemptuous glances from the females. She was talking nonstop, most of which I wasn't listening to. "He lied to me, and I believed him," she spat.

"Well, what did you expect, Rachel?" I said, looking at her face scrunching up in anger. "Did you honestly think he was going to leave his wife? Because you're more of an idiot than I thought if you did."

"He took advantage of me. How was I supposed to know? He strung me along until I gave him an ultimatum. And then he dumped me. Me, for her!!"

"She was his wife, the mother of his child," I replied, staring into her eyes. For a moment, she had the grace to look somewhat ashamed.

"Oh! I recognise this street; I was here with Johan today. He's a bit of a character, isn't he?" she gushed, changing the subject. I looked at my watch, only four or five more hours to go.

We met Sergio at the Torre de Oro. For some unknown reason, she tried to take hold of my hand, but I brushed it away. Sergio and Rachel immediately hit it off. Gay blokes, I had learned, love aesthetics, and Sergio embraced Rachel's with a zest. I felt like a spare part for the rest of the night, which was what I'd hoped for when I'd made the arrangements with Sergio.

He paraded Rachel around his gay friends like she was a new Ferrari car while I remained in the background. After a couple of hours, I left the club and sat outside on the terrace, knowing I wouldn't be missed. The night was still pleasantly warm. Music pulsed in the air from the surrounding bars, making the city feel alive. I could see the Giralda tower poking out of the skyline and smell the orange blossoms from the trees in the square. I was breathing it all in and as sober as a judge when I felt a tap on my shoulder. "Are you okay?" asked Sergio, his face full of concern. "It is a difficult evening for you."

"Yeah," I sighed. "I'll be glad when it's over. Thanks for tonight, Serg. I didn't have the energy to be alone with her."

"That's okay, my friend. She is very beautiful, no? Your ex-girlfriend."

"If you like that kind of thing," I shrugged. "And I used to, like that kind of thing, I mean." He pulled out his comb, did the Jimmy Dean flick, and thought momentarily.

"She is very much fun and very much, how you say? Empty? But for me, empty can also be fun. But for you, I think it is not fun anymore." I turned to look at him.

"No, it's not any fun at all. But the time has arrived to go and have a not-very-fun conversation."

Rachel was thoroughly enjoying herself, dancing with a couple of gay blokes. It was the same reason Sergio was attracted to her. Rachel's aesthetic was a great one, whatever taste you had sexually. On seeing me, she said something to them while pointing wildly in my direction. She blew a goodbye kiss with an extravagant hand wave, then strutted across the dance floor towards me. She bent her head close to mine, and the jojoba from her recent Meg Ryan choppy cut wafted into my nostrils. "We need to talk," I shouted above the music. Then, pointing to the exit, I took her by the arm and began to walk up the stairs.

Once outside, I walked over to the stone monument to escape the beat of the music and sat down on the steps of the square. Rachel perched herself next to me, her long legs flowing out of her mini-skirt. I wasn't remotely interested in them, though. It's funny how when you start a relationship, you can never imagine that moment when you would become sick of the sight of your loved one—even more difficult in Rachel's case—but I was firmly in that moment.

"Why did you come here, Rachel?" I asked, looking hard into her once seductive chocolate pools that now only seemed like mud that you could get stuck in.

"Isn't it obvious?" she asked, putting her hand on my arm.

"Actually, Rachel, no, it isn't. Not one bit," I replied, removing my arm. "So, tell me because I just don't get it."

"I still love you," she said, biting her bottom lip. "In spite of everything and the way you've treated me."

"The way I've treated you?" I gasped, almost at a loss for words and shaking my head from side to side. "Look, Rachel. I made a mistake back in England, I admit it. But I tried to tell you that it wasn't a shiny, new beginning. It was a dark, unfortunate ending. It's over between us. I have a job here, and I'm not coming back.

"Great," she said enthusiastically. "I'll come over. It'll be a new start away from all the things that happened. I'll get a job here, modelling if I have to."

"Rachel, you only like the idea of me. The fantasy of living here," I told her, waving my arms around. "What you don't do very well, Rachel, and what you aren't doing now is facing up to reality."

"But I know I could be really happy here. It's so hot and sunny and everything. I'd love it."

"You're not listening, Rachel," I said, grabbing hold of her by her arms. "The only word you understand is I. So, how can I spell it out? I don't love you any more. I don't know if I ever did. Moreover, I'm not even attracted to you anymore. You're not my type." I let her go at that. Her face seemed to register some understanding.

"And what, she is? That, that thing at the flat?" she scoffed in disbelief.

"I'll tell you what Maggie is: she is everything you're not. What she means to me has nothing to do with you. You lost those privileges when you shagged my boss," I replied angrily. "None of what we went through is important anymore. What's important is that I've changed, and you've stayed the same. You think that looking like you is enough. Well, it might be for lots of blokes. It was for me once, but not anymore. Look at me, Rachel, while I say this for the final time. I am not interested in getting back together with you, ever."

"And what are you interested in?" she sniffled, reaching into her Gucci bag and producing a tissue. I stood up, and her head followed me as her hand dabbed away at the chocolate pools.

"I'm interested in that very thing you don't have, Rachel. The very thing that's so obvious we should all be looking for it, but as Johan said, it is difficult to find. I'm interested in whether you're a nice person or not."

Maybe it was too harsh, I thought as she started to sob. But I didn't walk away, not because I couldn't have. I didn't walk away because a nice person wouldn't do that. I leaned down, helped her to her feet, and began to walk her through the streets of Seville.

The following morning, Rachel was packing when I returned from a morning stroll that had been purposely taken to avoid her. This was allied to the fact that the couch was not the comfiest for sleeping on. I went into the flat less to say goodbye to my ex-girlfriend and more to make sure that she was going.

As I closed the front door, I saw that Maggie was up and sat at the table in the Blue Duck Egg. She was banging away, typing a letter, or something, on the Amstrad. On hearing my entrance, she turned and gave me a sad little smile. I shrugged my shoulders and made eyes in the direction of my room. Maggie rolled her eyes up, then turned back and typed. I went to my bedroom door and tapped on it with my knuckles. I didn't get a reply but pushed it slowly ajar anyway. Inside, Rachel stood by the bed, pulling a top down over her exposed lacy bra. On hearing me enter, she hesitated, ensuring I got a view of her body before slowly flattening it out. It was the clearest of signs that some people never learn. It made me wonder if last night's waterworks were all just a show. "Sorry," she said, the smallest of grins twitching at the side of her mouth. "I didn't hear you knock."

"Are you ready?" I replied coldly. "You need to get to the airport. Seville check-in is not the most rapid process, and you don't want to miss your flight."

"Yeah," she said, fastening a couple of buttons on the side of her denim skirt. "Johan's friend Antonio's giving me a ride to the airport. He should be here any minute."

That'd be about right.

"Good," I said, watching her as she checked herself in the mirror. "Let me take your bag. I think I heard someone beeping." She placed hers on mine as I bent to pick up her case. We were both bent over. She kept her hand there.

"Are you sure, Andy?" she asked, switching the chocolate pools to Jacuzzi mode. "This is your Last chance."

"Do me a favour," I said, simultaneously moving the bag, my hand, and my eyes away. I turned around and dropped the bag in the living room. Not wanting to go through the same crap at the bottom of the stairs as I'd just been through in the bedroom, I left it there. It wasn't heavy, so she could carry it downstairs herself.

Rachel marched out of my bedroom for all the world, looking like a fashion marketing man's wet dream. She had more labels on her than a misdirected, round-the-world DHS parcel. Meanwhile, Maggie seated at the Armstrad couldn't have made a starker contrast. Dressed in the Blue Duck Egg, she looked like his worst nightmare.

Rachel's high heels clumped across the laminate floor until she reached the door. Once there, she shot me a disgusted look, bent her knees, and put her hand on the case. "You know, Andy? I can handle it that you don't want me anymore because of the way I treated you or because you've changed," she spat. "That's understandable, if not a bad decision on your part. What I can't believe is that you'd prefer that," she said, cocking a thumb in Maggie's direction, with one hand on her bent hip. "I mean, look at her! She, well, I'm not being unfair here, but she needs to keep off the old paella." In the moment of shock, all I could do was shout,

"RACHEL! You're out of order!!" But while I was reeling from Rachel's final outburst of outrageous behaviour, Maggie had calmly risen from the Amstrad. She padded across the room barefoot with silence and grace that compared so favourably to Rachel's ignominious exit. She moved over to where Rachel was standing, her bag on the floor, arms crossed and left knee bent as she'd just delivered the equivalent of Martin Luther King's 'I Have a Dream' speech.

Maggie stopped directly opposite her. It seemed clear that Rachel was about to get her comeuppance via Maggie. This would consist of a thoroughly deserved verbal onslaught from her razor-like tongue. I have to say I'd been waiting for it.

Instead, though, Maggie's right hand shot up like lightning and slapped Rachel hard across the face. The sound of Maggie's hand on contact made a loud cracking noise, and Rachel's head reeled slightly to the right. Blinking back tears, she quickly put her hand up to rub, to feel, and to check, as if she couldn't quite believe what Maggie had done.

'Shit!' my brain shouted at me. I was just about to rush forward to break up the catfight that I was sure would ensue when Maggie placed her hand with five fingers spread across my chest and said very calmly, "Andy, would you tell your friend here it's vulgar to talk about people, especially when they are in your presence. She doesn't appear to have any manners, and if I have to show her some again, I might not be so nice about it."

I looked at Rachel, who was wide-eyed but trembling now with her hand held up to her face. She made a pleading look in my direction to come to her aid. Maggie pulled on the belt of the Duck Egg, which had loosened around her waist, and glared at her. I moved towards Rachel. I could see from her face that she thought I was coming to do the damsel-in-distress routine. She was very wrong. I bent down, picked her bag up, and put it in the hall. "You heard the lady," I said, walking past her. Maggie held the door open.

"Adiós, as we say round here, darling. Now, get lost. You're so not his type anymore."

Rachel bowed her head. She didn't look at either of us but stumbled through the open door. Maggie leaned back against the wall and slammed the door shut. Even though it was closed, Rachel's heels could be heard clunking down the stairs in ever-diminishing tones. We were silent for ages as the heels continued their downward clunk until they could no longer be heard.

Maggie was now standing with her back pressed against the door as if Rachel might suddenly realise she'd been humiliated and charged back up the stairs. After what seemed like ages, we heard the downstairs door bang, and Maggie let out a huge gasp of air. "Oh, Andy! I can't believe I did that!" she screeched in hysterical laughter. Then she took in a couple of deep breaths to compose herself. "I'm so sorry. I can't believe I did that."

"Don't be," I said slowly. "She deserved it. She's had something like this coming to her for a long time."

"Maybe," said Maggie, stepping away from the door and into the dining room. "But I still shouldn't have hit her."

"How did you know she wouldn't start a catfight?" I asked. Maggie reached the couch and flopped onto it.

"Oh, I had to learn to stand up to girls like her at school. They rarely do."

"I think she's finally got the message," I sighed, sitting beside her.

"I'd ask you what you ever saw in her if it wasn't such an obvious answer," she giggled.

"I was beginning to wonder myself," I said, then raised my eyebrows. "If it wasn't so obvious."

"Did you see her legs in that skirt? I'd kill to look like that in a short skirt," she mused.

"You look just as good as her," I said sharply and more than a little defensively. "Like the time you wore that black dress at the Feria. You looked amazing."

"What? That time when you got all jealous?"

"I didn't get all jealous," I blushed. "But you did; you looked just as good but in a different way."

"How so different?" she asked, her face straightening.

"Err...you know? Maggie, stop it!" She started to laugh. "Maggie, you're so horrible to me at times." With that, she leaned over and pressed her index finger onto my nose.

"That's because I like you. And thank you for lying and saying I ever looked as good as her. It was lovely of you. I'm going to take a shower. When I come back, we could go to my room if you want to finish what we started." Her words made me blush again because I realised just how much I wanted to. She must have read it in my face as she got up and went to the bathroom.

"But I wasn't lying," I said softly.

Before she left the bathroom, I heard a key turn in the door, and Johan lumbered back into the flat from his exploits from the night before. He sat down on the couch opposite me, remarkably sober for that hour of the day. I heard the shower start up behind me. "What's new, amigo? I take it the very lovely Rachel has departed?" I smiled and proceeded to give him the details.

Five minutes later, Maggie exited the bathroom with a towel wrapped around her and the duck egg in her right hand. She saw Johan sat next to me. "Oh! Alright, Johan? Good night?" she asked. It was one of those rare moments when his English failed him.

"Goodnight to you too, Maggie," he replied. "Sleep tight." She looked blankly at me, gave a big grin, shrugged her shoulders, and tilted her head toward her bedroom. I raised my eyes to the ceiling. She blew me a little kiss and mouthed, 'Next time', and closed the door. Oblivious to everything, Johan slapped me on the leg. "Fancy a chicken burger breakfast?" he suggested.

"Sounds great," I said and gazed longingly at Maggie's closed door.

21 ALWAYS THE LAST TO KNOW.

Extract from a letter sent to the Orkney Islands on the 15th of May, 1992

'...it is, Mum. So I'm confused, to say the least. Maybe all your worrying about me has finally come to fruition. I have to stay here now. I've got this job, but I am worried I'm making a mistake.

Anyway, it looks like I'm going to lose something again.

Love,

Andrew xxx'

As the day of Maggie's departure came ever nearer, a feeling of helplessness enveloped me. I kept thinking I should do something to stop it, but knowing there wasn't anything I could do.

In the interim, Johan organised a night out on the town for Maggie, which crept ever closer. Before I knew it, the day had arrived. It was the last night we'd spend together before she left for the UK. We were caught up in the moment because we knew it was the end of something special, something we would never get back and could never be the same again.

Maggie's leaving do was immense fun for everyone, with the possible exception of me. We, naturally, started off at Unfriendly's, and there was another jaw-clanking moment when they brought out a cake. It appeared the Dark Lord and Maria had planned it. A couple of girls from Maggie's course with whom she'd become friendly drifted in and formed a gang with Sergio, Doug, and Ramon, who seemed like an item. Johan held centre stage, turning a very bad Flamenco routine to howls of laughter. A little later in the evening, Antonio made an entrance. Maggie sat with him, laughing for half an hour, and I didn't even get jealous once. That was because, although I didn't talk to

Maggie much, our eyes kept finding each other.

We proceeded in a rowdy manner to the gay area of Seville and, of course, ended up in Chicos. The night's highlight was the whole group going mad on the dance floor when 'Finally' came on.

Though eight or nine of us were on the floor dancing in a group, I felt like there was only really Maggie and me. We harangued the DJ to put it on again before we left, something he was reluctant to do until Sergio flirted outrageously with him. One of the greatest moments I'd ever had was standing in a circle with Maggie and all of my friends from Seville whilst screaming the words to 'Finally' out loud one last time.

When we all exited together, it was four in the morning. We stumbled down to the Isobella Puente and the flimsy wooden cabin selling chocolate con churros. We chatted loudly, speaking over each other whilst dunking sugar-coated churros into cups of hot chocolate. Maggie said some emotional farewells as splinters began to break away from the group. She cried a lot, hugged a lot, and laughed out loud even more. Me? I just felt sad and stood on the peripheries. When she'd said goodbye to the girls, some of them looked over and gave me disapproving looks. They hugged Maggie and presumably said whatever the Spanish equivalent of 'He's not worth it, love' was to her.

When we reached the flat at around five, it was just the three musketeers left. Amazingly, Johan was still with us. He'd promised to make an effort not to disappear and had lived up to his word for Maggie's sake. As we clambered up the stairs, Johan attempted to sing a lewd Swedish song, and Maggie jumped on his back to shut him up. In doing so, she made more of a racket than Johan's singing. She clamped her hands over his mouth, and we hustled him inside to the living room in a gigantic tangle of arms and legs. He broke free of Maggie's grapple, and we all fell onto the floor. Johan, with distinctly more practice than us at falling over, was the first to get on his feet. "Well, my dear. It is time we said our farewells, for I feel my bed is calling me."

"Johan," Maggie said, now scrambling up at him and throwing

her arms around his thick neck. "Thank you for being such an amazing flatmate. I don't think I could have spent my time here with anybody better than you and Andy." I was hanging back, and I could see what Maggie, who was holding him too tightly, couldn't, the tears welling up in his pale blue eyes. After a long time, he and Maggie let go.

"It was good to spend such an enjoyable party with two good friends such as yourselves," he blustered, trying to compose himself. "And you, Maggie, are such a wonderful English Rose." Maggie smiled at him as she wiped her eyes. "You have my address in Uppsala, young lady?"

"I do," she replied, hugging him once more. "And I promise to come over next summer."

"Well," he said, taking his glasses off with his right hand and wiping his eyes with his left. "Antonio will beep at ten. So it's goodnight and farewell. I shall not be getting out of bed until mid-afternoon."

"Of course not," she laughed. "I wouldn't expect anything else." He gave her a final hug and kiss, then winked at me and went to his room with his customary stagger. As his door closed, Maggie and I suddenly became aware of the moment. We turned to face each other. To my surprise, the awkwardness I'd been expecting never materialised because she reached out, took my hand, and led me to the couch. When we sat down, she placed my hand firmly between her two.

"Andy, I want to tell you some things before I go," she said, lightly sliding her fingers back and forth between mine while taking a deep breath. "Here goes. Andy, I just want to tell you that I love you."

"Maggie—"

"Shhhhhh! I'm talking, Andy, don't be rude," she said in a very cute voice. "I love you, but I know you can't give up this job. I know you can't follow me, and I understand why. I do, but it's important that you know. I think I've loved you from the very first moment I saw you stumbling around in that bar and throwing your drink all over me. You were so helpless, so good-looking, but so unaffected. It's just that I'm not very good at letting people know how I feel. Hence, all the pulling of pigtails and all the wisecracks. All defence mechanisms, really."

"Maggie—" I tried to interject again but to no avail.

"Will you shuuussshhh! It's my leaving do, so I get to say what I want, and you get to listen. Agreed?"

"Agreed," I sighed and tightened my grip on her hands.

"You know, Johan saw what I couldn't? He knew I liked you, but he saw that you liked me before I did. The only person who couldn't see it in the end was you. And now you do see it, it's too late. That's life. It never works out how you hope it will. I'm going, and you're staying. So there you go, I love you, and now you know." She giggled at accidentally creating a poem, but her eyes went solemn and held mine. She was waiting for me to say something. I thought long and hard before I answered.

"I don't know what to say, Maggie. Maybe I love you too, but even if I do, it's too big of a risk for me to take. To wager this job, this amazing opportunity, and everything else on a might-be. I've already blown three long-term relationships, and I thought I was in love on at least two occasions. And on the other one, I was in lust. I need to think about my future," I told her, pulling my hand away. "I'm sorry. I'd love it if you could stay here with me, and we could have a chance to see where it might go. I want more than anything for you to stay here with me. I'd ask you if I thought for one second you would." She kept her eyes on me, and I could feel them even though mine had left hers; they were gazing vacantly out the window. She reached over and took hold of my hand again. She was silent until I looked at her.

"I understand, Andy, but there are no guarantees with love, none," she said and then squeezed my hand hard. "If there was any way I could stay, I would. When I go tomorrow, I'll walk out of that door in love with you but with no hard feelings. But before I go, I want you to remember this." With that, she put her hands around my neck and pulled my mouth gently onto hers. She gave me a goodbye kiss that Bogart would have died for. She pulled away, held my hand, and led me to her room. I tried to stop her when I realised what she was doing.

"Don't, Maggie, I'll feel like I'm taking advantage." She put her finger to her lip.

"Shhhh! My leaving-do, so I get to make the rules. This is what I want," she told me, pulling me into her room. "So nobody's taking advantage of anybody. If anything, I intend to take advantage of you."

"Oh, you do, do you?" I smiled.

When I woke up a couple of hours later, she was lying asleep in my arms, her hair fanned out on the pillow behind her. She was naked and beautiful, and I'd just had the best sex of my life. I looked down at her; she was snoring lightly. It sounded cute, though. Like a tiny baby's rattle being shaken. Not a bit like I imagined a woman snoring might sound. After a little while, it stopped. I bent my chin to kiss her forehead and look into her face. Her eyes opened, squinting at the light, and then she looked directly at me. "I didn't have sex with him, you know?" she said softly.

"Who?" I asked, totally forgetting about that night.

"Antonio," she said again, barely audibly. "He's not my type. But he amuses me."

"I don't care," I told her. "You were free to do what you wanted. I'd no right to act like I did."

"I can't stay," she said and rolled away.

"And I can't go," I sighed.

"I know," she said softly. "So, kiss me once more and tell me you love me before you leave." I leaned over, kissed her soft mouth, and embraced her body against mine for the last time. I withdrew my lips without saying anything and stroked her hair back from her face, her green eyes not leaving mine for a moment. Then I kissed her again, gathered my things, and went to my room.

I didn't get up the following morning. I couldn't do another goodbye. When I heard the beep of Antonio's car in the street below and the door closed, I knew she'd left quietly. It was how she wanted to go. I then rolled onto my back, placed my hands at the back of my neck, and stared at the ceiling for about five hours.

A few days after that traumatic episode, I was at the airport saying goodbye to Johan. It was another emotional farewell. He had to return most of my clothes for a start. I say most because I'd let him keep the Nirvana T-shirt on the understanding that he bought a copy of the tape.

When we got to the Avis car rental stand near the departure lounge, we stood there looking at each other and grinning. The two of us standing there grinning was a fantastic encapsulation of our time together in the flat. In the end, I spoke first.

"Listen," I said, rooting around in my pocket, "when you return to Sweden, I want you to start taking it easy. Try and cut down on the drinking, please. I know I sound like a hypocrite, but it's only because I'm worried about you." He stepped forward, and I braced myself for the giant bear hug that followed.

"Old Bean," he laughed, letting me go. "I need to inform you that I don't drink alcohol in Sweden. I won't and shall not be drinking it on my return." I was stunned, and he saw it on my face. "Firstly, the state makes it too expensive, and I have never been one for catching the boat to Denmark. Secondly, when I get back, I need to focus on our company, which is my future, and I can't do that in the inebriated state that I have spent my time here in."

"I don't understand," I told him. "You're not normally pissed all of the time then?"

"No," he smiled and punched me in the arm. "My father came to Spain as a young man, before he went into the family business, and had a very...how do you say? A wild time here. He was very keen for me to follow in his footsteps and then to settle down in much the same way he did."

"Wow, great dad!" I replied, feeling a tinge of sadness and regret for obvious reasons.

"I think so, too," Johan agreed. "Anyway, you have my address, and you have made your promise to come and visit me. It has been a wild year, and now it is almost over. You have been a great friend to me here, Andy, and I won't forget you. I just hope that everything works out for you and you are happy with the choice you have made." I dropped my head but didn't say anything. So he stepped forward and gave me another Swedish bear hug. This one was the bear hug to end all bear hugs.

"Take care, Johan," I told him as he finally let me go.

"You too, my friend."

He turned, waved, and walked through the doors.

I stood there for a minute watching him go, and I'm not afraid to say there was not a dry eye in the house.

22 FINALLY.

Extract from a letter sent to Sweden on the 15th of April, 1995

'...great news that your dad has made you managing director. That's what dads are for.

You asked in your last letter if I am happy and if it all worked out for me. Well, the answer is yes and yes. I'm really happy here...'

I stepped out onto the street, and the warm Sevillian air hit me in the face. It felt so good. I looked at my watch and realised it was only twenty minutes to make my appointment at the university. It was not one for which I wanted to be late, so I stepped up my pace to the corner, bustling past chattering locals as I did so. The cacophony of Spanish voices shrilled out into the air.

Eventually, one of the many side streets brought me out onto the main drag. The heavy traffic rumbling along under the shadow of the great cathedral echoed through the air. I had to admit feeling nostalgic, even a little sad this morning. Sad about the choices that sometimes life forces you to make, which often means some things must be sacrificed for the greater good. I could have had my life here, or I could have had Maggie. It was not possible, the way things turned out, to have had both. Still, sad as I was this morning, I felt I had made the right choice. Did I have regrets?

Everybody has regrets.

I crossed over the roundabout as the pedestrian lights changed and made my way up the pavement towards the main university entrance. I remembered when I'd first come here. The magic of the building and the excitement it engendered in me as I made my way through the corridors to Johnson's office for my appointment, the appointment that would lead me to Saffron,

Johan, and eventually my old flatmate Maggie. If there was a small tear in my eye at that point, I'm sure I could be forgiven it. The Spanish have a word for the nostalgia that had engulfed me. They call it la añoranza, and, to my mind, it encapsulates the essence of that slightly sad, bittersweet feeling flowing through me far better than any word I can conjure in English.

I stood there and surrendered to la añoranza for a few seconds, letting it wash through me. I then looked at my watch again and was snapped out of my melancholy by the fact that I might be late for my meeting. I made my way through the central door arch. On the way in, I took a quick peek at the noticeboard. There were fewer intercambio cards than there used to be. A few people were even putting mobile phone numbers up. The times, as Dylan told us, they were a-changing. I took a left down the next corridor and wound my way up familiar stairs, looking around to see if I could see anyone. As I reached the top to look down the next corridor, I stopped. "Are you blind or what?" a voice behind me asked.

"I was distracted," I said, recognising it instantly and turning around to greet it. Maggie was standing there before me. She smiled, stepped forward, and reached up, kissing me lightly on the lips.

"Here. Grab these," she said, breaking away and thrusting four shopping bags into my hands. "What time did you leave the hotel? You're late."

"At twenty to four," I told her. "You said to meet here at four."

"I said three thirty," she reminded me, pushing a credit card back into her purse. "You're a right muppet at times, Andy McLeod."

"I know. I gave all this up for you," I said, waving the bags and my arms around. "So I must be."

"Don't start," she laughed, closing the purse and pointing to a door. "You know it was the best decision you ever made. Anyway, let's do this before you change your oh-so-clever mind."

"Do we have to?" I pleaded. "I want to do it; you know I do. I just don't want to do it here in front of all these people."

"All these people? There's hardly anyone around, and anyway, we agreed," she pressed. She was now bouncing around on her toes and making silly, wide-eyed faces at me. I reached inside my pocket and felt for the small box. I still had it. In the meantime, Maggie headed towards the bar, and I followed, carrying the bags she'd laden me with. As I trailed behind, I could see her curvaceous arse hanging out of her jeans, and I smiled at the fact that she still didn't give a damn. Just before we arrived, I passed an office in the Spanish department, and 'Dr.' was printed on the door. Saffron Morley – Departamento de Fililogía.

I smiled wryly to myself, remembering the call, telling Johnson I was sorry to let them down but that I couldn't take the job for personal reasons. I was pleased for Saffron when I heard they'd given it to her. But I didn't think us calling in to see her anytime soon would be a good idea.

Maggie was now at the entrance, waving at me to come into the bar. We went inside and piled all the bags of presents and clothes on the tables. She turned towards me and flicked her hair back in a mock Miss Piggy gesture. "Do you remember this is where we met?" she asked, looking all around.

"How could I not?" I replied. "Spilling that drink all over you in front of your dad."

"How romantic you were," she giggled. "And talking of romantic, let's be having you on your knees then. And say it like you mean it and in exactly the same way that we agreed." Thankfully, there were only a few curious people sitting at scattered tables to see me as I bent down onto one knee. I took the diamond ring out of the box. She held her hand out, and her face lit up like Blackpool in November as I took it. "Maggie, even though you are not my type, will you marry me?"

Why did I choose Maggie over the job and my dream life in Seville? Simple: I realised I loved her. How do you realise that you love someone? Less simple. I think each of us realises we are in love differently. The books tell you what it feels like to be in love, but it didn't work out that way for Maggie and me. That was because Maggie didn't make my heart skip a beat when I first met her, she didn't make my pulse race whenever she walked into the room, and she didn't keep me tossing and turning all night (well, not always)—at least, not until she'd gone. Only then did I realise I loved Maggie.

I missed her. I missed her like I couldn't believe I could ever miss anyone. Missing someone is a golden rule they should write down in the books. It only took a day or two of being in that flat with her gone to make me realise I could no longer be happy without her. When I told Johan I was leaving to follow her because I realised that I loved her, he said, "About fucking time."

He came to see me off at the airport and left Seville a week after me. He is currently the teetotal managing director of a family logging business in Uppsala, Sweden.

Doug and Sergio were disappointed I was leaving but understood. They're both great friends now, perhaps better friends than ever I was with either of them. Considering Doug could hardly speak Spanish when he arrived in Seville, his Spanish is now as good as mine. He works as a tour guide and loves taking handsome Americans around the back of the cathedral to see the views (double-entendre alert), though he still hasn't met that special someone.

My mum's doing really well with the new hip. She met Maggie last year, and they got on brilliantly, though she told me behind Maggie's back that she still liked the one who became a lesbian best. She didn't.

The last I heard of Rachel was from one of Doug's ex-colleagues who worked for the Greater Manchester police. He told me she was dating a Rugby League professional from Leeds. The guy recently had assault charges against him dropped after the alleged victim, one Brian James Cruikshank decided he didn't want the publicity of a court case and all that might bring out into the open.

A wise Swede once said, 'If you look in all the wrong places, you'll find all the wrong things.' I guess it is fair to say that while I was in Seville, I was looking in all the wrong places. I went to Seville to find something special and discovered that the first place I needed to look was inside myself. Are you looking for the wrong things? If you search for what's important in life, you will have a chance of finding the things or the person that will make you happy. It just might come in a different package from the one you imagined.

I went to Seville thinking, no, knowing that something wonderful was waiting for me. There was, but in the end, I had to leave Seville behind to find what it was I was really looking for.

Life forces us to make choices, and I had to make a difficult one. To relinquish a job and a new life in a city that I had come to love, or the woman with whom I had fallen in love. But if you have to choose between a city or a woman, there is no choice really, or there shouldn't be.

I currently teach Spanish Literature at a faculty in Northern England, and life is great. I get to visit Doug and Sergio once a year and then go over to Johan in the Swedish summer. And I'm with the woman I love, and do you know what?

I think she's lost a bit of weight lately.

Steve's other novels, 'Love, Sex and Tesco's Finest Cava' and 'These Things Take Time,' are also available on Amazon Kindle and in paperback.

ABOUT THE AUTHOR

Steve Carter

Steve and writing partner Julie live in the beautiful Highlands of NE Scotland.
There, they live in semi-retirement and walk their Golden Retriever, George, in the surrounding forests.

BOOKS BY THIS AUTHOR

These Things Take Time

Steve and Julie's 'These Things Take Time' is an epic, sprawling love story spread over 40 years.

Love, Sex And Tesco's Finest Cava

Steve's first novel was a surprise smash hit, charting at No1 in romance and comedy.